happily letter after

RECEIVED
JUN 05 2021
BROADVIEW LIBRARY

NO LONGER PROPERTY OF
SEATTLE PUBLIC LIBRARY

OTHER TITLES BY VI KEELAND AND PENELOPE WARD

Dirty Letters

Hate Notes

Rebel Heir

Rebel Heart

Cocky Bastard

Stuck-Up Suit

Playboy Pilot

Mister Moneybags

British Bedmate

Park Avenue Player

Other books from Vi Keeland

Inappropriate

All Grown Up

We Shouldn't

The Naked Truth

Sex, Not Love

Beautiful Mistake

Egomaniac

Bossman

The Baller

Left Behind

Beat

Throb

Worth the Fight

Worth the Chance

Worth Forgiving

Belong to You

Made for You

Other books from Penelope Ward

Just One Year

The Day He Came Back

When August Ends

Love Online

Gentleman Nine

Drunk Dial

Mack Daddy

Stepbrother Dearest

Neighbor Dearest

RoomHate

Sins of Sevin

Jake Undone (Jake #1)

Jake Understood (Jake #2)

My Skylar

Gemini

happily letter after

VI KEELAND
PENELOPE WARD

This is a work of fiction. Names, characters, organizations, places, events, and incidents are either products of the author's imagination or are used fictitiously.

Text copyright © 2020 by Vi Keeland & Penelope Ward
All rights reserved.

No part of this book may be reproduced, or stored in a retrieval system, or transmitted in any form or by any means, electronic, mechanical, photocopying, recording, or otherwise, without express written permission of the publisher.

Published by Montlake, Seattle

www.apub.com

Amazon, the Amazon logo, and Montlake are trademarks of Amazon.com, Inc., or its affiliates.

ISBN-13: 9781542025133
ISBN-10: 1542025133

Cover design by Caroline Teagle Johnson

Cover photography © 2019 S. Tong Photography

Printed in the United States of America

To Luna—this book is almost as special to us as you.

CHAPTER 1

SADIE

> Do: Tell your date how nice she looks.
>
> Don't: Tell your date how much she resembles your ex-fiancée . . . but with a little more meat on her bones.

This week's article was an easy one. All I had to do was summarize the time I'd spent with Austin Cobbledick last night. No, I'm not kidding. That was actually his name—smart move going by Austin Cobb on Match.com. Anyway, the name wasn't the worst of it. The guy was just awful. I could have written this week's *Do's and Don'ts of Dating* column on at least a half dozen things the guy did wrong. Let's see . . .

I stared unfocused at the computer monitor on my desk and tapped my finger to my bottom lip, pondering the other choices.

> Do: Close your mouth when you sneeze.
>
> Don't: Get food particles from the meal you just chewed with your mouth open all over your date's

> Burberry coat. (Which, by the way, I dropped at the cleaners this morning. I should send Cobbledick the damn bill. No wonder there's an "ex" in front of the word "fiancée" when he says it.)

Though an article about getting sneezed on probably wouldn't fly. The twenty-one to twenty-eight-year-old demographic that reads *Modern Miss* magazine tends to be a bit squeamish. Perhaps they'd be more interested in another article about Cobbledick:

> Do: Order a beer, soda, water, or glass of wine during your date.
>
> Don't: Order a Shirley Temple and use it as a prop to show off your ability to tie a knot in a cherry stem when you've known a woman all of five minutes.
>
> Total sleaze bucket.

My ruminations were interrupted by my coworker Devin coming to deliver mail. She dropped a stack of envelopes in the in-box on the corner of my desk and said, "Want Starbucks? I'm going on a run."

Mind you, she still had an unfinished venti cup in her hand.

Devin was one of the fashion editors for the magazine. Yet sometimes, when I looked at her, that made me scratch my head. Today she had on a white baby-doll dress, silver sparkly sequin jacket, yellow rubber boots, and a colorful scarf that wrapped around her neck and hung to almost the floor . . . and it wasn't even raining out. I bit my tongue. She had, after all, just picked up my mail from the mail room and was now offering to go fetch me coffee. I knew enough not to bite the hand that fed me. Plus, Devin was one of my best friends.

I opened my desk drawer, dug my wallet out of my messy purse, and pulled out a ten-dollar bill. "I'll take a grande iced sugar-free vanilla latte with soy milk. And yours is on me."

She wrinkled up her pert little nose. "Is there even coffee in that?"

"Espresso."

"Oh. Okay. Be back in a few." She turned around and started to walk, then stopped in the doorway to my office. "By the way, how was your date last night?"

"He turned into an article five minutes in."

She laughed. "Maybe you should go back to eHarmony?"

Over the last two years, I'd tried Match, Plenty of Fish, eHarmony, Zoosk, and Bumble. I'd even tried Jdate, the site where Jewish people looked for other like-kind religious people to date, even though I wasn't actually Jewish. My bad luck at dating sucked for me but worked well for the weekly columns I had to write in my position as a magazine staff writer.

"I'm thinking of trying Grindr, actually."

"I thought that site was for gay, bi, and transgender people?"

"I might reconsider my options after my date last night."

Devin laughed, thinking I was kidding. But any more dates like the last few, and I might have to seriously reconsider how much I liked penis.

I decided to wait until she returned with my coffee before going back to work on the article I needed to finish. To pass the time, I grabbed the new pile of mail and started to sort through it.

Advertisement.

Advertisement.

Résumé from someone who wanted to do an internship at the magazine.

Layout proofs from the copy department.

Advertisement.

Letter from a woman who disliked my use of the word "panties" in last week's article. It was a full page back and front, typed. Obviously she had too much time on her hands.

I stopped at the next-to-last envelope. This one wasn't addressed to either Sadie Bisset or to the editor. It was addressed to Santa Claus. Seeing as it was June, I looked at the postmark, thinking maybe the letter had gotten lost in the mail. But . . . nope. The postmark was just three days ago. Each of the staff writers here at *Modern Miss* had set weekly columns to write, but we also had to run one seasonal or holiday-related feature. I was in charge of the *Holiday Wishes* article that ran during November and December. So it wasn't actually all that unusual for me to receive a letter addressed to Santa. Though the timing was obviously odd. We hadn't even put the mailing address in the magazine since last December. Nonetheless, I sliced open the envelope and settled back into my seat, curious about this person who was too impatient to wait a few more months.

> Dear Santa,
> My name is Birdie Maxwell, and I'm ten and a half years old.

The first line made me smile. At what age did I stop saying *and a half*? Technically, I was twenty-nine and a half. But I certainly didn't want to lean any closer to thirty than I had to. These days, I preferred to say *late twenties* rather than my actual age. Birdie, on the other hand, likely wanted to sound more mature. I did at that age, too. I went back to reading, curious about what the little girl's wish might be.

> Even though I'm writing this letter, I'm not sure I believe in you anymore. I know that sounds dumb, since here I am writing and all. But I have my reasons. You let me down. If there really is a you. Maybe

this letter will never even be opened because you don't exist. I don't know.

Anyway, four years ago, I wrote you a letter and asked you to make my mom better. She was sick with cancer. But she died on December 23rd. When I cried and said you didn't exist, Dad told me that Santa was only for kids, and it didn't work to ask for things for adults. So the next year, I asked for a blue Schwinn with a white basket with pink flowers, a bell that made a quacking sound, and a license plate that had my name. Nothing ever comes with the name Birdie. Not magnets, or coffee mugs, and definitely not bicycle license plates. But you came through. My bike is super awesome, even if Dad says my knuckles are starting to drag on the ground when I ride it.

Then last year I asked for a puppy. I really, really wanted a Great Dane named Marmaduke, one with one blue eye and one brown eye. But you didn't bring a puppy. Dad tried to tell me that Santa doesn't bring live gifts. He didn't know that Suzie Redmond, the *most* annoying girl in my class, asked for a guinea pig and got one from so-called Santa. Anyway, like I said, I'm not sure if you're real. Or if any of the rules Dad told me Santa has to follow are even true. But I thought this might be a good way to send my list for this year. Well, it's not really a list but one big thing that I want . . .

If you're really Santa, can you please bring my dad and me a special friend? Sort of like a mom, but not a mom because I only have one mom, and she's gone. But maybe someone who can make Dad laugh more.

And if she can do braids, that would be super cool. Dad is *really, really* bad at them.

Thank you!

Birdie Maxwell

P.S. I know it's summer. But I thought it might take a while to find the right special friend.

P.P.S. If you're real, Dad can use some black socks. The ones he wore today had a hole in the big toe.

P.P.P.S. And if you're really real, can you send me olives? The big black ones that come in a can. We ran out and Dad finally lets me use the can opener. I like to put one on each finger and eat them in front of the TV.

I blinked a few times, taking it all in. It was the sweetest, most selfless letter to ever cross my desk. The fact that the little girl lost her mom at only seven made my heart hurt. I'd been six and a half when my mom died of cancer. And *oh my God* . . . I'd just thought back to the last time I'd seen my mom and realized how I recalled my age—six . . . *and a half.*

Oh, Birdie. I totally get you. The years after my mom died, my dad rarely smiled, too. My parents had been high school sweethearts. On Valentine's Day in ninth grade, he'd given her a diamond Ring Pop while standing in front of the pizza place down the block from their school. Five years later, he brought her back to that exact spot and proposed with a real ring. Their love had been the things little girls dream about. Though inspiring, their romance had a downside. My parents had set such a high bar for what a relationship should be, I refused to settle.

Sighing, I reread the letter. The second time around, I had tears in my eyes when I was done. I wasn't sure what I could do for Birdie, but I had the sudden urge to call my dad. So I did.

Like a typical New Yorker, I didn't go food shopping so much as visit the tiny grocery store around the corner from my house on my way home every day. Cairo, the guy who worked behind the counter, had moved here from Bahrain with dreams of becoming a stand-up comedian. He treated his customers like we were his test audience.

I started to unload the items from my basket onto the counter.

"Last night, I told my wife that she was drawing her eyebrows too high. She looked surprised."

I chuckled and shook my head. "Cute, Cairo. But you know me, I like the dirty ones."

Cairo looked around and then motioned for me to lean in close. "A girl noticed she started to grow hair between her legs. Not knowing what it was, she got nervous and asked her mom if it was normal. Her mom responded, 'It's normal, sweetheart. That's called your monkey. It means you're becoming a woman.' The girl got excited. That night at dinner, she boasted about it to her sister. 'My monkey has hair now!' Her sister smiled. 'Big deal. Mine's already eaten a dozen bananas.'"

I laughed. "Keep that one in the act."

Cairo pointed down the aisle behind me. "Did you see? I got more of those chocolate wafer cookies you like so much."

I groaned. Hazelnut-filled Pirouline wafer cookies were my weakness. I was lucky that most of my weight went to my ass, and junk in the trunk was en vogue right now. "I told you to stop ordering them."

He smiled and waved his hand. "Go. My treat."

I sighed. But yet I made my way back down the aisle. Because . . . well . . . cookies. Cairo's little local store had no rhyme or reason to the product placement. Sponges were stacked next to spaghetti and on the other side of that were the Piroulines. I grabbed the front canister, and as I went to turn away, I noticed a stack of cans next to where I'd just grabbed the wafer cookies from. *Black olives.* I smiled, thinking about Birdie, and started to walk back to the register. I made it only three steps before I turned around and grabbed two cans of olives off the shelf.

Cairo proceeded to tell me three terrible olive jokes while I finished paying for my purchases. I left with two bags of groceries, and I had no idea what the hell I was going to do with the olives, but for some reason, I hummed "Jingle Bells" all the way home.

CHAPTER 2

SADIE

"What the heck are you doing?"

The next afternoon, Devin came into my office and found me with a roll of Christmas wrapping paper laid out on my desk and a can in the middle. I shrugged and started to cut the paper. "Wrapping olives."

"Uh. Why?"

I reached into the plastic bag sitting on my chair and held up the item I'd bought on my lunch hour. "How do you think I should wrap these? I don't have a box."

Devin's bushy brows drew together. "You want to wrap men's black socks?"

I set down the scissors and folded the red-and-white candy-cane-striped wrapping paper around the can. "Well, I can't send the olives looking festive and not the socks."

She plucked the socks from my hand and rolled them into a ball. "I have two brothers. My dad used to give me twenty bucks to buy each of them a gift at the holidays. Every year they got socks from the sale rack for a buck, and I used the rest of the money to buy makeup. They wrap best folded like this, into a ball."

"Oh. Smart."

Devin leaned against my desk and moved the tape dispenser closer to me. "So who are the olives and socks for? New guy I don't know about?"

I shook my head. "No, they're for Birdie."

"*Ohhhhh.* Birdie." She nodded as if it all made sense. "Who the hell is Birdie?"

"She's a little girl who wrote to the *Holiday Wishes* mailbox. I want to make some of her wishes come true."

"And she wished for men's black socks and olives?"

"Yep. And a special friend for her dad. Her mom died of cancer a few years ago. So sweet."

Devin frowned. "That sucks. But what's her dad look like?"

"How should I know?"

She shrugged. "He's single. And is about to have clean socks. That's better than half the men you've gone out with lately already."

I chuckled. "True. But I don't think so."

"Suit yourself. His kid sounds like an odd duck anyway. Who asks Santa for olives?"

I stopped wrapping and looked at her. "When I was seven, I asked for a rooster because I wanted fresh brown eggs."

"But . . . roosters don't lay eggs."

"I didn't say I was the smartest seven-year-old."

Devin laughed as she walked out of my office. "I think you just made a case for why you *should* google Birdie's dad. Sounds like maybe you're a match made in heaven."

I never ended up googling anyone. In fact, after I sent Birdie the olives and socks, I wished her well in my mind and never gave it a second thought. That is, until another envelope showed up at the magazine about a week later. When I noticed her name on the return address, I immediately dumped the other mail and ripped that envelope open.

A photo fell out of the letter onto the floor. When I picked it up, what met my eyes was a beautiful little girl with golden hair and a bright smile that melted my heart. It was a wallet-size school photo. Wow. *This is her.* It felt surreal to be looking at the actual Birdie. She was so pretty, with kind eyes and, from everything I knew, a beautiful soul to match. I put the photo aside and read the letter.

> Dear Santa,
> Oh my God. Oh my God. Oh my God! You *are* real. You're really real. I got the olives and socks today. The holes fit on my fingers! Not the holes in the socks. The holes in the olives. The socks didn't have holes. My daddy's socks don't have holes anymore. They were so nice and soft. You should've seen him when he found the socks in his drawer! He still doesn't know how they got there. He said today must have been his lucky day because he found them. And I laughed. It was so funny! And then he took me to the ice-cream place next to his restaurant to celebrate our lucky day. I couldn't tell him that I was too full because I just ate a can of olives.
>
> Did I tell you my dad owns a fancy restaurant? People wear high heels to go eat there. I prefer to eat in my feetsy pajamas. But Dad makes me wear a dress on date night. That's on the first Tuesday of every month. Mom used to go with him. But now I do. It's my favorite day of the month. Not because I like to look all fancy and eat at Dad's restaurant but because after dinner, Dad comes home with me. He usually works really late.

Oh! And I also didn't tell him I wrote to you. He would've told me it was too early to write to Santa and that I shouldn't be greedy.

Last night, I told my dad that I really want someone else to braid my hair besides him. He doesn't know how to do it right. Then I caught him watching a YouTube video on how to braid. I told him I want the kind of braid that goes across the top of my head. The fancy one. He was watching someone make that kind of braid. If he tries to braid my hair like that, then I'm going to feel bad and let him do it. And I'll look silly.

Anyway, I just wanted to thank you for showing me that you're real.

Birdie Maxwell

P.S. I am sending you one of my school photos. They gave me a lot, and I have no one to give them to besides Dad and my grandmas.

P.P.S. I added something to my Christmas list. Did you ever hear of 23andMe? In school we made these big trees that showed all our parents and grandparents on all different branches. Mrs. Parker told us all about how you can spit in a tube and find people related to you going back hundreds of years. I want to add branches to my tree, enough to cover an entire wall in my bedroom! My tree was one of the skinniest in school because I don't have any sisters or brothers.

P.P.P.S. That wasn't me dropping a hint. I don't want you to buy it for me. My aunt always buys me dresses that I don't like, so I'm saving that for her to get me this year!

I let out a long breath and kept staring at the photo. Birdie really could have been me at her age. We had so much in common, from our blonde hair to . . . well, our dead moms.

And her note about the braids totally brought back memories of my own dad trying in vain to do my hair way back when. He'd get so frustrated and give up. Then I'd end up going to school looking like Pippi Longstocking.

Yup. Her dad reminded me of mine. We were both lucky to have men like that in our lives. I felt for Mr. Maxwell, whoever he was—someone doing the best he could to make his daughter's life as normal as possible.

When I returned to my desk with the mail, I attempted to work on my article for a bit before my mind began to wander. I started to think about Birdie again and suddenly switched my screen over to Google and typed in: *Birdie Maxwell.*

No.

Delete.

A few seconds later, temptation once again won out. I typed: *Birdie Maxwell New York, New York.*

I deleted it again.

What am I doing?

Just leave well enough alone.

Why do you need to know more about this poor girl and her father?

My heart raced as I typed again: *Birdie Maxwell New York, New York.*

Not sure what I was expecting, but the very first result was something I wasn't prepared for.

It was an obituary. I clicked into it.

At the top was a photo of a beautiful brown-haired woman with her arm around a little blonde girl—a younger Birdie.

Amanda Maxwell, age 32, of New York City passed away on December 23.

Amanda was raised in Guilford, Connecticut, and enjoyed summers growing up alongside her many cousins, all of whom grew up along the Connecticut shoreline. She enjoyed hosting large family parties at the home she shared with her husband and daughter.

Amanda attended Guilford High School before graduating from New York University, where she majored in business. It was there that she met the love of her life, Sebastian Maxwell. Amanda worked as a business analyst in Manhattan for several years before attending culinary school. She and her husband, Sebastian, eventually opened a five-star Italian restaurant in Manhattan.

Despite her successes, there was nothing Amanda loved more than being a mom to her darling daughter, Birdie, who was her entire world.

Amanda is survived by her husband, Sebastian, and young daughter, Birdie Maxwell of New York City; her mother, Susan Mello of Guilford, Connecticut; brother Adam Mello of Brooklyn, New York; sister Macie Mello of New Jersey; and many loving aunts, uncles, and cousins.

Amanda requested an intimate burial and funeral in Guilford. The family wishes to thank all of those who surrounded her with love during her last days. For

> those who wish to celebrate Amanda's life, visitation will be held at Stuart's Funeral Home on Main Street in Guilford on January 2 from 4 pm to 9 pm. In lieu of flowers, the family asks that you make a memorial donation to St. Jude Children's Research Hospital in Amanda's name.

Devin's voice startled me. "Are you crying?"

I wiped the tears falling from my eyes. "No."

"What happened?"

I grabbed a tissue and said, "It's that little girl . . . Birdie."

"What about her?"

"She . . . sent a thank-you letter with a school photo of herself. And I should've just read the letter and stopped there, but I ended up googling her name, and the first thing that popped up was her mother's obituary. The whole thing just hits really close to home."

"Ugh. I can imagine. I'm sorry." Devin looked at my screen, then scrolled up to the photo in the obituary, taking a few seconds to examine it.

I clicked on the icon at the top to exit out of it. "It's okay. Anyway, I need to just stop thinking about her and get to work."

"What did her letter say? I take it she got your olives?"

I reached for the envelope and handed it to her.

After Devin read Birdie's letter, she said, "Oh my God. She sounds so sweet. And the dad . . . looking up videos on how to braid hair? Swoon. I bet he's hot, too. I mean, the mom was so pretty."

Feeling oddly defensive, I said, "Will you stop with that?"

"Why?"

My reaction to her talking about the dad—like he was some piece of man candy—sort of caught me off guard. I think I was putting myself in Birdie's shoes. This whole thing was just such a sensitive subject. Was I sad for me? For Birdie? I didn't even know anymore.

You know how sometimes you merely think of something and suddenly you see ads all over social media for it, as if the advertisers somehow got inside your brain?

A few days after Birdie's letter came, I started seeing ads in my feed for these braided headbands made out of synthetic hair. Then once you click on the ad, forget it—they never stop showing them to you. Anyway, this headband looked just like a braid across the top of the head—the exact type of braid Birdie said she wanted.

Before I knew it, a week later, a box with the braided headband inside had arrived at my office address. I'd examined Birdie's photo to match the headband to the closest shade of blonde.

Taking the candy-cane-striped wrapping-paper roll out from under my desk, I wrapped the braid before addressing the box and sending it on to Eighty-Third Street.

CHAPTER 3

SADIE

Some days I worked in the office, and other days my assignments took me out. For my upcoming online dating feature, titled *Best Out of Ten*, I scheduled two dates a day for five consecutive days. To minimize the variables involved, I met all ten men at the same exact restaurant, even sitting at the same exact table. The idea of the piece was to determine whether quantity amounted to quality—whether you could find at least one good apple out of ten online prospects.

The answer for me, unfortunately, was no. Not a single one of my ten dates was someone I could see myself meeting again. One of the guys let me foot the entire bill after I offered to pay my half. Never even took out his card. When I asked if he wanted to split it, he informed me that *"funds are tight at the moment."* Another guy asked me if I minded letting him smell the inside of my shoe. Apparently, he had a foot fetish. The other eight were no better, each one displaying some characteristic that was a hard no for me.

So at the end of this particular week, I was more exhausted than usual when I stopped into the grocery store at the corner of my street. Days like this, I wished Cairo stocked alcohol in here, because I was too tired to make a separate stop at a liquor store tonight.

Perusing the aisles, I grabbed a bag of cheese puffs, Devil Dogs, a large bottle of Coke Zero, some Sour Patch Kids, and a frozen pepperoni pizza. It was going to be that kind of night.

When I got to the register, Cairo's eyes widened at the sight of my junk-food extravaganza.

As he rang up my stuff, he started to smirk like he always did while his mind was cooking up a new joke.

"Whaddya got for me tonight, Cairo?"

He came out with it. "What did the horny pizza say to the pepperoni?"

"What?"

"I like you on top." He laughed.

"Ah. Nice." Not sure if it was my mood today, but I found that one more annoying than amusing.

"You staying in tonight?" he asked. "No hot date?"

"I've had ten hot dates this week, if you can believe it, except they were more like hot messes. I've never been happier to spend a Friday night alone in my life." I ran my credit card through his machine and smiled. "Have a good weekend, Cairo."

As I carried my handle-less paper bag out of the grocery store, my text notification chimed. I reached into my purse and took out my phone as a breeze blew my skirt up, nearly exposing me to people passing by.

Devin: You never came back to the office after your assignment today, so I picked up your mail. You got another letter from that little girl, Birdie. I took it home with me if you want me to drop it by.

Shit. Did I want to get into that tonight? I knew it would make me emotional. I was better off just escaping into some Netflix and calling it a night. Yet, even though I knew what was best for me, I typed the opposite.

Sadie: Yeah. That would be great. I bought some junk food if you're down. Bring a bottle of wine.

Later that evening, Devin and I had finished off the pizza, half of the other snacks, a bottle of wine, and three episodes of *Stranger Things* before I decided to open the letter.

> Dear Santa,
> Thank you for sending the braid. I wasn't expecting to get anything else. I don't want you to think I told you about wanting a braid on the top of my head so you would send me one. I didn't even know they made braid headbands! It's so cool! You can't even tell it's not my hair!
>
> The first time I wrote to you, I only wanted to know that you're real. And you are. That's why I asked for olives. (But I did want socks for Dad.) The braid made me really happy. My dad saw me wearing it and asked me where it came from. I told him I got it from a friend. It's not really a lie. He seemed happy he didn't have to learn how to braid my hair anymore.
>
> I saw Dad talking to a lady the other night. It was weird. I was hungry, so I got out of bed to steal cookies, and he was on the couch, and there was a woman talking to him through the computer. I ran back to my room, because it scared me a little. I don't know why. He didn't see me. I know I was supposed to be in bed, but I wanted Oreos. I had them for breakfast instead.
>
> Anyway, I'm not gonna ask you for anything anymore. Not until Christmas.
>
> But I want to know if you can tell me something. Since the North Pole is pretty high up there, can you see heaven from where you are? Can you tell me if

my mom is okay? Can she see me? I talk to her all the time, but I don't know if she can hear me or see me. I asked her to send me a sign, but maybe she can't do what I asked for. Like, if I ask her to send me a butterfly or a bird, they are everywhere, and how do I really know it's her? My mom used to ride horses before she got sick. She rode this really pretty girl horse named Windy—because she ran like the wind. She was all black and had long blonde hair on her head and tail. Maybe I could ask her to show me a black horse running like the wind? That would be a way for me to know for sure Mom was okay. Can you see if you can get that message to her?

Thanks again, Santa.

Love you lots!

Birdie

P.S. I didn't give you my mom's name! It's Amanda Maxwell, and she has long brown hair (before she lost it, but she probably has it again), and she smells like the perfume Angel.

The wine I'd consumed wasn't beginning to help me process this one in the least. I didn't know whether to laugh or cry this time. So I was just—in shock.

Devin noticed the look on my face and said, "What does it say?"

I handed her the letter and let her read it for herself.

She handed it back to me. "What the hell are you supposed to do with this?"

I sighed. "I don't know."

"You know, you've really gotten yourself into something crazy here, Sadie. It's cute and all, but maybe you should've stopped at the olives, you know? Maybe you write her back and nicely close things off so she doesn't get hurt?"

"The thing is . . . I don't *write* to her. I've only *sent* her things. I don't know if it's a good idea to start corresponding back at this point. Honestly, it's been kind of fun brightening her days. Not sure I would change anything. I wouldn't have minded sending her more things, either, if it made her happy. But a black horse with long blonde hair running like the wind? I just can't make that happen."

As much as I thought I'd meant the words I'd just spoken, the wheels in my head were already turning.

I'd never been what I considered normal. I liked my hot dogs wrapped in white bread with crushed Doritos on top, rather than on a bun with ketchup. When I'm on a date and bored, I plot imaginary escape routes in my head—often envisioning myself hurdling a nearby table or springboarding over a car in the parking lot like an action hero. And don't even get me started on the insane lies I make up to strangers when I'm on a plane—once when I got bumped to first class, I told a woman I was a duchess of Belgium. But today, today might have taken the cake. At least I was going to have a future article in the bank—*Five Ten-Minute Dates*.

I'd told each date to meet me at a different location, starting at eleven o'clock.

Sam met me at Prospect Park in Brooklyn first. I'd presold each of them on the concept. We'd meet, set our phone alarms for ten minutes, and say goodbye at the beep. If either of us was interested, we'd wait twenty-four hours and send a text. If the recipient of the text didn't respond, they weren't interested. No fuss, no phony excuses . . . clean and simple. The only thing I hadn't mentioned to my five Sunday dates was the reason I'd picked each place.

Anyway, Sam was cute! The smile on my face as we walked around the park was genuine. Sure, I had an ulterior motive, to write an article and do some Birdie research—two birds, one stone. But finding true love was never out of the realm of possibility. So imagine my disappointment when I started walking with cute Sam and he spit. *Spit!* Not like *Oh my God, a bee flew into my mouth, get this thing out of here*. But he *hocked a loogie* and power shot it onto the ground in front of us.

Ugh.

What was next? Holding one nostril and blowing his nose onto the grass?

Our date was only ten minutes. He couldn't wait to do that? Maybe until like . . . *we were married* and I'd already found thirty-four special reasons to love him that overshadowed this major flaw?

Sayonara, Sam!

Date two took place at the Bronx Zoo, followed by date three at Bryant Park, then date four at Hudson River Park. Let me summarize those for you.

Dud. Dud. And dud.

I'd also not had any luck on what I'd dubbed Birdie Quest.

My fifth and final date for the day was to occur in Central Park. I was meeting Parker. I stood in front of Bethesda Fountain at exactly 5:00 pm. It was a crowded afternoon, but I didn't see a six-foot-tall man looking around for the woman of his dreams. As I waited, I took out my phone and called up a picture of Parker to make sure I remembered what he looked like. They were all starting to blur. After a few more minutes, I sat down and began to scroll through Instagram. At 5:20, I called it an afternoon. I'd officially been stood up. Four out of five wasn't bad, I suppose. Plus, I was anxious to check out my last stop on Birdie Quest for the day.

I walked the distance of around a dozen city blocks through the park and arrived at the ticket booth.

"Can I buy one ticket, please?"

The young kid behind the glass shook his head. "Closed. Last ride was at five. I'm just sorting things out for the day."

I looked over at the carousel. "Could I . . . just go inside and look at the horses for a minute?"

The kid didn't seem fazed by my request. He shrugged. "Whatever. But you'll have to hop the fence. Security locked it up already."

I glanced back at the carousel once again. There was a three-foot fence around it. It had been a long time since I did something like that. But hey, why not? "Okay."

Somehow I managed to scale the fence without ripping my jeans. I started to walk around the colorful carousel, looking for what was beginning to feel more like a unicorn than a black horse with long blonde hair. I made it almost halfway around when I stopped in my tracks.

Oh my God.

There it was.

It was perfect! I clapped my hands together. Not only was it a black horse with a blonde mane, but all four of its hooves were raised in the air like it was midgallop—running like the wind.

I hopped the fence a second time and ran back to the ticket booth. The kid was just locking up the door.

"Can I please buy a ticket?"

He frowned. "Told you. It's closed."

"I don't want to ride it now. I just want to buy a ticket. Two, actually."

"I already closed out the register."

I was so excited to have found my unicorn that I got a little carried away with myself. "I'll give you fifty dollars for two tickets."

The kid pointed to the sign stuck to the glass. "You know they're still only three twenty-five a ticket, right?"

"I do. But I really need the tickets. Do they expire?"

He shook his head. "Don't expire."

I opened my purse and pulled out a fifty-dollar bill. Flashing the cash always worked to close a street deal in New York. Well, either that, or they stole your wallet when you took it out, and then they bolted. But that had happened to me only once. I held up the fifty-dollar bill between two fingers.

"Fifty dollars. Won't take you more than a few minutes to open the register back up, I'm sure. Change is yours."

The kid plucked the bill out of my hand. "Be right back."

I felt like I'd won the lottery . . . overpaying for two carousel tickets by forty-three dollars and fifty cents.

Yup, I'd lost it.

After seven hours of traveling through three boroughs, four bad dates, and being stood up, I was giddy as I left the park with the tickets securely in my purse. I felt like I'd won a battle. But really, it was only half a battle. Because how the hell was I even going to get little Birdie to Central Park?

CHAPTER 4

SADIE

I decided to leave the rest up to fate. I know, I know . . . after all that searching for the black horse and bribing a ticket taker at the park, something still felt wrong about writing to this little girl. So I placed the two carousel tickets into a box, wrapped them with the candy-cane-striped Christmas paper, and mailed them off to her. If she went, she went. And even if she did go, there was no guarantee that she'd figure out what I'd been trying to lead her to see. With no letter and almost two weeks having passed, I figured perhaps my days of playing Santa were over for the summer.

Until . . . I saw Devin walking down the hall. She'd become almost as invested in the crazy Santa-Birdie saga as I was. Every day when she brought me my mail, she checked for a letter before she left the mail room. Her long faces told me nothing had come before she stepped foot into my office. But today . . . she was literally skipping to my office wearing a full-tooth smile.

"It's here!" She held up the envelope and waved it back and forth. "It's here!"

What the hell is wrong with the two of us?

I wasn't sure. But figuring it out was going to have to wait until I read the damn letter. I tore it open, and Devin came around my desk to read over my shoulder.

> Dear Santa,
>
> I love Central Park! I didn't know there was a carousel! I asked my dad if he could take me last weekend, but we didn't get to go because of the flood. Something happened to a rusty old pipe in the kitchen of his restaurant, and Magdalene had to come over. Magdalene's my babysitter. She asked me if I wanted her to take me instead, but I really wanted to go with Daddy. Last week, my teacher for next year mailed all the kids in my class a welcome letter, so I told him the teacher included the tickets with her card. Anyway, I go to dance class at nine every Saturday morning, and Daddy said we could go right after. So I'll get to go this weekend! Thank you for sending me the tickets for us.
>
> Also, I wanted to tell you something. Remember Suzie Redmond? The girl you gave the guinea pig to? I told you how she is the *worst* in my first letter. Well, it was me who cut her hair. She sits in front of me in class . . . and, well, I had a pair of scissors. But I only cut some of it off from the back. It's not even that much. She might not have noticed it if she hadn't found some of the red pieces that fell on the floor. Anyway, she deserved it. On Tuesday, I wore these pretty pink Crocs that Dad bought me. Suzie was standing in a big circle with all her friends when I walked up and she said, "Are those Crocs? I can't

believe your mom let you out of the house like that. Oh, wait. No wonder. You don't have a mom."

You might be wondering why I'm telling you about Suzie. You see, Dad makes me go to these religion classes on Sunday mornings. Last week, we talked about confession. You go to church, and you tell the priest all the things you did wrong, and then he tells you to say a few prayers, and it makes everything okay again. I was hoping you sort of worked the same way. Because I don't want you to find out and not bring Dad our special friend.

Thanks!

Love you lots!

Birdie

P.S. I also kept some of Suzie's hair, and it's in my jewelry box.

I started to crack up about three seconds before Devin.

"Oh my God. I freaking love this kid!" I said.

Devin laughed. "She thinks Santa works like the Catholic Church. Go murder someone, and Saint Pete still opens the pearly gates. Cut off a girl's hair and still get gifts from Santa!"

I had to wipe tears from my eyes. "Maybe I should write back and tell her to sing three 'Jingle Bells' and two 'Silent Nights.'"

We both had a good laugh, then Devin sighed. "God, that Suzie is a real piece of work, saying that to Birdie. I bet her mom is a real bitch, too."

"I know, right? What a little evil brat. I wish I were really Santa. I'd fill her stocking with coal this year and bring her nothing."

"And poor Birdie's dad. That guy can't catch a break. Dead wife, no taste in footwear, burst pipe." Devin's eyes went wide, and she held up her finger. The only thing missing from the picture standing before me was the bubble over her head with a light bulb. "I have an idea!"

I chuckled. "You don't say . . ."

"Let's go to Central Park on Saturday and stake out the carousel for Birdie and her dad. You'll get to see Birdie's expression if she notices the black horse, and I'll finally get to check out her dad. I just know he's going to be hot."

"We can't do that!"

"Why not?"

"Because . . . it's . . . I don't know. Creepy."

Devin leaned against my desk. "Ummm. Did you or did you not make me go with you to follow that guy Blake you went out with a few times home from work? The one who kept getting texts from someone named Lilly, and he told you it was his mother."

"It wasn't his mother! He was freaking married!"

"My point exactly. Sometimes being a creeper is necessary."

I shook my head. "I don't know. Following a child just feels icky."

"So pretend you aren't following Birdie. You're following her hot dad, like me!"

"I almost want to do it just to prove you wrong about her father." I pictured a guy sort of like my dad looked at the time my mom died. Yet for some reason, Devin thought he was going to be a supermodel.

She knocked her knuckles on my desk. "Prove me wrong, then. I'll be over at nine so we can get to the park by nine thirty. How long can dance class be? Forty-five minutes? An hour at most?"

"I don't know . . ."

Devin walked to my door and stopped. "See you tomorrow morning. And if you don't answer your door, I'm going all by myself."

"I cannot believe we are doing this."

Devin and I took the C train to Columbus Circle and stopped at Starbucks before walking over to the carousel. My partner in crime came dressed for surveillance, wearing head-to-toe black, dark sunglasses, and a wool cap . . . in *July*. We were lucky it was New York or she might look like the weirdo she is. I, on the other hand, had on jeans and an Aerosmith T-shirt. Because . . . you know . . . Steven Tyler and those *lips*. I didn't even care he was probably pushing seventy. I'd still suck on those babies.

We took a seat on a bench located to the right of the carousel—not directly in front of it but where we could still see everyone who walked in and out. As we got into position, I started to feel *really bad* about what we were about to do—invade little Birdie's privacy.

"Maybe we shouldn't do this."

Devin put her hand on my shoulder and applied pressure—just in case I tried to get up. "We're doing this. Don't even try to make a run for it."

I slouched back onto the bench. "Fine."

We sat for the better part of an hour, sipping coffee, gossiping about work, and looking around for a little girl and her dad. When I caught the time on my phone, I said, "It's after eleven. I don't think they're coming."

"Let's give it until eleven thirty."

I rolled my eyes. But screw it, we were in this far—I might as well go along with the rest of the ride. Otherwise, Devin would never let me hear the end of it. At eleven thirty on the dot, I stood. "Let's go, Lacey."

"Who?"

"*Cagney & Lacey*. It was a show my mom used to watch when I was little. It had two women detectives."

"Well, which one was hotter? Maybe I don't want to be Lacey."

I laughed. "You can be whichever one you want to be."

I turned to throw out my coffee cup in the basket next to the bench and was just about to start to leave when I spotted a little girl and a man who had just turned into the entrance of the park. They were pretty far off, but I thought it could be Birdie. "Oh my God. Sit! Sit! I think that's them."

The two of us planted our asses back on the bench at the same exact time. Devin leaned forward and squinted. "Are you sure?"

I grabbed her arm and pulled her to sit back. "Don't be so obvious."

We watched, while completely failing at looking casual, as the man and the little girl moved closer. The man was tall, broad-shouldered, and had on a pair of jeans and a T-shirt. He was holding the hand of the little girl. And she had on . . . a bodysuit and tutu. It was definitely Birdie!

"Oh my God. It's them!"

Neither of us said a word as the father and daughter approached the carousel. When they got close enough so I could finally see their faces, I gasped. "Oh my God. He's . . ."

Devin grabbed my hand. "I call dibs. I want to have his babies."

I couldn't believe my eyes. While I was expecting a modern version of my dad twenty years ago, the man standing before me was anything but. For the record, my dad is awesome, and he's not too shabby-looking. But this man . . . was . . . drop. Dead. Gorgeous. *Wow.* Just . . . yeah. Wow.

Sebastian Maxwell had dark hair, bone structure *to die for*, and full, beautiful lips. I'd joked how Devin thought the guy was a supermodel, but this man could actually *be* a supermodel. He had that longish, messy hair—the kind that he could drag a hand through, and it would look like he'd been both thoroughly fucked and just finished a photo shoot. Yeah, that was him. I was absolutely, positively speechless.

I'd been so preoccupied with ogling her father that I almost forgot the real reason I'd agreed to come—to see Birdie's reaction when she found the black horse. It took almost all my willpower, but somehow I managed to refocus my attention on the sweet little girl. The two of them gave the ticket collector their tickets, and I watched as they walked through the gate and toward the carousel. They made it about a quarter of a way around when Birdie pointed to a white horse and smiled. Her father lifted her into the air, climbed up onto the carousel, and swung her over the horse to plant her into the saddle.

Shit. She hadn't even passed the black horse to notice.

I felt deflated.

Though I got a boost to my morale . . . or something . . . when Birdie's dad bent to buckle his daughter onto the ride.

What an ass. I was a little jealous of the denim that hugged the curve of that tight derriere.

Sebastian hopped onto the horse next to his daughter, and the two of them proceeded to laugh as they waited for the ride to begin. Birdie giggled at her dad pretending to fall off his horse, and she petted the mane of her own plastic ride.

Once the carousel started to turn, Devin and I sat back into our seats. In all honesty, I forgot my friend was even sitting next to me for a few minutes.

"I think I'm in love." Devin covered her heart with her hand.

"You should probably let the man who put that obnoxiously huge rock on your finger know, then."

She smiled from ear to ear. "Say it. Devin Marie Abandandalo was right."

I rolled my eyes. "I guess he's kind of cute."

Devin burst into laughter. "You are *so* full of shit. You wish he was riding you right now instead of that plastic horse."

Well, it had been a while. "Shut up."

She grinned. "Sadie and Sebastian sitting in a tree. K-I-S-S-I-N-G. It even sounds great, doesn't it? Sadie and Sebastian. There's a ring to it. Like it could be a TV show, even. Sounds better than dumb *Corey and Lacey*."

"Cagney," I corrected.

Devin shrugged. "Whatever."

I sighed. "Birdie didn't see the black horse with the blonde mane."

"Eh. You'll send her a stuffed one and a live hamster to make up for it. Let's go back to talking about the hot dad."

The carousel ride lasted about five minutes, and when it slowed to a stop, the black horse was directly in front of me. I tapped Devin's arm. "There it is!"

"Maybe she'll notice it on the way out."

Birdie and her dad were nowhere in sight, so I figured the ride had stopped with them on the other side. The exit gate was only about two horses to the right, so if they came from the right, she wouldn't have a chance to even see the black one. I watched as people got off the ride and started to walk toward the gate. Unfortunately, when Birdie and Sebastian appeared, they were walking from the right side. They were the last two people to exit from the group they'd ridden with, and it looked like my attempts to play Santa Claus and God had all been for naught.

Until . . . a butterfly flew by Birdie as she was about to exit. She smiled and ducked under her dad's arm to chase it. Sebastian called after her as she took off, but she'd already run pretty far. When he called after her a second time in a deeper, more stern voice, she froze . . . directly in front of the black horse.

I literally held my breath.

I swear, the entire thing happened in slow motion after that.

Birdie turned around, seeming like she was going to walk away. But she must've caught sight of the black horse as she did. Her head whipped back, and her eyes grew as wide as saucers. Both hands came up to cover her open mouth. She stood there frozen for a long time. At least it felt like a long time. Until her dad walked over and grabbed her hand.

She said something to him I couldn't hear, and then they started to walk away. Birdie made it about three steps before she wiggled out of her dad's grip, ran back to the plastic horse, and kissed the mane on the horse that ran like the wind.

CHAPTER 5

SADIE

Watching that butterfly lead Birdie right to the horse had been truly magical. It was like the universe had intercepted to prove to me that if I thought I could control everything, I had another think coming.

Perhaps, somewhere up there, Amanda Maxwell was looking down on me and shaking her head. Maybe she thought it was about time she intervened to show me who *really* was in charge.

A part of me hoped that Birdie didn't write back, because it was starting to feel like I was playing God. I didn't want to have to continue to mislead her as much as I never wanted to disappoint her, either. This was honestly a great time to walk away from the situation—on a very happy note.

The Sunday afternoon after I'd seen Birdie in the park, I'd taken the train to Suffern to visit my father. It had felt like the perfect time to visit Dad. He was always good at offering insight when I felt stuck on something. Maybe he could give me his opinion on whether I'd taken things too far. Well, I *knew* I'd taken things too far, but I still wanted his opinion. And if I was being honest, I also wanted to pick his brain about what being a single dad had really been like all those years ago. There were certain things I would have never had the courage to ask him when I was younger. But now that I was older, I was curious about whether he dated more than I realized back then. I knew he'd had a couple of girlfriends in recent years, but had there been women I didn't know about growing up?

I suppose my curiosity stemmed from seeing Sebastian yesterday. A man like that must have had women throwing themselves at him left and right. Yet from what I could tell from Birdie's letters, he tried to be discreet so as not to interrupt their lives.

My father lived in the same house I grew up in. It was still brown on the outside, although the paint was flaking a bit now. The house had a large front porch with hanging plant pots. While our house certainly wasn't the biggest in town, we had an incredible amount of land. Dad had the most amazing garden, and this was the time of year he'd be pawning tomatoes off on all the neighbors because he had so many, he didn't know what to do with them.

Dad would always calculate the exact time it would take for me to arrive based on my train. As usual, he was standing at the door waiting for me.

He gave me a huge hug. "How's my Sadie?"

Looking up at something dangling near the top of the door, I said, "I've been really good. I see you made a new contraption?"

My father loved to create instruments that he believed could predict the weather. Even though there was plenty of technology in this day and age to do so, he preferred to build tools from scratch that he swore were just as good if not better than the best Doppler radar. He would give them cute names, too.

"What's this one called?" I asked.

"The humbug."

"What does that stand for?"

"The 'hum' comes from the fact that the strip of paper right there expands when it becomes more humid. The more it expands, the more chance for a storm. The 'bug' just sounded good with 'hum.'"

"You're so funny." I smiled.

The interesting thing was, I remember the weather-instrument hobby starting not too long after my mother died. It was his way of keeping his mind occupied, perhaps, so that it didn't wander to things that were too painful.

"I just put on a fresh pot of coffee," he said as I followed him inside.

"Ohhhh, a fresh pot," I teased. "To what do I owe this honor? I must be someone special."

I always joked with my dad whenever he made a fresh pot of coffee, because normally he made only one large pot in the morning for himself and poured from the same carafe throughout the course of the entire day. He'd just nuke it in the microwave. But he knew I liked my java fresh, so he'd suck it up and dump out the old coffee before making a new pot whenever I came over. I tried to buy him one of those Keurig machines once so that he could have fresh mugs of coffee all day, but he said he didn't mind his coffee a little burned and stale and preferred not to contribute to the environmental hazard of plastic waste.

On the counter was a gigantic bowl of tomatoes in varying shades of red, green, and orange along with a lineup of cucumbers and peppers on some paper towel.

"Let me guess . . . cucumber and tomato salad for lunch?"

"With feta and olives." He winked. "And warm pita bread from the bakery."

My stomach growled. "Mmm. That sounds so good."

There was nothing like the comfort of home. Even though this house brought about painful memories, there were many good ones. Lazy lunches on a Sunday with my father definitely fell into the good category.

He sat down across from me. "So what brings you home early? I thought you weren't coming until next weekend?" he asked as he poured a mug of coffee and handed it to me.

"Yeah, well, I've sort of had an issue at work that made me think of you."

"Hope it wasn't one of those foolish men you date."

"No." I laughed. "Although *that* situation really hasn't improved." I sighed. "This came from the *Holiday Wishes* column. You know, the one I normally get assigned around the holidays?"

"Yeah, sure."

"Well, there's this little girl who sent a letter in to the column even though it's summer, and it's set off a chain of interesting events."

Over two cups of coffee, I spent the next several minutes telling my father the story of Birdie and her letters. He listened intently and, as expected, found the entire thing quite endearing.

He shook his head as he poured more coffee for himself. "I can't get over that adorable name. It sounds like something I would name one of my weather instruments."

"Yeah . . . she's adorable like you would imagine a Birdie to be, too." I shook my head. "I'm very confused, though."

"Are you wondering whether you should keep it going if she writes back?"

"I'm definitely torn over that. The other thing is, this whole situation has actually got me thinking a lot about my own childhood. Because of how similar Birdie's and my situations are."

"It's definitely eerie that she lost her mother around the same age as you."

"Yeah." I sighed, then after a few seconds of inner debate, I decided to bring up the subject I'd been very curious about. "She mentioned in one of her letters that she'd gotten up in the middle of the night and caught her dad chatting with a woman on his laptop. She said it scared her, and she ran back to bed. It made me wonder whether you used to date when I was small. I always assumed you weren't with any women at the time, because you didn't do it in front of me. I suppose that might have been naive."

My father looked down into his cup and nodded. "I'll never love anyone like I loved your mother. You know that. No amount of dating in those years was gonna erase that." He looked up at me again. "But loneliness does set in eventually. And there were times I'd tell you I was going to play poker with the guys or that I was heading over to your uncle Al's when I'd really be meeting up with a lady."

I nodded, taking that revelation in for a moment. "Around what age was I then?"

"It was probably about four years after Mom died, so maybe ten? The first couple of years, I hadn't been able to even consider looking at another woman. But once I hit that three-year mark, well, it became about a man having needs. It had nothing to do with wanting to move on from your mother. You know what I mean?"

It was hard to imagine my dad having sex, but unfortunately, I knew exactly what he meant. "Of course. I understand that now. And it's not like you could have explained casual sex to me back then. If I'd seen you with a woman, I would've assumed you were trying to replace my mother. It would've upset me."

"Well, that's what I figured. So . . . I tried not to open up a can of worms. But honestly, if I had found someone special, I might have brought her around eventually, because it would've been nice for you to have a positive female influence in your life."

I stared off, thinking about the fact that I did definitely crave a female influence the older I became. "There did come a time, as I got into my early teen years, when I really did wish that you could have found someone . . . not only for you but for me."

"It wasn't in the stars. I had the great love of my life, even if it wasn't for long enough. And now . . . I don't need anyone else besides you." He smiled and knocked a few times on the table with his knuckles. "And I beat cancer. What more can I ask for?"

When I was a teenager, my father had been diagnosed with colon cancer. I remember thinking his diagnosis was the end of my life, because if I had lost my father in addition to my mother, how could I possibly go on? He was my everything. Thank God, by some miracle, the treatments worked and my father remained in remission to this day.

Dad got up and walked over to the nearly empty carafe, then lifted it. "Want another cup?"

"No. Unlike you, I can't drink an entire pot of coffee without repercussions. Pretty sure if they popped a needle in your vein, all that would come out is Maxwell House."

Maxwell House.

Maxwell.

That had just hit me.

The can had been sitting on the counter this whole time, but I'd only now made the connection between Birdie's last name and the brand of coffee my father always used.

Maxwell House.

I wondered what the real *Maxwell house* was like. Then, of course, my mind wandered to Sebastian Maxwell—his gorgeous face and hair. The way he'd doted on his daughter at the park. Birdie said he owned a restaurant—I wondered what that was like.

"You still with me?" my dad asked, snapping me out of my daydream.

"Yeah. I was just thinking . . ."

"About Birdie?"

"Indirectly, yeah." I drank the last drop of coffee and sighed. "Anyway, I hope she doesn't write back. As much as I loved making those little wishes come true, I can't keep doing it forever—playing God."

He smiled. "Speaking of God, I don't pray for much besides health these days, but I do pray that one of these losers you take for a ride as part of your job actually ends up surprising you and turns out to be a decent man. I don't want to have to worry about you when I'm gone someday."

"I can take care of myself just fine. I don't need a man."

"It's not about finances. I know you're a strong, independent woman, honey, but the truth is . . . everyone needs someone. The only reason I was okay after your mom died was because I had you."

"Well, it's a good thing my daddy isn't going anywhere anytime soon." I winked.

My visit with Dad lasted a few hours. After I'd stuffed myself with the yummy food he'd laid out for me, I called a car to take me back to the train station. Since Dad and I had shared a bottle of wine over lunch, I didn't want him driving me.

When my father walked me out to wait for my Uber, he looked up at his weather apparatus.

He scratched his chin. "Hmm."

"What?"

"Humbug says it's gonna rain."

Sure enough, as I traveled home that afternoon, the storm my father predicted came through, pelting the windows of the train. Then, after, a beautiful recurrence of the late-afternoon sun shined over the New York City skyline in the distance, filling me with hope and, much to my dismay—continued thoughts of Sebastian Maxwell.

CHAPTER 6

Sadie

I typed.

Sebastian Maxwell restaurant.

The keys clicked as I immediately deleted the words.

No, I can't go there.

After a few seconds of staring at Google, I typed again.

Sebastian Maxwell restaurant New York.

This time, instead of deleting it, I hit "Enter."

The *About Us* section of a website popped right up in the search results.

Bianco's Ristorante.

I read it.

> Bianco's Ristorante was founded in 2012 by Sebastian Maxwell, a New York City entrepreneur and his wife, Amanda, a master chef. The Maxwells were heavily inspired by Sebastian's paternal grandmother, Rosa Bianco, who emigrated from Northern Italy in 1960. Over the years, Sebastian saved all his nonna's recipes and today, together with head chef Renzo Vittadini, has crafted one of the most decadent menus in all of

> the tristate area, boasting old-world recipes infused with a modern flair. Bianco's top-notch cuisine coupled with its dimly lit, rustic ambience makes your night out more than just a meal—it's a culinary experience.
>
> From intimate dinners to private events, contact us to make a reservation.

I clicked over to the menu tab.

Each entrée was named after a person. Renzo's Ricotta Pie, Nonna Rosa's Chicken Parmesan, Birdie's Pasta Bolognese, Mandy's Manicotti.

Mandy.

Amanda.

Sebastian's Saltimbocca.

They had an extensive wine list.

"Whatcha doin'?"

I jumped at the sound of Devin's voice from behind. "You scared me."

"Why did you tab over to another screen just now?"

"No reason. You know . . . I'm not really supposed to be goofing off."

She smirked. "What's Bianco's?"

Great. She'd caught the name at the top of the tab.

I let out a long breath but tried my best to still sound nonchalant. "It's Birdie's dad's restaurant."

"Nice!" She laughed, all too pleased with my apparent weakness. "You know I'm down with the stalking—especially the stalking of that amazing-looking specimen."

"I know you fully support it. But I feel stupid doing it."

"But a part of you can't help it, right?"

I shrugged. "He's intriguing."

Her eyes filled with excitement, like a giddy kid who'd just found out the carnival was coming to town. "So when are we going? I'm suddenly craving a nice big bowl of al dente pasta."

"Oh, no. That's where I draw the line. Online stalking is one thing. That's a leisurely pastime. Innocent, even. But showing up in person? No." I shook my head. "No, no, no."

"It's a public restaurant. How is that stalking?"

Rustling some of the papers on my desk, I said, "Devin . . . drop it."

"Would you care if I checked it out, then? Armando and I have been looking for a new place to try."

"Are you going to tell your fiancé that the real reason you're taking him there is to check out the hot owner?"

She waved her hand dismissively. "He doesn't have to know that. He loves food. He'll be thrilled." Devin leaned over to my computer. "Can you make a reservation online?"

"I don't know. I didn't check because I had no intention of going."

"Let me see," she said, grabbing my mouse and maximizing the screen before perusing the site. "Ah." She grinned.

"What are you doing, Devin?"

She proceeded to type in all her information. "The only opening was 5:00 pm on Saturday. Looks like everything beyond that is taken. Good thing I love early-bird specials like an old person anyway."

Shaking my head, I said, "You're nuts."

She winked. "I'll let you know if I spot him."

Two weeks passed, summer was coming to an end soon, and no more letters from Birdie had arrived. Devin and Armando ended up having that amazing and very expensive dinner at Bianco's—with no sign of Sebastian Maxwell whatsoever. *That's what she gets for trying to stalk him.*

Because it had been a while, I'd been pretty convinced that I wouldn't hear from Birdie again.

Then one afternoon, much to my surprise, in the middle of my usual stack of mail was a letter from my little friend.

My pulse raced as I ran to my desk, dumped the rest of the mail down, and ripped open the envelope.

> Dear Santa,
> Did Mommy tell you she came to visit me at Central Park? I know you gave her my message because there was a black horse like I told you about on the carousel. She sent a butterfly to lead me to it. I don't know if she sent a butterfly or if the butterfly was really her? Anyway, it was so amazing. I miss her so much.
>
> But can you ask her why she isn't trying to come see me anymore? I keep looking for her, and she hasn't given me any more signs. Now that you reached her and she found a way back, I thought she would want to spend more time with me.
>
> I'm worried she might be mad at me now that she can see me. Maybe she knows what I did to Suzie's hair or that I sometimes steal cookies in the middle of the night.
>
> Can you just tell her to send me one more sign so I know she's not mad? Even if she can't stay?
>
> I'm sorry to bother you again, Santa. This will be the last time. I promise.
>
> Birdie

As I folded the letter while tears streamed down my cheeks, I realized that maybe Birdie wasn't the only person who needed help anymore.

It had been a long time since I'd visited my shrink, Dr. Eloisa Emery. Her office overlooked Times Square, which I always found ironic, since the view from her window was just about the most chaotic thing I could imagine. Definitely not a relaxing atmosphere for a therapy appointment. During my sessions, I'd stare out at the massive, ever-changing digital billboard as I attempted to gather my thoughts.

I'd been suspecting I needed my head checked for some time, and today I was taking that literally, sharing the story of Birdie and hoping that Dr. Emery could help me move past everything.

I'd just finished telling her about our letters and ended on the most recent one I'd received.

"The tone of this one seemed more panicked," I said. "She was truly worried that she'd done something to keep her mother's spirit away. There was no usual P.S. at the end, either, so the overall tone was a bit short. It made me realize that I had really made things worse in setting her up to find that horse, even if it was the butterfly that ultimately led her there."

She pulled off her glasses and set them on her leg. "So you're feeling lots of guilt."

"Yes, of course. Now there's an expectation for more from her mother when there *isn't* anything more. I started a mess. Her mother's dead, and any implication that Birdie could still communicate with her is misleading."

Dr. Emery put her glasses back on and scribbled a few things down in her notebook before looking up at me again. "Sadie, I think it's going to be important for you to learn to accept the fact that you can't change anything you've done thus far. You know now that playing with fate the way you have, as charming as it was, is really not the wisest idea. So I do think you need to really rip the Band-Aid off here."

My hands felt sweaty as I rubbed them along my legs. "What do you mean by that exactly?"

"You seem incapable of not engaging whenever she contacts you. I think on some level, you're so invested because she reminds you of yourself, so it's almost like you've been given this opportunity to do for someone else what wasn't done for you. And that was hard to resist. You're also connecting with your inner child a bit. But now you know that engaging is harmful. And the more you engage, the harder it's going to be to stop. So perhaps, if she contacts you again, you should not open the letter at all."

Shaking my head repeatedly while staring out the window, I said, "I can't do that."

"Why not?"

"Because I have to at least know she's okay . . . even if I don't engage."

"She doesn't know you exist. She doesn't know you have developed feelings for her. Therefore, your feelings, no matter how strong, do not impact her. If you're not communicating back with her and if you've vowed to no longer interfere by pretending to be Santa Claus, then you mustn't involve yourself in any way in her life. That includes reading her letters." She tilted her head. "Can you do that? Can you cut all ties for your own good and, ultimately, the good of this little girl?"

I gazed out at the billboard and watched it change approximately three times before I finally said, "I'll try."

CHAPTER 7

Sadie

It had been almost a month since my last letter from Birdie. I'd followed Dr. Emery's advice and not written back to my little friend, even going as far as putting Devin on mail patrol—asking her to weed out my daily delivery of any new letters that Birdie might send. Though I'd broken down on more than one occasion, demanding to know if any had come, and Devin swore that she hadn't had to intervene. Lately, I'd even stopped dwelling on whether my letters had done more harm than help. But today wasn't one of those days, though for good reason.

I had an appointment on Eighty-First Street with a professional matchmaker—not for me personally but research for the magazine. Next month, I planned to write an article on the pros and cons of using a service, and today was my first interview. Kitty Bloom ran the agency I'd visited and gave me tons of great information for the piece. She'd also given me a free thirty-day membership—which went for a staggering $10,000. Although if I wanted to give it a whirl, I'd have to submit a ton of personal information—from medical clearances and a psychological profile to financial statements and a detailed questionnaire that asked about everything from my hobbies to my fetishes and sexual appetite. I accepted the gift but wasn't sure I wanted someone poking their nose into my business.

It was a beautiful evening, so I decided to take a walk. The matchmaker's office was on the ground floor of a block filled with beautiful brownstones, and the Upper West Side was one of my favorite neighborhoods that I could never afford. I was on the corner of Broadway and Eighty-First Street, and Birdie lived somewhere on Eighty-Third Street, which could be close by.

I really shouldn't.

I'd been so good lately.

But . . . I'm already here . . .

What harm could it do just to pass by?

I'd taken an Uber uptown because I'd been running late, but I could grab the train back downtown from a few different nearby stations. So it wasn't like I'd really be going out of my way if I strolled for a bit in any direction. I could just walk up Eighty-Third, and if I happened to pass Birdie's house on my way to the train, then that was fate. I remembered her house number, only because it was my parents' anniversary, February 10, or 210, but I had no idea what block it crossed with. So it really was up to chance whether I passed it or not. If I reached a train before I came upon Birdie's house, then I'd get to see her house. Big whoop-de-do.

Yet . . . it felt so wrong.

Especially as I turned down Eighty-Third Street and caught the number on the first house I passed: 230.

Oh my God.

Eighty-Third Street ran forever. It had to be at least a half mile on the west side alone, from Central Park down to near the Hudson River . . . yet the very first block I turned onto happened to be the one that Birdie lived on.

It sort of freaked me out a little bit.

My blood started to pump faster with every step.

228.

226.

224.

It was one of the next eight or so houses up ahead.

Damn, the neighborhood was really nice. Birdie lived on a tree-lined street of brownstones worth some serious money. I didn't know why, but I had envisioned her living in an apartment building, cramped for space like the rest of us in the rat race, not in such a luxurious home. These things went for millions. Even if they didn't own it and only rented a floor out, it would still be big bucks.

I started to slow down as I counted the addresses.

220.

218.

216.

Birdie's house was only three more away.

When I came right upon hers, my heart started to beat so fast. I slowed my walking speed and tried to get a look inside the windows. But it was about ten steps up to the front door from the sidewalk, and I couldn't really see much from down here. Disappointment came over me. A few steps after passing the staircase that led up to Birdie's front door, I forced myself to stop staring like I'd been casing the place for a potential robbery. As I looked down, something shiny caught my eye out of my peripheral vision, sitting on the bottom step of the stairs.

Is that?

No . . . it couldn't be.

I looked around—no one seemed to be paying any attention. So I backed up and bent down to take a closer look.

My eyes widened.

Oh my God.

A silver hair barrette was lying on the bottom step, the kind a little girl would wear to clip back her hair when her father sucked at making braids. And . . . it had a silver butterfly on it.

Butterflies.

Birdie.

There was no doubt that the two went together.

Without thinking, I picked it up.

Only . . . what the hell was I going to do with it once it was in my hand?

I supposed putting it somewhere safer would be the right thing to do. The pretty little clip could just blow away out here on the last step. Or, at the very least, someone could step on it and break it.

It didn't look like anyone was home in the Maxwell house anyway. I could just leave it at her front door.

Yeah . . . that was a good idea.

The fact that I might get a better look inside the windows from up at the top of the stairs was just a coincidence. I was doing the right thing, after all, making sure Birdie's little barrette didn't get broken. She could be attached to this thing, for all I knew. Glancing around again, I noticed there was also a door underneath the main staircase, a few steps down from ground level. Maybe the Maxwells lived in the basement apartment? Though my gut didn't think they did.

So I took a deep breath and started up the brownstone stairs. My knees wobbled a bit as I climbed to the top one. God, I really was nervous.

From the sidewalk, I hadn't realized how tall the front doors were—the double set of ornate glass doors had to be at least ten feet, maybe more. Looking to my left, I could see right into the front window, which gave me a partial view of a big living room. A man's suit jacket was lying over the top of a chair across from the sofa, and I wondered if it belonged to Sebastian. I stood there staring for a long moment, trying to pick up any small details I could see—the titles of the books on the bookshelf, the photos inside the frames on the mantel—until suddenly the curtain moved.

Someone was home!

I felt all the color drain from my face.

Oh my God.

I need to get the hell out of here!

Panicking now, I looked for a place to leave the hair clip. Finding nowhere suitable, I balanced it on the top of the doorknob, thinking someone would either see it or, if they didn't, it would fall to the floor when the door opened and snag their attention.

Then I started to haul ass back down the stairs. My heart was pounding so fast, it felt like I was running from the scene of a crime instead of doing a good deed returning a little girl's favorite hair clip.

I made it only a few steps when I heard a clanking sound from behind me—the sound of a lock opening. Freaking out, I kept going . . . until a deep voice stopped me in my tracks.

"Hey. You. What are you doing?"

Oh. My. God.

I closed my eyes. *That voice.* Of course, I'd only heard Sebastian Maxwell speak briefly at the carousel, yet I was 100 percent positive it was him. That deep, rich, sexy baritone rasp totally went with the rest of the package.

When I didn't respond, he snapped again. The second time louder.

"I said, where are you running to?"

I took a deep breath, realizing I was going to have to face the consequences of my actions, and slowly turned around.

Jesus Christ. Sebastian was even better up close. It looked like he'd just gotten out of the shower. His hair was wet and slicked back, and he had on a simple white T-shirt and gray joggers. Standing so close, I became mesmerized by the color of his green eyes—they were so unusual, not hazel or the green color that most people have, which resembles jade or moss, but the bright color of a brilliant emerald, and the areas surrounding his pupils were filled with flecks of gold.

"You're late," he barked.

"Uh . . ."

"The bell isn't working. I have to fix it this weekend. So you're going to have to knock a little harder and be on time if you want this job. I have to leave for work in five minutes."

"Job?"

"You are the dog trainer, aren't you?"

His beautiful eyes were boring into me, and it made me more than a little nervous. In the moment, I felt like he could see straight through me and was going to think that I was some sort of a crazed stalker of his ten-year-old daughter. I mean, I was, of course, but there was no way I wanted him to think that. So I panicked.

"Umm. Yes. Sorry I'm late. Umm. Traffic."

What the hell am I doing?

He motioned toward the house. "Well, hurry up. Let's go. I don't have all day. I'll introduce you, and then you're on your own. Have him back in an hour. The babysitter will be here by then, and she'll take him when you return. Whatever commands need to be learned for homework, teach them to Magdalene. She's here more than I am anyway."

I hesitated but began to walk back up the stairs again. My knees shook more and more with each one. When I got to the front door, Sebastian was already inside. I took a few cautious steps into the vestibule, and out of nowhere, I was attacked.

Alright. So "attacked" might not be the right word. But I was suddenly knocked on my ass, with two giant paws pressed to my chest holding me down. And the biggest tongue I'd ever seen began to slurp the side of my face.

"Marmaduke," Sebastian yelled. The giant black-and-white-spotted Great Dane looked over his shoulder and practically laughed at the big, angry man looking down at him. He then proceeded to go back to licking my face.

After the shock wore off, I was somehow able to push the behemoth off me. I wiped the saliva from my face and climbed to my feet, only to find Sebastian looking not so happy. *What the hell?* I was the one who had just gotten pillaged, not him.

He put his hands on his hips. "I seriously hope that wasn't a demonstration of your training skills. You had less control over him than I do."

I got annoyed. "What do you expect? He knocked me over without warning. Nice of you to extend a hand to help me up, by the way."

Sebastian scowled. "You don't look German."

I dusted off my pants. "Well, that's probably because I'm not."

He squinted at me. "Then why do you teach your training commands in German?"

Oh shit. "Umm." I blinked a few times before pulling an answer out of my ass. "Please don't start questioning my methods already. If you don't want me to train your dog, who clearly needs training that you're not capable of providing, then say so, and I'll just be on my way."

The corner of Sebastian's lips twitched upward. "Fine. I'll get his leash."

Seriously? What the hell was I doing? I had needed a visit to Dr. Emery to discuss my actions surrounding a little girl who had written to Santa. What did pretending to be a dog trainer who taught commands in German warrant, then? Being institutionalized? Lord, how the hell did I get myself here?

Sebastian came back with the leash and handed it to me. I was surprised when he softened his tone and extended his hand. "I apologize. I didn't introduce myself. That dog just gets the best of me sometimes. I'm Sebastian Maxwell, and I assume you must be Gretchen."

Gretchen. Of course! Because the woman *not* from Germany who trains in German would logically be named Gretchen. I put my hand into his large one and shook. The minute my skin made contact with his, my pulse took off like a runaway train. When his grip tightened around my hand, it sent a shock of electricity up my arm. Great, more unsettling behavior to discuss with Dr. Emery—though it did make sense that I lit up like a Christmas tree, since I was damn Santa Claus. I'd need a loan to pay for my therapy sessions after today.

Pulling my hand back, I focused on getting the hell out of there. Apparently, I'd be taking my new student with me. I managed to clasp the end of the leash onto Marmaduke's collar and did my best impersonation of a professional animal handler. "Okay. So I'll be back in an hour." I tugged at the giant dog's collar, and amazingly, he followed. Just to solidify that I was totally losing it, I turned back at the top of the steps and smiled at Sebastian Maxwell. *"Danke."*

After I said it, I started to question whether that was even German for "thank you" or not. Oh well, too late if it wasn't. Marmaduke bolted down the stairs, and I had to run to keep up. At the bottom, I stood my ground and yanked hard on his leash.

"Whoa . . . ," I said.

Shit. Whoa? That was for a horse and in English, wasn't it? I looked over my shoulder and back up the stairs, hoping Sebastian had gone back inside and hadn't heard me. Of course, I had no such luck.

Sebastian stood at the top of the stairs watching me. He looked really damn skeptical.

Yeah, you and me both, dude. You and me both.

Marmaduke and I went to a nearby park that had a doggy run, which meant I could let him off the leash in the fenced-in area while I googled *dog training.*

I spent a good half hour reading up on the basics of schooling a dog on obedience and then asked Google for reasons to train a dog in German. Surprisingly, it was more common than I would've guessed. Many people trained dogs in the native language of the breed. And who knew . . . a Great Dane wasn't actually Danish—it was of German descent. So that made sense, I guess. Plus, training in a foreign language made it easier for the animal not to get confused when others used common words near them. I also looked up a couple of words for basic training in German. *Sitz*, pronounced *zitz*, meant "sit." *Platz*, pronounced *plah-tz*, meant "down," and *nein*, pronounced *nine*, meant "no." I figured Marmaduke desperately needed those three words in his life.

The one good thing about a big puppy with a lot of energy was that he wore himself out pretty fast. Once he seemed more subdued, I took him out of the doggy area and went and found a quiet tree to sit under and work on training him.

He laid his enormous body across my legs. I petted him as I spoke. "So, Marmaduke, tell me about the people you live with. Is Sebastian as much of a jerk as he seemed like back at the house? He's definitely not anything like I'd expected him to be after hearing about him from Birdie." When I said "Birdie," Marmaduke started to wag his tail. I wanted to see if it was a coincidence or not. So I waited until his tail stopped wagging and then talked to him a little more. "Yeah. So I expected a really nice guy, maybe soft-spoken, even though he's clearly a big dude like you. But Sebastian's kind of a meanie, isn't he?"

Nothing. Marmaduke just kept looking at me, but his tail didn't budge.

"I really hope he doesn't talk to *Birdie* like the way he spoke to us."

The minute I said "Birdie," the dog's tail took off wagging. I smiled and scratched his ears. "Yeah, I get it, buddy. I could tell she was really special just from her letters. I'm glad you're there to protect her."

Birdie had written in one of her first letters that she'd asked for a dog for Christmas and Santa hadn't brought her one. So I couldn't help but wonder what made her father get one now. Was some stalker lurking around the neighborhood, and he felt she needed some protection when he wasn't home? Well, some stalker other than me, that is. I hoped that wasn't the case.

I really needed to teach this dog something today, because it was almost time to bring him back already. But most of the training information I'd read said you needed dog treats. So I improvised. I dug around inside my purse for whatever I had that might be a decent substitute. Unfortunately, I didn't come up with too many choices—only one stick of gum and a KIND bar, which was mostly nuts. Since half the world seemed to be allergic these days, I googled *can dogs eat nuts* to be safe. They could but needed to avoid macadamia and walnuts. After checking out the ingredients of my KIND bar, I shoved the stick of gum in my mouth and stood. Marmaduke stood right along with me. I broke the KIND bar into a few pieces and showed him one.

"Sit," I said sternly. "Oh wait, no. *Sitz.*"

The dog just looked at me. I sighed and called up one of the better articles I'd read on dog training and scanned for the section on teaching a dog to sit.

Step one. Kneel directly in front of your pet.

Great. Grass stains on my white pants. I took a deep breath and dropped to my knees anyway.

Step two. Holding the treat in your hand, let your dog see their reward, then bring it to their nose.

That seemed kind of mean. I hoped Marmaduke wouldn't lunge for my fingers and take a few of those along with the KIND bar for taunting him. But he didn't. Hmm . . . maybe the person who drafted this article was onto something. So I continued.

Step three. Tuck the reward into your hand and raise your hand upward. Tell your dog to sit.

I tucked the chunk of nut bar into my palm, then spoke in a stern voice. *"Sitz!"*

Holy shit.

Marmaduke sat.

He actually sat!

I gave him the treat and scratched behind both of his ears. "Good boy. You're a good boy."

By the time I left the park to head back to the Maxwell house to return my prized student, he'd followed my command at least five times. The very last time, I didn't even have a treat in my hand. The moment I raised my arm, he simply parked his ass on the grass. I couldn't believe it. But while I'd managed to accomplish one small task, I definitely was not a professional trainer. And I needed to nip this craziness in the bud. My meddling in Birdie's life had already caused enough damage. I was supposed to be stepping back from interfering, not diving into it headfirst. Though I had to admit, I was really excited to get to meet the sweet little girl. And the fact that I was returning to the sitter and not Sebastian made me feel way less stressed than I would've been if I'd had to face him again.

I arrived on Eighty-Third Street a few minutes later than the time I was supposed to return. Stopping to take a few deep breaths, I recomposed myself and headed up the flight of stairs to the Maxwell brownstone. I rang the bell and waited, but no one came to the door. After a minute, I remembered what Sebastian had said about the bell being broken and that I needed to knock loudly. So I did.

A pleasant-looking woman who was probably in her midfifties answered the door. With her warm smile, she wasn't nearly as intimidating as the guy I'd had to deal with earlier.

"You must be Gretchen," she said.

I nodded. "Yup, that's me. Gretchen the dog trainer."

She stepped aside. "Come in. I'm Magdalene. Mr. Maxwell said I should learn anything that we need to work on at home to help with Marmaduke's training."

I looked around as I entered. The house was quiet. No sign of either Sebastian or Birdie. "Umm. Is Mr. Maxwell home? Everyone is welcome to join in on the training."

She shook her head. "No. He left for work. He works nights. But his daughter and I are anxious to work on the training. He's her dog."

My heart did an unexpected little flutter at the mention of Birdie. "His daughter's dog. Oh, okay. Can she join us?"

Magdalene shook her head. "No, she's out with her Girl Scouts troop doing a fundraiser in front of the supermarket. But I'll teach her whatever you think we should work on."

I felt deflated. *No Birdie.*

Swallowing a sigh, I nodded. "Okay. Well, today we worked on sit, but his commands are in German. I'm out of treats—would you have any so that I can demonstrate?"

"Sure. Just a moment. They're in the cabinet in the kitchen. Please, make yourself at home while I grab one."

A part of me felt so guilty about what I was doing, yet another part of me couldn't help but look around, given the opportunity. The uglier part won out when I saw the framed photos on the mantel above the big fireplace that I'd spotted earlier from the window. My heart squeezed when I picked up the first one. It was a picture of Sebastian and his wife bundled up in winter coats and hats, in front of a snow-covered mountain. They both had on skis, and Sebastian held Birdie up in the air with one arm—and she had a snowboard strapped to her little feet. She couldn't have been more than five or six in the picture. Her chubby cheeks were all red, and she wore the biggest, happiest smile I'd ever seen. Even though Sebastian looked super handsome, it was Birdie's smile that I couldn't peel my eyes from.

Magdalene returned before I could stop staring. Seeing what had captured my attention, she smiled sadly. "That's Mr. Maxwell and his daughter, Birdie." She made the sign of the cross. "And his beloved wife, Amanda. She's gone now. God rest her soul."

I felt myself starting to get all choked up, so I coughed to clear my throat and set the frame back down. "Well, they're a very beautiful family."

Magdalene nodded. She handed me the dog treat, and I returned my attention to Marmaduke. I hoped like hell he remembered what he'd learned. Following what we'd practiced, I let him see the treat and then held up my hand with it tucked inside. *"Sitz,"* I said. Miraculously, Marmaduke sat right down.

Magdalene smiled. "Oh my goodness. You're very good at your job. This big boy doesn't listen to anyone."

As nutty as the entire situation was, I still felt proud of what I'd accomplished. "Thank you." I smiled. "Or *danke*." I almost laughed after I said that last comment, but I couldn't help getting into the act. After my demonstration, I gave Magdalene some tips I'd picked up from the internet, and then it was time to go.

"Okay. Well. Good luck with him. He's a sweet dog."

Magdalene walked me to the door. "You'll be back next week, right?"

"Umm. Well . . ."

"Birdie is going to be so upset she missed today. To be honest, we'd forgotten all about your coming when she made these plans with her troop. I'm sure she'll be standing at the door waiting for you next Tuesday."

Standing at the door waiting for me.

I pictured Birdie with her nose pressed to the glass, excited to work on the dog's training.

I couldn't let her down. Could I?

One more week won't hurt too much, will it? I mean, I was already this far in—how could I end things without at least meeting little Birdie now? Plus, she'd be so disappointed if the trainer quit after the very first day.

"You know what, sure. I'll see you next Tuesday."

I walked outside and took a deep breath.

Shit. Here we go again.

CHAPTER 8

SADIE

"Bleib."

Ruff!

"Bleib."

Ruff!

"What the hell are you listening to?" Devin had once again caught me goofing off at work. "Is that German . . . and barking?"

I pressed the "Pause" button as fast as I could. I'd been watching another YouTube tutorial on German-language dog training. They were all I'd been watching lately whenever I had any spare time. In fact, German dog training had consumed me, to the point where last night I'd dreamed I was on trial for some crime, and the entire courtroom was filled with dogs shouting at me in German.

"No." I shook my head and lied. "No German. I don't know what you thought you heard."

"No? What was it, then?"

There was no way I was getting out of this one.

I conceded. "Okay, it was."

"I know it was . . . because my grandma Inga is German. Are you taking a trip soon?" She beamed at the prospect of my traveling abroad.

"An international dating piece! I'd totally be down to be your assistant on that one!"

Devin had no clue about the mess I'd gotten myself into. But I was going to burst if I didn't tell someone. If anyone would understand and not have me committed, it would be Devin. *Only Devin.*

"No international dating article." I sighed. "But I have to tell you something, and you'd better sit down for this."

Devin couldn't even stand to sit anymore. She paced excitedly across the space between my cubicle and hers. "Oh my God. This is too good to be true."

"It's a mess is what it is! And it's ending after this next visit."

She stopped for a moment. "So you plan to play German dog trainer one more time and then what?"

I tapped my pen and blew out a long breath. "Then I have to come up with a way out of this."

"Wait . . . what happened to the *actual* dog trainer?"

That's the question of the year, isn't it?

"I have no idea. That's the other problem. As far as I know, *Gretchen* never showed up yesterday, but I have no idea why or if she'll come back into the picture."

"Let's hope not." She sighed. "This is fate, Sadie. The butterfly barrette, the fact that he opened the door right at that moment, the way the dog just listened to your asinine German instructions like you're some kind of expert! This is your window in. Why give it up after one more visit?"

I couldn't believe her suggestion, although I shouldn't have found it surprising.

"My window into what, exactly, Devin? And don't say Sebastian Maxwell's bed."

"I was actually going to say . . . your window into Birdie's life. You can see her now, check in on her, and not have to make unattainable wishes come true while playing Santa Claus." She paused, then smirked. "And it could potentially lead to amazing sex with Sebastian Maxwell, yes."

I stood up from my seat. "One more time and I'm done, Devin. I mean it. I can't lie to that little girl's face. That's the only thing worse than playing God from afar."

"You're not lying. That's the beauty of this. You're . . . *you.* You just also happen to be training that dog—in German. You *are* the dog trainer. You're earning this. Who cares how you got there?"

"And my name is *Gretchen*? That's not a lie?"

She shrugged. "Small detail."

I pulled on my hair. "How do you say 'fraud' in *Deutsch*?"

It was a beautiful, sunny late-summer day on Eighty-Third Street. The perfect day for a picnic at the park or a stroll with a cup of coffee. There were a ton of things I could have been doing today—anything besides continuing this facade. But with my heart pounding, I made my way up the stairs of the Maxwell brownstone and proceeded to knock on the door.

From behind the door, I could hear Marmaduke's paws scratching against the wood floor as he frantically raced to greet me.

When the door opened, there he was, immediately jumping all over me. Who had even opened the door? All I saw was him. It was as if he'd opened it to let me in himself.

I turned my cheek, trying to avoid getting slobber in my mouth. "Whoa. *Sitz. Sitz.*"

Apparently, he'd forgotten everything he learned last time. *Sitz* had done *zilch* to keep him from standing on his hind legs and attempting to french-kiss me.

"Come in," Magdalene said from somewhere behind Marmaduke. "So sorry about his energy today. As you can see, he's being very rambunctious, so it's perfect timing for another lesson."

I'd been expecting that Birdie would be waiting at the door like Magdalene had said she might, but there was no sign of her.

As Marmaduke trailed behind me, I followed Magdalene inside as I looked around in search of Birdie. Magdalene led me into the kitchen. My eyes eventually landed on Birdie's blonde locks.

There she is.

She looked like she was hurrying to put something back into the cupboard. When she turned around, her cheeks were filled like a chipmunk's.

"Are you alright?" Magdalene asked.

She nodded fast and mumbled with her mouth full. "Uh-huh."

Did Magdalene not know what she was doing? Because it didn't take a rocket scientist to know that Birdie had taken the opportunity of Magdalene going to answer the door to steal cookies. I laughed inwardly. *My little cookie thief. She strikes again.*

She turned around briefly with her back to us, and when she faced me again, her cheeks were hollow. She'd apparently swallowed the cookies. Now that I wasn't distracted any longer by her cheeks, I really got a look into her beautiful baby blues. Birdie was a stunning little girl, and looking into the eyes of the kid who'd charmed my heart for so long from afar was truly surreal. I couldn't stand to look into those eyes and lie to her. So I decided I would try my best to be as honest as possible under the circumstances.

"Birdie, this is Gretchen, Marmaduke's dog trainer," Magdalene said.

"Actually, Gretchen is only my work name. You can call me Sadie."

Birdie had a confused look on her face. "You have two names?"

I paused. "Yes."

"I want two names! I'm gonna think about another name."

Smiling, I said, "It's kind of fun, I suppose."

"Are we taking Marmaduke to the dog park?" Birdie asked.

"Yeah, I was thinking I'd let you watch me run through some commands with him, and then I'd have you both try them as well."

Birdie bolted out of the room. "I'll get my sweater." With his tail wagging, Marmaduke followed her down a hallway.

After she returned, Birdie, Magdalene, and I walked together to the park. Well, it was more like Marmaduke ran to the park and took me along with him while Birdie and Magdalene ran behind us. I needed to figure out how to teach him "slow down."

When we got to our destination, we went in search of a good spot to run our lessons.

Birdie turned to me and asked, "Are you German?"

"No, I'm not."

"Then how do you teach Marmaduke in German?"

"I taught myself the important words, and I'm going to teach you, too, so that you don't need me anymore. The goal is to get him to listen to you, and to Magdalene and your dad."

"Can you teach him not to jump on my daddy's face in the morning? That's how Marmaduke wakes him up, and he gets so mad. I'm afraid if he keeps doing it, Daddy will want to give him away."

"I don't think your father will do that."

I probably shouldn't have made that promise on Sebastian's behalf. At least I hoped he wouldn't break his daughter's heart in such a way.

This time, I came armed with a bag full of treats I'd brought. Having the right kind of reinforcements would hopefully make this easier than last time.

I demonstrated *sitz* (sit) and *platz* (down) a few times myself before handing over some of the treats to Birdie. As usual, Marmaduke's tail was wagging like crazy whenever Birdie took the helm. The level of excitement he had for this little girl was unlike anything else. Birdie squealed in delight the first time the dog listened to her command for a treat. It was truly miraculous how this dog-training thing seemed to be coming together. I really hadn't thought I could pull this off, but it seemed I was—for now.

But from everything I'd read, proper dog training typically lasted more than just a couple of sessions. There was no way I could just bail after two times without a good reason. So I was going to have to come up with an excuse after today as to why I couldn't return. Even the thought of that was daunting.

Ironically, we were working on the command for stay, *bleib*, when Marmaduke did just the opposite after he became distracted by a puppy who'd entered the doggy area. No amount of shouting *bleib* was going to convince him not to chase after the little animal. It took the three of us to rein Marmaduke in and lead him to the quieter area away from the other dogs. After enticing him with a few more treats, we were able to take a rest with him under a tree. Even though it was cooler out, I was definitely breaking a sweat.

"So, how did you get into this dog-training career?" Magdalene asked.

Oh, you wouldn't believe.

"It's not my career. It's just something I literally fell into. I do it on the side. I have another job."

"You have two jobs and two names!" Birdie laughed.

Magdalene smiled. "May I ask what your other job is?"

"I write a column for a magazine."

Her eyes went wide. "Oh, that sounds so fun. What's the subject?"

"Dating, actually. I sometimes go on dates and write about them."

Birdie scrunched her nose. "Ew. You have to kiss them?"

I laughed. "No. Definitely not."

"Good. The only boy I want to kiss is my daddy."

"And I think your dad will be perfectly fine with that for as long as possible," I said.

Magdalene and I grinned at each other.

"I bet a lot of the boys want to kiss you," Birdie added. "You have pretty blonde hair and a nice smile."

That was sweet.

"Why, thank you, Birdie. Can I tell you a secret?"

She leaned in curiously. "Yes!"

I lowered my voice for effect. "Most days, I'd rather kiss a frog."

She gasped. "And then he'd turn into a prince! My mommy read me a story like that once."

My heart clenched. "Yeah?"

"Yeah. I don't remember it too much. But I know there was a frog and a kiss and a prince."

"That sounds like a cool story, though."

She fell silent for a moment before she said, "Do you know my mother died?"

"Yes. I did know that, actually."

Guilt crept up. Magdalene had told me about Amanda last week, but little did they know I knew *way* more than anyone could have ever imagined. Suddenly I was reminded of the fact that I was an imposter.

"She died when I was seven."

I'd promised myself I would do everything in my power not to bond with this little girl today. I needed to let the urge to do that go. Unfortunately, the need to show her that she wasn't alone was even greater.

"I lost my mom when I was around your age, too."

The look on her face transformed from one of sadness to wonder. "You did?"

It was as if she'd never heard anyone say that before.

"Yes, I did."

"What happened to her?"

"She died of cancer."

"Mine too!"

My heart felt so heavy that I could have sworn it was weighing me down. She looked so relieved to know that someone had been through what she had. It made me happy I'd chosen to open up.

"Did you ever stop thinking about her? I'm afraid I'll forget her when I get older. I only remember a little now."

Trying to reassure her, I said, "I never forgot the things I remembered when I was your age. Because those memories are so important and precious that they are branded into us. And I have a great dad who also made sure I never forgot her, either. But you know the number one reason you'll never be able to forget her?"

"What?"

I pointed to my heart. "Because she's right here. Always. She's a part of you and you carry her inside your heart every day. You can't forget your own heart and you won't."

Birdie closed her eyes and whispered, "Yeah. Okay."

This moment was one I would never forget. Even if I never saw Birdie again, at least I knew I was able to make her feel a little less alone in this world. The entire time she'd been communicating with me as Santa, the one thing I'd always wanted to say to her was: "Me too. I know how you're feeling."

"I'm really happy I met you. I've never met anyone who lost their mom young like me."

I couldn't help but smile. "Well, maybe we were meant to meet, so you could know there are other people out there just like you."

Magdalene's eyes were glistening.

When I realized I might have taken things a bit too far emotionally, I hopped up. "Well, let's get back to training Marmaduke, shall we?"

The dog looked like he was half-asleep, enjoying the breeze with his tongue hanging out.

Birdie and I got him up and once again took turns reciting the commands in German and rewarding Marmaduke as he earned the treats. Everything was going as normal until that puppy from earlier entered his line of sight again. Then it became clear that perhaps our luck in trying to tame him this afternoon had run out.

We led him out of the park and began the trek back to Birdie's house.

◆ ◆ ◆

Once back at the brownstone, Magdalene insisted I stay for a few extra minutes before leaving so that I could taste a dish that she'd been cooking all day in the Crock-Pot. The three of us were at the table and had just finished up the stew when we noticed an odd noise coming from Marmaduke in the next room.

When we got up from our seats, it didn't take long to realize he was choking on something.

He's choking.

The dog is choking.

Full-fledged panic set in.

Everything from there on in happened so fast.

I had just been watching a video the other night on what to do if a dog started choking. YouTube had recommended it because it was related to my dog-training search results. I remembered thinking maybe it would be good to watch it, since I'd be taking the dog out one more time. But good God, I never thought I'd have to use any of those skills.

I struggled to remember the instructions from the tutorial as I stepped into action, standing behind the dog and placing my arms around his body.

Think.

Think.

Think.

Making a fist with my left hand, I placed my thumb against his stomach and with my other hand, I pushed upward toward Marmaduke's shoulders. Unsure if I was doing it correctly, I kept repeating this motion until I heard Magdalene yell, "It's out!"

"It's out! It's out!" Birdie echoed, tears streaming down her face.

Magdalene went to pick the culprit up off the floor. It was a tiny rubber ball, no bigger than the size of a half-dollar.

I'd never been so scared in my life. Poor Birdie was so frightened. I hadn't really had any time to think about what almost happened.

"You saved Marmaduke's life," Birdie cried as she wrapped her arms around the dog's neck and pressed her cheek against his face. The dog seemed unfazed by what could have happened to him.

I bent down to comfort her. "I only did what anyone would've done in that situation."

Magdalene had her hand on her chest, seeming more rattled than any of us. "I wouldn't have known what to do, Sadie. Thank goodness you were here."

The baritone voice from behind literally shook me. "What the hell is going on? Why is Birdie crying?"

No one had noticed until he'd spoken that Sebastian had come home.

Birdie ran to her father. "Daddy, Sadie saved Marmaduke's life! He was choking on a ball, and she did the hymen remover."

Did she just say "hymen remover"? Clearly, she meant *Heimlich maneuver*. I would've laughed had he not been giving me the death stare.

Sebastian squinted in confusion. "Who's Sadie?"

She pointed to me and started talking so fast. "The trainer! She just uses Gretchen for work. Her real name is Sadie, and Marmaduke swallowed the small ball I'd gotten out of the gumball machine at the supermarket the other day. Sadie did this thing to him and it came out. I was so scared. I thought he was gonna die."

"It was really pretty amazing, Mr. Maxwell," Magdalene said.

Sebastian looked to me and then back at Birdie before bending down to rub the dog on the head, seeming a bit shaken now that he'd fully absorbed what had just happened.

He looked up at me. "You used the Heimlich maneuver on him?"

God, I didn't even know *what* I did. I just remembered the steps from that video and stepped into action.

"Something like that, yes."

Still kneeling down, Sebastian wrapped his arms around his daughter. "You okay?"

She nodded. "Yes."

My eyes focused on his strong hands as he rubbed her back.

"Why don't you go into the kitchen with Magdalene and have her give you some cookies and milk." He looked at me as he stood up straight. "Can I have a moment with you, please?"

"Me?" I stupidly said.

"Yes."

Who the hell else?

"Sure." I turned to Birdie. "In case I don't see you again before I leave, it was great meeting you, Birdie."

"See you next week, Sadie. Don't kiss any ugly boys."

I didn't have the heart to tell her that I might not see her next week.

Wait . . . "might"*?* Now I was doubting whether I was going to cut things off after today?

I followed Sebastian into his office. It was as intimidating as he was, with dark wood and a dark-brown leather chair behind his large desk.

We stood a good few feet across from each other, and before he could say anything, I started to stammer.

"S-she was just . . . I write for a dating column. I told her that. She . . . That's why she said that about kissing boys." I cringed over my own words.

"You're a writer?"

"Yes. The dog-training thing is . . . extra."

It's extra, alright.

He nodded and contemplated my admission for a moment before rubbing his eyes.

"The last thing I needed in this house was that dog. I'd put my foot down for years about not getting one. I work too many damn hours and can hardly keep my daughter alive and healthy, let alone bringing what's closer to a horse into this house."

"I understand. It's a lot of responsibility."

"My daughter had been asking for a Great Dane named Marmaduke for I don't even know how long. I had no intentions of making that dream come true. But a few weeks back, for some reason, she became convinced that her dead mother was mad at her for some things she'd done. I honestly don't know where she gets some of these ideas. All I know is that the one thing she really wants most, more than a dog, more than anything . . . I'll never be able to give her. And that's to have her mother back."

He paused. Tears were starting to form in my eyes, but I did my best to fight them as he continued.

"So I did something that probably in retrospect was a very stupid thing. I got her the exact dog she wanted. I'd looked everywhere for the right black-and-white-spotted Great Dane—minus the different-colored eyes—she wanted. I told her that her mother had come to me in a dream, that she'd told me to get the dog but to let Birdie know that just because she's not getting signs doesn't mean her mom's mad." He stared off and shook his head. "I basically lied to my daughter to take away her sadness. I've somehow convinced myself that lying for the good of making someone happy cancels the lie out."

Wow.

And that, Mr. Maxwell, is precisely why I am standing before you at this very moment.

"I understand that more than you know," I said, swallowing.

"Anyway, things have been better with her since that damn dog arrived, aside from the fact that he wakes me up with a sticky face every day. But that's my problem. My point is . . . I can't imagine what we would've done if anything had happened to that animal today. Not only for the dog's sake but for my daughter's. I'm very grateful you were here."

My cheeks felt hot as he stared into my eyes. The power of his emotions was almost too much for me to handle.

I cleared my throat. "Like I told Birdie, anyone would've done the same thing."

His eyes seared into mine, seeming to challenge my feeble attempt to downplay what had happened.

"I doubt Magdalene would've known what to do. The fact that you were here saved that dog's life."

"Well, I'm really glad I was . . . here, then."

He chewed his bottom lip a bit, then added, "I also want to apologize for being short with you when you arrived last week. I was having a bad day for more reasons than one. But that's no excuse."

"Well, I was . . . late, so I understand."

He said nothing as he slipped his hands into his pockets and continued to look at me. His apology came as a surprise. It proved Sebastian was definitely not the insensitive jerk he appeared to be during our initial meeting. He had a vulnerable side. I could see that now. He was a man who wanted to protect his daughter from having to experience another tragedy.

I got the urge to comfort him, to assure him that I understood how difficult it was for a widower dad to take on the responsibility of single fatherhood. After all, I'd lived that life through my father's eyes.

But I wouldn't say anything. Because at this point in time, I was simply overwhelmed by the power of his stare and felt the need to flee.

"Anyway, I'd better get going."

He nodded. "I'll send your payment to the PayPal address you gave me."

"Thank you."

As I walked out of his office, I still had no clue how I was supposed to break it to them that I wasn't coming back. Before I exited out the door, though, I did feel compelled to turn around and say one last thing to him.

"For the record, Mr. Maxwell, from the small amount of time I've seen you and gotten to know your daughter, I can tell you that I think you're doing an amazing job. I'm not just saying that, either. You have an incredible daughter, and that's undoubtedly due to the kind of father you are."

He blinked a few times, and I didn't think he was going to respond, so I continued my way out the door.

His voice stopped me.

"Sadie."

I turned around. "Yeah?"

"Call me Sebastian." He paused, then flashed a genuine smile. "And . . . *danke*."

CHAPTER 9

Sadie

Number of times per week you enjoy coitus.

I chewed the end of my pen while I mulled over yet another tough question. *That really depends, doesn't it?* I mean, is he good and gets me to my happy place before crossing the finish line himself? I had to assume that, since I was seeking my ideal mate, they were asking about how things would be with him and not some three-pump chump. My mind wandered to Sebastian. That man had a definite edge to him. There was no way he wouldn't deliver the goods.

I sighed. I'd decided to take advantage of my free matchmaking trial to get my mind *off* Sebastian Maxwell. Yet he seemed to pop into my head as I pondered every intrusive question.

Describe your ideal mate's physical appearance.

I closed my eyes and thought about what type of man I was attracted to, then jotted down the description that came to mind. Tall, broad-shouldered, green eyes, chiseled jaw, strong forearms, and a wide alpha-male stance. *Good God.* The only thing missing were the gold flecks in Sebastian's eyes. I really needed to hop off the Maxwell train.

Preferred primary residence location.

Duh. A brownstone on the Upper West Side, of course. Though, in my defense, I would've answered that one the same even before meeting a certain someone.

What song did you last sing in private?

Oh jeez. I might have to lie about this one. I'd been feeling a little down this morning, so before I went in the shower, I cranked up an oldie but goodie and twerked to Sir Mix-a-Lot while I shampooed my hair. I was pretty certain we all *liked big butts*, but it didn't make a very appealing match profile. So I went with something a little more mature—Lewis Capaldi's "Someone You Loved" and then wasted time thinking about what type of music Sebastian might like. For some reason, I pegged him as a country fan—all those songs about lost women and dogs seemed to fit him. Though, oddly, I got the distinct feeling that Sebastian would be more intrigued by a woman who sang Sir Mix-a-Lot rather than Lewis Capaldi.

Complete this sentence: I wish I had someone with whom I could share . . .

My immediate response was to write *everything*. But I thought that might make me sound too needy. So I toned it down a little, yet still went with something that was true and had a bit more personality sprinkled in: *cold pasta and laughs at two am.*

The *clickety-clack* sound of a woman's heels alerted me that Devin was coming down the hall, so I quickly hid the matchmaker questionnaire under some papers.

"Coffee time." She breezed into my office. "You want the usual?"

"Yeah. That would be great. I'm really dragging this afternoon."

"Oh? Do anything interesting last night?"

Since I didn't categorize watching dog-training videos as interesting, I shook my head. "Nah. Just woke up early and couldn't fall back asleep."

Devin looked down at my desk. "What are you working on?"

"Copyedits for next month's articles."

"Mm-hmm." She squinted at me. "Okay . . . well. It's my turn to pay for coffee, so I'll be back in a jiff."

"Sounds good, thanks."

Devin turned toward the door and then back to me. "Actually . . . I forgot my wallet. Can I borrow twenty dollars?"

"Yeah, sure." I got out of my chair and walked over to the cabinet under the window where I kept my purse. As soon as I dug in to find my wallet, Devin snatched the pile of papers from atop my desk.

My eyes narrowed. "What the hell are you doing?"

"Copyedits my ass." She started to riffle through the papers in her hands. I attempted to grab them, but she pulled back too quickly for me.

"Give me that!"

She dug a few pages down into the pile and then yanked out a page. "*Aha!* I knew you were doing something you didn't want me to see."

"You're crazy."

She started to read the paper aloud. "Bloom Matchmaking Services. Boutique services for elite singles." Devin rolled her eyes. "Let me translate. 'Boutique' equals 'expensive.' 'Elite singles' equals 'a bunch of stuffy assholes who think they're too good for Match.com or the bar scene.'"

"It's research for an article."

"So why did you just lie to me and tell me you were working on copyedits?"

"Because of exactly what you're doing at this very moment. You blow everything out of proportion."

Devin was too busy scanning the sheet for clues to even hear my defense. She smirked when she looked up. "The description of your ideal mate sounds very familiar."

"I've always liked tall with dark hair."

She arched a brow. "With good bone structure, green eyes, and a wide stance?"

"Who *doesn't* like that?"

"Uh-huh. So you weren't describing Sebastian Maxwell on this form?"

"Absolutely not."

She flipped over the page and looked at the questions I'd answered earlier this morning. "How many children does your ideal mate have? Zero to one? Since when are you in the market for a single dad? This is the first time I've heard about this."

I grabbed the papers out of her hands. "Don't you have a job to do? Or coffee to mainline into your vein or something?"

"You need to just ask him out and you know it."

"Yes. That's exactly what I need to do. Because the foundation of any good relationship starts off with a series of lies about . . . let's see . . . my name, occupation, and relationship with his only child. It was obviously meant to be. We'll probably be married by Christmas."

Devin sighed. "Why don't you just come clean, then? Tell him the truth."

"And then what? Ask him out on a date?"

She shrugged. "Sure. Why not?"

"Because he'll go ballistic on me if he finds out. He bought an unruly Great Dane that is driving him crazy because his daughter suddenly became convinced her dead mother was mad at her for something she'd done. That was *all my fault*, Devin. I made a child think Santa Claus had a direct line to a dead woman."

"But you meant well."

"I'm sure Sebastian Maxwell won't see it that way."

"Well, you'll never know unless you tell him, will you?"

I sighed and shook my head. "I could really use that coffee."

Devin nodded. "Fine. I'm going. But think about it, Sadie. There're eight million people in this little city of ours and somehow you wound up meeting this guy. Maybe it started out wrong, but maybe there's a reason you two met."

After Devin left, I crumpled up the matchmaking application I'd been filling out. The truth of the matter was, I had no desire to go on any date. Devin was right. I had a real thing for Sebastian. And it wasn't just that he was ridiculously handsome. He had a soft side that he reserved for his daughter. I was certain that his wife had been privy to that side of him, too. There was something just so beautiful about a man who saved the best parts of himself for the women in his life. I knew . . . because he reminded me of another man I adored. God, Freud would have a damn field day with me.

I decided to come clean. Shockingly, Devin had been right. Since the very first letter from Birdie, something had felt like kismet. Like I was supposed to meet her and her father for a reason. Of course, it helped that once I did, the man was insanely handsome. But a part of me truly felt like even if Sebastian Maxwell hadn't turned out to be gorgeous, I'd still be drawn to him. My attraction went deeper than the surface. I was also well aware that I was bringing parts of my own history into my fascination with his little family—but isn't that how life works? Our hearts are made up of all different broken pieces that belong to others, and when we find the right one, they show us how they can all fit together again.

Maybe I was reaching too far and being too philosophical, but the bottom line was . . . I'd run the dating gauntlet enough times to know that when someone comes along and makes you feel butterflies, you need to chase them. Because it doesn't happen very often.

So I decided that after today's training session, I was going to ask Sebastian to speak to him privately and then come clean. Chances are he'd freak out and never want to see me again. But at this point, I couldn't keep up the lies anymore. It wasn't fair to me, or to him and his daughter. And if there was a shot in hell that maybe something could happen between us, I couldn't have that built on a foundation of lies.

My palms started to sweat as I got closer to the Maxwell brownstone. I was so damn nervous. A part of me hoped that Sebastian wouldn't be around today, just so I could delay going through with it. Last time I'd trained Marmaduke, only Magdalene and Birdie had been home. When I arrived at the house, I took a deep breath and prayed that was the case today.

The walk up the stairs to the front door felt a lot like walking the plank. I shook out my tingling hands and then forced myself to knock. A few seconds later, I saw shadows on the other side and held my breath as the handle started to turn.

Unfortunately, it wasn't Magdalene.

"Mr. . . . umm . . . Sebastian . . . I didn't expect you to answer the door."

He folded his arms across his chest and squinted at me. "No? Why is that, *Sadie*?"

Was it me or did he just say my name weird? Or maybe my nerves were getting the best of me. Picking imaginary lint off my pants to avoid his intense stare, I cleared my throat. "I . . . uhh . . . thought you'd be at work. Last time I came on this day, Magdalene was here."

His mouth slid to a wicked smile. "I took the afternoon off. Thought you and I could have a little training session. Just the two of us."

A giant lump formed in my throat. *Shit.* Now I had no choice but to come clean. I'd left it up to fate, and fate couldn't smack me in the face more than it was doing right now. This man who worked six days a week had miraculously taken the day off to spend time with me. Alone. "Umm. Okay. That's good."

He stepped back, opening the door wide. "Come in. I'd like to start the training inside today, if that's alright with you."

It wasn't. Not at all. Stepping over the threshold made me feel claustrophobic. At least being outside, I had a place to run. The door suddenly slammed closed behind me and I jumped.

Sebastian flashed another wicked smile. "Sorry. Slipped."

If I didn't know better, I'd think he was intentionally making me feel on edge.

Luckily, Marmaduke came to my rescue. He charged at me and nearly knocked me over in an attempt to lick my face. "Hey, boy." I scratched behind his ears. "It's nice to see you, too."

When I looked up, I found Sebastian's eyes searing into me. He held a folded sheet of white paper in his hand that I hadn't noticed before.

"Where did you say you got your training from again?"

Uh. I hadn't that I remembered. Looking around the room, I felt a panic come over me. I could have just ripped off the Band-Aid and come clean right then, but my heart was racing out of control, and I just wasn't ready. So what did I do? Of course, I dug myself deeper. The hallway we were standing in had a large round table. On top of it was a set of keys. "I went to the Key Training School."

"The Key Training School . . ."

He glanced at the keys on the table and back to me with narrowed eyes. "Where is that located exactly?"

"Umm . . . downtown."

"I'll have to look them up. See if they have a comments section so that I can give you a good review. Is it K-E-Y Training?"

Shit. "Yes . . . but they're closed now."

"Closed today or closed for good?"

"For good."

"That's a shame. Since they clearly produced such a qualified *dog trainer*."

What the hell? Was he mocking me? We'd ended on such a nice note after I'd saved his dog's life, and now suddenly I felt like we were back to square one.

He tilted his head. "Why did they close?"

"Umm. I think because the rent is so high in the city."

He squinted so tightly that I could barely see the whites of his eyes. Then, without another word, he turned his back to me and started to walk into the living room. "Follow me."

Like a puppy, I trailed behind. Marmaduke had walked ahead and was busy doing something in the corner. Sebastian turned to me and pointed to the dog. "This is new. Perhaps we can start today's session with you demonstrating how to stop my dog from doing that to my daughter's stuffed animals."

Leaning in for a closer look, I saw that the giant animal was humping a stuffed turtle. *Ugh.* His lipstick was out and everything. I scrunched up my nose. "He's humping a turtle."

"Is that what he's doing? I wasn't quite sure. Perhaps you get a lot more practice than I do."

My eyes widened. *Did he just call me a whore?* I blinked a few times. "Excuse me?"

"Well, you told my daughter that you write about your dating life for a living. So naturally I assume that means you go out with a wide variety of men."

I was getting more pissed off by the minute. I might be a liar, but I was certainly not promiscuous. My hands gripped my hips. "Just because I date a lot doesn't mean I'm off humping anything I can get my hands on like your dog. Perhaps you should look inward—maybe your dog gets his hobbies from his master. What exactly is *your* dating life like?"

Sebastian practically snarled at me. *Screw this.* I snarled right back.

My attention was again distracted when Marmaduke started to really go to town. While before, he had been gently gyrating his hips in a haphazard motion, now he was pumping away like a man on a mission. Or a dog. A dog on a mission, I meant. I yelled at him. "Marmaduke. No!"

Shockingly, the big dog froze. He stood there midpump, looking like he hadn't even realized anyone was watching, and now he'd been caught red-handed. While he was flustered, I marched over and slipped the stuffed turtle from beneath him. *Ugh.* It was . . . wet. I didn't even want to know what type of canine bodily fluids I was touching. I held the tail between two fingers and looked at Sebastian. "Where is your washing machine?"

"The laundry room is off the kitchen."

I knew which way that was, so I helped myself. I walked the offending turtle to the kitchen and opened a bunch of doors until I found the one that contained a small laundry room. Lifting the top of the washer, I tossed the plush toy inside and turned to Sebastian, who was watching from the doorway.

"What else is he humping?"

"A few of my daughter's other stuffed animals."

"Go get them."

Sebastian disappeared and came back with three more small plush toys. He handed them to me, and I tossed them all into the washer. "Do you have any vinegar?"

His brows furrowed. "I think so."

"Go get it."

Once again, he surprised me by doing as I instructed without question. When he returned, I had the washing machine filling up with water, and I added two capfuls of the vinegar. "Puppies don't reach puberty until six to eight months, so he isn't humping for sexual pleasure. It's usually just a playful game they find out is fun for them. Animals tend to pick things that smell good. A little vinegar in the wash might do the trick to stop him."

Thankfully, I'd been reading a lot and stumbled on an article on humping. For a minute there, I almost sounded like I knew what the hell I was talking about.

Sebastian nodded, seemingly knocked down off whatever high horse he'd been on when I arrived. I brushed past him to exit the laundry room and went back to the living room to find Marmaduke sitting. It looked like he was waiting for me to return.

"You said you wanted to do some indoor training today. But I think it's best if I take him for a walk before we attempt that. He has a lot of energy and follows commands best when he's a bit tired."

"Fine. I'll join you."

I held up a hand and showed him my palm. "I prefer to go alone." Not wanting to tell him I needed a minute to gather my wits, I pulled yet another bullshit lie out of my ass. "It's bonding time for me as Marmaduke's trainer."

Sebastian's eyes roamed my face, as if he was debating what I'd said. Eventually, he gave a curt nod. "Fine. I'll wait here."

You know how you're calm during the seconds of a narrowly averted disaster, only for your heart to start pumping like crazy after the situation is under control again? That's exactly what I felt like as I walked down the front stairs of the Maxwell residence with Marmaduke. My legs shook with each step, and I had to gulp a few mouthfuls of air in order to catch my breath. What the hell had gone on in there? I replayed the last ten minutes over in my head—the mocking way Sebastian had spoken to me, how he'd seemed to challenge every word that came out of my mouth, the way he'd questioned my dating habits. But by the time I'd walked around the block a few times, I'd calmed down and convinced myself that my own guilt had me reading into things that hadn't really been there. It was like the telltale heart beating under the floorboards—with every minute I was in Sebastian's presence, I heard the thumping louder, and it had started to feel like the room was closing in on me. But really, there had been no beating heart under the floor. The entire crazy encounter had been a figment of my imagination.

Yeah, that was it. It had to be. I mean, sure, Sebastian was a tough nut. But he had no idea who I really was. If he did, he would have called me out on it immediately. So it had to be all in my head.

Twenty minutes later, I finally garnered the courage to walk back to the house. I took a deep breath and lifted my hand to knock, but the door swung open before my knuckles could connect with the wood.

"It's about time."

"Marmaduke had a lot of energy today."

"I was beginning to think you were going to take off with my dog."

I sort of laughed at that notion. Who the hell in their right mind would take off with this out-of-control animal? Only a person who was nuts, obviously. *Oh. Wait.* Maybe I did qualify, then. I guess I could see his point. "Sorry. I'll stay a bit longer so you get your full hour of training time, if you'd like."

Sebastian stepped aside, and I noticed that he again had a folded-up piece of white paper in his hand. Only this time, I wasn't going to let my imagination get the best of me by thinking whatever it was contained some ominous evil thing to expose me as a fraud. So I lifted my chin high and ignored his hand as I walked inside.

Back in the living room, I felt Sebastian's presence all around me. It was uncomfortable yet oddly arousing at the same time. I cleared my throat. "Is there something specific you wanted to work on today?"

He watched me intently. "Yes. Jumping over people."

My brows drew together. "Excuse me?"

"Your website said it's one of the tricks that you teach. I thought my daughter might enjoy that type of thing, so I'd like you to teach the dog how to jump over people while they're down on all fours."

"You want me to teach Marmaduke how to jump over people who are down on all fours?"

Sebastian looked around. "Is there an echo in here?"

"No. But I just . . . It seems like a better use of our training time might be spent teaching Marmaduke some basic commands. Not something so . . . advanced."

"Are you not capable of teaching him an advanced trick?"

Uh . . . no . . . I hadn't gotten that far on YouTube yet. "Of course I am."

Sebastian flashed a cynical smile and sat down on the couch. He stretched both of his arms out across the top and kicked his feet up onto the coffee table in front of him. "Good. Now down on all fours, Ms. Schmidt."

"Schmidt?"

"Oh, is that not your real last name? Your website said *Gretchen Schmidt*. But yet you told my daughter your real name is Sadie? So what is it now? Are you Sadie Schmidt, or is there yet another name?"

I started to feel my cheeks heat. "Umm. No, it's Schmidt. Like I told your daughter, I just use Gretchen for work purposes."

"Right. Because it sounds more German."

"That's right."

"Alright then, *Ms. Schmidt*. Why don't you get started? What's the German word for 'jump'?"

Oh God. I totally panicked and said the first jumbled syllables that I could force out of my mouth. *"Flunkerbsht."*

Sebastian's brows jumped. *"Flunkerbsht."*

"That's right."

I could have sworn I detected a hint of a smile at the edges of his lips. But then it quickly disappeared. "Ready whenever you are . . . *flunkerbsht*."

CHAPTER 10

SADIE

It was the longest ten minutes of my life. Seriously. Every second that passed was excruciating as Sebastian just watched with his arms crossed as I made a fool of myself.

I tried in vain to get this horse of a dog to jump over my back with a made-up command that meant absolutely nothing. It was looking like I'd have a greater chance of turning water into wine.

How the hell do you teach a dog to jump over your back anyway? I tried everything, from demonstrating the act myself while jumping over an end table shouting *"flunkerbsht"* repeatedly . . . to grabbing another one of the stuffed animals from Birdie's room and jumping over that. He ended up going after the toy and humping it.

I'm a flunkerbsht, *alright. A* huge *flunker shit.*

In a last act of desperation, I tried getting down on all fours and yelling *"flunkerbsht"* while nudging my head, hoping that by some miracle, Marmaduke would take that as a sign to jump over me. He'd either lie down with his chin on the floor or, worse, climb up on my back and try to stay there. At one point, I became pinned under him. Then, after I flipped around, he started licking my face as I struggled to get up.

How had I gone from getting ready to tell Sebastian the truth just this morning . . . to this?

I needed to end it.

Now.

I needed to tell Sebastian everything.

When I finally got Marmaduke off me, I stood up.

Brushing off my pants, I said, "Sebastian, we need to—"

"Stop it, Sadie. Just stop." His tone was jarring and his eyes—they became filled with so much anger as he said, "Don't say another word. It won't matter. Because it'll just be another lie."

My heart pounded, and the room started to feel like it was spinning.

What's happening?

He unfolded the paper he'd been holding and faced it toward me. It was a photo of a woman and some words. It looked like a bio maybe. The woman had long, curly red hair.

"Who is that?" I swallowed.

"It's the real dog trainer Gretchen Schmidt. She contacted me recently to apologize for not showing up a few weeks ago due to a family emergency. Gave me the link to her new website, where I found her bio."

Oh no.

I knew I should've said something at that point, but the words wouldn't come.

He continued. "And what do you know . . . she trained in Munich while spending a year abroad, not at the . . . what was it you said? The Key Training School? Apparently, all they teach at the latter is how to lie through your teeth!"

I was seriously going to throw up.

"I can explain—"

"That's good to know, but unfortunately, there's nothing you could say at this point that I would believe. So, what I need you to do right now is to get out of my house and never come back."

This is so bad.

So very bad.

"I'll leave. But can I please just explain first?"

"Not unless you want to explain to the police."

The police? He had to be kidding me. Was impersonating a dog trainer even a crime? I didn't have enough legal background to figure out if I was in any kind of serious trouble here. So, rather than take a chance and make things worse, I decided to do as he said and headed for the door.

He might as well have told me not to let the door hit me on the way out, because I swore I felt it hit my ass as he slammed it shut behind me.

The New York air never felt colder, the skies never looked grayer as I made my way down the stairs and onto the sidewalk, feeling like a piece of tossed-out trash that had been fucked worse than Birdie's stuffed turtle.

A mix of emotions pummeled through me. It wasn't just the shock of having been outed but also an inexplicable sense of loss—not only the loss of Birdie but losing a sense of belonging that had come along with this experience. I hadn't even realized it had been missing in my life until it was ripped away.

Two weeks after that horrible day at the Maxwells', I still hadn't gotten over it. The one thing I was grateful for was that Birdie hadn't been there to witness any of it. I certainly hoped Sebastian never told her what really happened with me. It would break my heart if I thought Birdie saw me as a malicious person.

My heart was truly broken, and I'd spent many sleepless nights weighing whether or not I should try to find a way to explain myself to Sebastian again. He'd specifically said that he wouldn't believe anything I had to say. Telling him the truth could also make things worse. Then again, how much worse could things get?

Dr. Emery was out of the country for a few months, so I couldn't even run this situation by her. It didn't matter how many times I went back and forth over it, I would always come to the conclusion that it was better to just leave well enough alone.

But of course, life has a way of sometimes coming around and making decisions for you.

One afternoon, I checked the mail to find that Birdie had sent "Santa" another letter. It had been a long time since she'd written, and I truly hadn't been expecting her to write back ever again.

Given the circumstances, nothing could have kept me from ripping that envelope open.

Dear Santa,

I wasn't going to write to you anymore, but now that it's getting closer to Christmas, this can be like my one Christmas letter.

I have a dog named Marmaduke now. He's a Great Dane like I've always wanted. I love him so much. Mommy brought him. Well, not Mommy herself, but Daddy said that she sent him a message to bring Marmaduke to me. That's how I knew she wasn't mad at me for stealing cookies. (I still steal cookies. You know that, right?)

Mommy hasn't sent me any more signs. But that's okay. I know she's busy being an angel.

I met someone who lost her mom when she was six like me. I never met someone else who had a mom die from cancer before. She was really nice. Her name is Sadie. Well, she has two names: Sadie and Gretchen. She's the reason I have two names now: Birdie and Muffuleta. Anyway, Sadie was Marmaduke's dog trainer. She taught him to sit and other stuff in German. Oh and she saved his life, too. I thought maybe you had answered my wish for a special friend when she first came. But then Sadie disappeared. I don't know what happened. Daddy just said she wasn't coming anymore. He said he didn't know why. But he acted weird when I asked him about it. I think maybe it was my fault that she left. Maybe I made her sad because I lost my mom. Maybe it reminded her about hers? I wish I knew why Sadie left without saying goodbye. Why does everyone leave me?

Anyway, I don't know if you can find Sadie and tell her that I'm sorry.

Thanks, Santa.

Love, Birdie

(AKA Muffuleta)

I ended up having to leave work early that day. Even though I'd wanted to hit the liquor store, I knew I likely wouldn't have been able to know when to stop drowning my sorrows. I went straight home instead.

It didn't matter how many times I reread that letter, the answer of what I needed to do next was now abundantly clear.

Sebastian had paid me for my services via a new PayPal account I'd set up before he realized the truth. So I had his email address associated with that payment.

Before I could change my mind, I opened my laptop, generated a new email from my real account, and started typing.

Dear Mr. Maxwell,

I opted to send you this email instead of trying for an in-person meeting, because I doubted you would agree to see me. I urge you to please read

> this and save your judgment until you've gotten to the end. I promise it will fully explain why I was at your doorstep that first day.
>
> My name is Sadie Bisset. I'm twenty-nine years old and, like your daughter, I lost my mother to cancer when I was six (and a half). As part of my job, I answer a column where people write in their holiday wishes. The column is normally published during the holiday season, but your daughter, Birdie, first wrote in to us over the summer.

The email to Sebastian was probably one of the longest diatribes ever written. I explained each of the letters I'd received from Birdie, the wishes I'd fulfilled, and also how much I struggled with whether to respond each time. Eventually, I got to the part where I explained how I ended up being the dog trainer.

> I'd never intended to show up at your door. I happened to be in the neighborhood and stopped when I realized it was the same address from which your daughter's letters came. I'd noticed a butterfly barrette lying on the stairs and walked over to pick it up and place it closer to the door so that no one would step on it. That's when you opened the door and assumed I was Gretchen. I was a little shell-shocked in that moment. Perhaps my judgment was hampered by the fact that, by that time, I felt personally invested in your daughter's well-being. To you, I was a stranger. But because Birdie had opened up to me, I felt like I not only knew her but that I knew you as well. I made the hasty

decision to go along with your assumption. It was clearly the wrong decision and one I deeply regret. Despite that, I spent many hours studying the art of German dog training and truly intended to do the job justice, to perform the duties you thought you were hiring me for. But if I'm being honest, the real reason I stuck around after that first day was to see with my own eyes that Birdie was really okay.

That brings me to the reason I decided to write this letter today. Birdie wrote in to "Santa" again. This time, she mentioned the sudden absence of the dog trainer—me. She somehow suspects that something might have gone awry, even though you never told her why I'd stopped coming. (Thank you for that, by the way.) She has good intuition. But she drew a very wrong conclusion: that I left because she did something to make me sad, that perhaps being there reminded me of my own mother's death. It's killing me to think that she's blaming herself for the fact that I disappeared. I'm not really entirely sure how to fix that. I just wanted to make you aware.

I know I made a huge mistake. But I'm human, and please know I would never have done anything to intentionally hurt you or your daughter. I only wish the best for you both.

I want to remind you of something you told me once. You explained your reasoning behind telling Birdie that her mother had sent Marmaduke. You said that you convinced yourself that lying to take away your daughter's sadness canceled the lie out. My lie might appear to be leaps and bounds away from yours, but the intention was the same. It was pure.

If you've gotten to the end of this message, thank you for taking the time to read it.

Best,
Sadie Bisset

CHAPTER 11

Sebastian

Nights like this, I thanked God my daughter was here sleeping. If Birdie wasn't home, I might have drunk the entire bottle of scotch or made some other reckless decision. The biggest mistake I made tonight was checking my damn email right before bed. Because now there was no chance of getting any sleep.

I must have read Sadie's message over ten times, but it never got easier to comprehend the fact that my daughter would sooner unload her fears onto a stranger than talk to me. It was a wake-up call. I knew I hadn't been there for Birdie in the way she needed. As much as I tried my best to make her happy, I'd been emotionally unavailable, and my daughter knew it. That was the way I'd always dealt with Amanda's passing, by bottling up my pain and keeping busy.

Sadie Bisset.

There had been something about her from the very beginning. She was a knockout, but I'm not referring to her obvious good looks. There was something oddly familiar about her. I could never figure it out. Now that strange air of familiarity made sense. Even though I didn't know her, in an indirect way, she knew *me*. And she certainly knew Birdie.

Her pretending to be the dog trainer was asinine, though. There was no doubt about that. But everything else? I still didn't know what to make of it.

In some ways, what she'd done for my daughter was endearing, and in other ways, a little insane. But the more I processed that email, the more I did believe Sadie meant no ill will, that her intentions had been good. And there was no way she was making this story up, because she simply knew too much. Everything she mentioned that Birdie had said matched up. It was a relief to know that the dog-trainer act hadn't been malicious. Because of my own anger, I'd given her no chance to explain herself that day. Not knowing who the hell she was and where she'd come from had been haunting me, made worse by the fact that I blamed myself for my poor judgment. Now, at least, everything made sense.

When it hit me, I started to laugh deliriously. The socks.

The fucking socks.

The next morning, I did something I rarely did. I made pancakes. Or I *tried* to make pancakes. Saturday was Magdalene's day off, which meant Birdie's breakfast normally consisted of whatever sugary cereal she'd pull from the closet. Cookie Crisp was her favorite.

But today I vowed to give my daughter a proper breakfast and to have a chat with her when she got up.

Birdie had slept later than usual. She walked into the kitchen rubbing her eyes, her blonde hair a knotted mess.

I flipped the pancake using just the pan to turn it over. "Morning, sunshine."

Her little voice was groggy. "Daddy . . . are you cooking?"

"I sure am."

"Are you sure you should be using the stove?"

That made me laugh. My little girl officially had no faith in her father's cooking skills. But I'd really given her no reason to.

"Hey, now. Your dad is a restaurateur. I know a thing or two about food."

"You know how to burn it." She giggled.

I quickly flipped the pancake I'd been making around again to hide the somewhat overdone side. Then I plated it with the good side up before handing it to her.

"Does this pancake look burned to you?"

"No." She laughed. "Thank you for making it, Daddy."

"You're welcome, sweetheart. I'm making plenty more, too. Go grab the syrup and whipped cream."

After Birdie sat down, I made two more pancakes before grabbing myself a mug of coffee. Then I took a seat across from my daughter. She ate quietly and seemed to be enjoying the flapjacks. Her mother used to make them into Mickey Mouse heads. I was afraid to even attempt that.

Resting my chin in my hand, I said, "Hey . . . I know it seems like I'm always busy. But I want you to know that I'm never too busy for you. If you're ever worried about something, there's nothing you can't tell me. I want to know what you're thinking. Promise me you'll come to me if something is ever bothering you."

Her chewing slowed as she looked up at me with her big eyes. "Okay."

"You mean that?"

She resumed devouring the pancake. "Yes," she said with her mouth full.

After a minute of watching her eat in silence, I tilted my head. "Anything bothering you in this moment that you want to talk to me about?"

She lifted her milk and swallowed it all down in several gulps, then wiped the top of her lip with her sleeve. "No, Daddy," she finally said.

I'd been hoping that she would open up to me about her concerns regarding Sadie. Then I would have had the opportunity to assure her that the situation wasn't her fault. But she said nothing. I realized that despite her assurance that she'd tell me what was bothering her, she still had no intention of opening up to me. And that gutted me. But you can't change old habits overnight. In that moment, I vowed to be more on top of things moving forward, to not let her drift away from me any more than she already had.

"Thank you for making me pancakes."

"My pleasure, baby girl."

She got up and put her plate in the sink before running some water over it.

"Where are you going?" I asked.

"To play in my room."

I frowned but didn't fight it. "Alright."

As she was about to head down the hall, I stopped her.

"Hey . . . I'll let you play for a half hour. But how about we take Marmaduke to the park after? Toss around a ball with him."

She shrugged. "Okay." Then she headed back down the hall to her room.

I knew I couldn't be everything she needed. A girl her age needed her mother, and that was the one thing I couldn't give her. Still, especially after what I now knew, that she sought the help of a stranger, I needed to try harder to fill that void as much as I could.

I deserved a gold star for parenting today. I'd stuck to my promise to not check my business emails or my phone and spent the entire day with Birdie. After we took the dog to the park, we brought him back home before heading for ice cream.

Later, we played Scrabble together before I cooked one of the only things I knew how to make for dinner: spaghetti and meatballs. Normally, we did takeout. It was certainly ironic that the owner of one of the best Italian restaurants in the tristate area couldn't cook for shit.

Birdie and I ate together, then sat down and watched a movie, *Matilda*. I'd remembered Amanda saying that she thought Birdie might enjoy it someday. It was strange that I'd remembered that film randomly today, as if my dead wife had whispered the title in my ear as I was perusing the movie selections online. *Jesus.* Now I was starting to sound like my daughter.

Anyway, every time Birdie smiled or laughed at parts of the film, it both warmed me and cut like a knife. I'd debated whether to tell her that her mom had suggested the movie but ultimately didn't want to make her sad tonight. She seemed off today overall, and I couldn't help but think it had to do with what Sadie mentioned, that Birdie still blamed herself for Sadie's absence. Guilt was a bastard, and when you keep it inside, it festers. It's bad enough when it's warranted, but in this case, it was a complete waste of my poor little girl's time and energy.

After Birdie went to sleep that night, I lay in bed, trying to decide whether I should respond to Sadie's email.

The problem was that I didn't know what I wanted to say to her. A part of me was tempted to give her a piece of my mind for manipulating my daughter with trickery. But a bigger part of me knew that was bullshit. It hadn't been her intent to hurt Birdie. It just made me angry that a stranger playing the role of something that doesn't exist was able to make Birdie happy in a way that I couldn't. And while Sadie's lying was in poor taste, to me that wasn't the issue.

I knew I wouldn't be able to sleep unless I responded to that damn email. So, without overthinking it, I pulled up her message and hit "Reply."

Dear Sadie,

I appreciate you taking the time to explain everything to me. To say that I was shocked to hear the extent to which you had been interacting with my daughter—albeit from afar—is an understatement.

And while I don't fully understand the reasoning behind your decision to let me assume you were the dog trainer, I no longer believe that you intended any malice. So let's just forget about the latter.

The fact of the matter is, your unexplained absence has put my daughter in some kind of funk. I don't even care whether or not the damn dog can jump over your back or whether he sits or humps a turtle. I just want to see my daughter happy. And it's apparent that your being here, even for that brief time, made her happy, as she'd found someone she could relate to. I can't believe I'm about to say this. In fact, I may need to get my head checked . . . but would you consider coming back a few more times to "train" Marmaduke? That way you could plan your eventual exit more gently than the one I forced upon you. We could tell Birdie that you just had to take some time off and that you've returned to finish the job.

I realize that perhaps the crazy has rubbed off on me a bit with this suggestion. I will certainly understand if you don't wish to return, especially after the way I kicked you out. But hopefully, you understand why I did it, given what I was led to believe at the time. In any case, I'm sorry for being so harsh and for not allowing you a moment to explain.

Let me know if you'd be willing to take me up on my offer. I'd pay you double or triple for your time. You'd basically have to do nothing more than keep Marmaduke alive. Given that you've saved his life once already, I trust you can handle that. (That was my best attempt at making light of things and moving forward.)

Sincerely,
Sebastian Maxwell

CHAPTER 12

Sadie

I might've been more nervous than the first time that I climbed these stairs. Though today I didn't really have a reason to be. Everything was out in the open now. Sebastian and I had exchanged a few emails, and he'd invited me back to the house. Yet for some reason, I had a *really* bad case of the jitters.

I took a few deep, cleansing breaths and knocked. A minute later, Birdie opened the door. Her entire face lit up, and she practically knocked me over wrapping her arms around my waist in a hug.

"Sadie! You're back!"

Though we hadn't discussed it, I had just assumed that Sebastian would tell his daughter I was coming today.

"Hey! Yes, I'm back. Didn't you know I was coming?"

The voice that answered wasn't Birdie's. "I thought it would be a nice surprise for her, so I didn't mention it."

Well, I guess we were both surprised, then. Because I thought for sure Sebastian wouldn't be home today. I bent to hug Birdie and looked up at him. He smiled, though I could see the hesitancy in his face.

"Hi. I didn't expect you to be here."

"Disappointed?"

Just the opposite. Although I wasn't sure I could go through with impersonating a dog trainer in front of him now that he knew I wasn't one.

I shook my head. "No, not at all."

Marmaduke squeezed his way between Sebastian and Birdie and jumped up on me. He licked my face with his giant, wet tongue, which made Birdie giggle. The sound felt like a salve for a wound that I'd been nursing the past few weeks.

I scratched Marmaduke's ears. "Hey, buddy. It's good to see you, too. I think you grew two feet in a few weeks. You're getting so big so fast."

Sebastian tugged at the dog's collar. "Down, Marmaduke. *Platz!*"

Shockingly, he listened.

"Uhh. Sorry about that." His eyes dropped to my chest. "His new hobby is digging in the plants. I guess that's what he was doing right before he came to the door."

I looked down to find two giant dirt paw prints, one right over each of my boobs. I attempted to brush them from my white T-shirt. "It's fine. It will come out in the wash."

Sebastian's eyes stared at the mess again. He shook his head and mumbled something under his breath before opening the door wide. "Come in."

Once we were in the living room, he spoke to Birdie. "Sweetheart, why don't you go get yourself dressed?"

"Okay!" She literally skipped to her room.

Sebastian caught my gaze. "She's excited to see you."

I smiled. "The feeling is mutual."

His eyes roamed my face, and I got the feeling he was gauging my sincerity. Seeming like he found what he saw acceptable, he nodded. "Thank you for agreeing to come back."

"I know I've said it in emails. But I really am sorry for everything that happened. One little lie just spiraled into another and before I knew it, I didn't know how to get myself out of it. But I promise you. My intentions were never anything but good when it comes to your daughter."

Sebastian arched a brow. "Just my daughter? Does that mean you have bad intentions with me?"

Uh, yeah. I have very bad intentions when it comes to you. I felt my cheeks start to heat. Luckily, Birdie ran back out and gave me an excuse to hide my face.

"Sadie, do you know how to braid?"

"I do. Would you like me to braid your hair?"

She jumped up and down. "Yes, please!"

"What kind would you like?"

Sebastian's forehead wrinkled. "There's more than one kind of braid?"

I laughed. "There are hundreds of kinds." Turning back to Birdie, I asked, "What about a fishtail braid? Those are my favorite."

She nodded fast. "I love fishtail braids!"

"Why don't you go grab a brush?"

When she ran back out of the room, I noticed Sebastian was staring at me. I put my hand on my chest. "Oh my God. Did I overstep? I should have asked you if it was okay."

He raised his hand. "No. No. It's fine. I appreciate it. Her hair has always been something I struggle with."

"Oh, okay. If you'd like, I could show you how to make the braid while I do it."

"That would be great, actually."

When Birdie came back out with a hairbrush, I took a seat on the couch, and she sat between my legs. Sebastian sat next to me.

God, he smelled so good. I wondered what cologne he wore. It had a woodsy but clean smell . . . perhaps with a little leather thrown in and some . . . what was that . . . eucalyptus? I bet he kept it in the bathroom. Maybe I could . . .

Jesus, Sadie, what the hell is wrong with you? I internally scolded myself. *You're here for Birdie. The last thing you need to do is get caught exploring the medicine cabinet.* I forced myself to ignore the pheromones wafting through the air and focus on Birdie's hair.

After brushing out the tangles, I gathered her hair into a pony and then divided the hair into two equal sections. Lifting one, I explained, "You just take a small section from here." I demonstrated as I spoke. "And you flip it like this before adding it to the inner side like this."

"Okay."

"I'll show you a few more times, and then you can give it a try."

Sebastian looked on as I weaved sections of hair into a symmetrical pattern. I kept going until he could start to see how the braid resembled a fish's tail.

"I get where it got its name now," he said.

I smiled. "Birdie, do you mind if we take a few extra minutes to do this? I'm going to unbraid you and let your dad take a shot."

She laughed. "He braids worse than he makes pancakes. But okay."

I reversed the weaving I'd done and ran my fingers through her hair while talking to Sebastian. "Birdie told me you own a restaurant. How do you not make great pancakes?"

His face grew solemn. "My wife was a chef. I ran the business end of the restaurant."

I frowned. "Oh. I'm sorry."

He nodded.

"Alright, well, let me scoot over, and you give it a try now." I made room for Sebastian to sit behind his daughter and then leaned close to watch and give him step-by-step directions. "Separate the pony into two, and take a small section and flip it before you add it to the inside, like I showed you."

Sebastian took Birdie's hair and separated it, but that was as far as he got. He held on to the pieces of her hair and chuckled. "I have no clue what the hell you just did."

Smiling, I reached over and covered his hand with mine so that I could guide his movements and he could get the feel of the motion of weaving the braid. The gesture was innocent enough, but my hands hugging his felt absolutely electrifying. It rattled me so much that I forgot how the hell to make the damn braid myself. "Umm. You put this one over here . . . No wait . . . that's not right . . . this goes over there." Honestly, I needed to let go of him if I had any chance of Birdie walking out the door without looking like a rat had nested on top of her head.

Sebastian tried in earnest to continue without me, but he was just lost.

Eventually, he sighed. "Why don't you just do it, or we might be here all day."

"Yeah, maybe that's best."

As I went to move back to sit behind Birdie, Sebastian and I stood so we could switch places again. We both attempted to pass each other on the same side and wound up banging into each other.

"Sorry," he said.

"My fault." I smiled.

I moved to my left, and Sebastian moved to his right, which meant we did the same thing again. This time, his eyes flickered to my lips before we managed to figure out how to step around each other.

Was I imagining that just happened? I didn't think so.

He cleared his throat after I sat back down behind Birdie. "I'm going to . . . give Marmaduke some water before we head out."

If what I'd thought just happened had really happened, Birdie seemed oblivious. "See, I told you," she said. "Worse than pancakes."

With Sebastian out of the room, I was able to do Birdie's braid in just a few minutes. She ran to a mirror when I finished. "It's so pretty. Maybe you can teach me how to do my own. I don't think Dad's going to be very good at it."

"Sure. That might be a better idea."

Sebastian returned from the kitchen. "Something came up at the restaurant, and I need to make a few calls. Why don't you two take Marmaduke for his walk, and I'll join you for the training session when you get back."

"Okay, Daddy!"

I had no idea why, but I got the distinct feeling that something hadn't really popped up at work for Sebastian. Though the man *had* let me back into his life, so I wasn't going to do anything stupid. I smoothed the wrinkles from my pants. "We'll be back in about twenty minutes."

Outside, I took Marmaduke's leash, and Birdie walked alongside me.

"I didn't think you were coming back," she said.

"I'm sorry about that. Something . . . unexpected came up. I didn't mean to disappoint you when I had to stop coming."

She shrugged. "It's okay. I'm just glad you're back."

"So what's new? How has Marmaduke been the last few weeks?"

Birdie giggled. "He ate the blanket off Dad's bed, and there were feathers all over the place. Like, a million of them."

"Oh boy. How did he handle that?"

"He was angry. That night, I heard him telling the lady that he wanted to bring Marmaduke to a farm somewhere."

"The lady?"

"My dad talks to this lady sometimes at night. He does it from his room because he thinks I don't hear him."

We got to the corner, and I put my hand out to make sure Birdie didn't keep walking at the red light. While we waited for the crosswalk sign to change, I dug a little deeper.

"Is the lady a friend of his?"

"He got her from the internet."

I had to stifle a laugh. "From the internet? What do you mean?"

Birdie frowned. "I think he's looking for my new mom. This girl Suzie at school said her dad bought his new wife from Russia."

My eyes widened. "He what?"

"She said that her mom said that her dad got his bride through the mail." She shrugged. "From Russia."

"Honey, I think maybe Suzie's mom is saying that facetiously."

"Fay-sheesh-ly?"

I smiled. "Facetiously. It means sort of saying it as a joke to be funny."

"Oh. So her dad didn't buy a wife from Russia, then? I guess that makes sense. Because if he was going to buy one, he'd probably get one his own age, right? Suzie's stepmom is really young."

Or . . . maybe Suzie's dad did buy his bride. Either way, this conversation had taken an odd turn. "What made you think your dad was looking for a new wife?"

"A few weeks ago, I was listening by his door at night, and I heard him tell her he wanted to be up-front with what he was looking for—that he's not looking to date."

Uh-oh. "Did he say what he was looking for?"

"No. But what else would he want if he didn't want to date the lady?"

I wasn't touching this one with a ten-foot pole. Perhaps it was time for a change of subject. I knew from her letters that Suzie was a girl in school who had been mean to her. So I thought maybe it might be an opportunity to see how things were going in that department.

"Is . . . Suzie a good friend of yours?"

Birdie's little face scrunched up like she smelled a rotting fish. "No way. She's the worst."

"Why is she the worst?"

"She makes fun of everyone. About what they wear, their hair, even the books people pick out in the library during quiet time."

The light changed, and the three of us crossed the street. "Do you know why Suzie is mean to people?"

"Because her soul is black?"

I laughed. "Where on earth did you learn about black souls?"

"In religion class. Well, they didn't teach us about black ones. But they said good people have pure souls. And white is kinda pure. So I figured hers must be black."

Well, her logic was pretty damn good. But I wanted to steer the conversation back to the real reason some kids were bullies.

"Actually, usually kids who are mean don't really like themselves. They put other people down in an attempt to make them feel better about themselves."

Birdie guffawed at that notion. "Suzie likes herself a lot. She thinks she's the best at everything."

"That's what Suzie *wants* you to believe. But I bet you deep down, she's really struggling."

"I don't know . . ."

Clearly Birdie wasn't sold. "Let me see if I can guess a few things about Suzie."

"Okay . . ."

"Is she overly concerned with what she looks like? Like, is her hair always done just right, and she wears nice outfits every single day instead of just throwing on a pair of sweats and a wrinkly T-shirt sometimes, like the rest of us do?"

"Yeah. She's *always* perfect."

"And does she belong to a clique of girls, and they all sort of travel as a pack—all together?"

"Yeah."

"Does she start rumors about people at school?"

Birdie's head whipped to me. "How did you know that? Last week she told everyone that Amelia Aster still wears pull-up pants to sleep because she pees her pants. But she doesn't. I'm good friends with Amelia, and we've had sleepovers."

"You see . . . I knew all that because those are all the classic signs of the mean girls who don't like themselves very much."

"Did you have mean girls in school?"

"I sure did. And you know what I found out worked best to make them stop picking on me?"

"What?"

"Smiling."

Birdie looked confused. "Smiling?"

"Yup. Whenever a bully said anything mean to me, I would just smile back at her. After a while, when my bully stopped getting a reaction from me, she left me alone."

A stray cat ran out from nowhere in front of us. Unfortunately, Marmaduke saw it before I did, so I wasn't prepared when he took off running. My hand had been looped through the leash, and he tugged me along for the ride.

"Marmaduke! *No! Stop!*"

He didn't listen. I ran past six or seven houses screaming like a lunatic and trying to keep up. The damn dog was pretty fast.

Birdie caught up to me and yelled, *"Nein!"*

Marmaduke instantly halted.

My hand covered my racing heart. "Oh my God. Thank you. I can't believe he listened to you."

"I've been working with him every day."

"Wow. Well, that's great. Obviously you've done really well with him."

Birdie beamed. "Thank you."

The rest of our walk was uneventful, and we returned to the Maxwell house after about twenty minutes.

"How was your walk?" Sebastian asked his daughter.

"Good. Marmaduke tried to chase a cat."

Sebastian looked over at me and frowned. "How'd that go?"

"Well, to be honest, it wasn't going too well. He caught me off guard, and I couldn't get him to back down. But Birdie here got him to stop."

She shrugged. "It was no big deal. Sadie was the one who taught him the word. I just yelled it."

Sebastian smiled warmly at me. It made my stomach do a little flip.

God, I'm wound tight today. I unclipped the leash from Marmaduke's collar, and he took a few steps before sprawling out on the area rug. It looked like he might go down for a nap. "I think the pup is sufficiently tuckered out now. So I guess we should get started? I was thinking that today we could work on 'stay' and 'down.'" Lord knows I'd watched about a hundred hours of different videos to learn training techniques for just those two commands.

Sebastian stayed in the room, but he took a seat off to the side and left the training to Birdie and me. Every once in a while, I'd look over and see him watching us. After more than an hour of training, he looked at his watch and stood.

"I think you went over on your session time."

"It's okay. They did great today, don't you think?"

Sebastian walked over. "They sure did." He crouched down to his daughter. "I think all your hard work deserves some ice cream. What do you say we hit Emack & Bolio's before I have to go to work?"

Birdie flashed a toothy smile. "Yes!"

"Alright. Why don't you go get washed up . . . and use soap, okay?"

"Okay, Daddy!" Birdie looked at me. "Sadie, do you want to come? They make this purple ice cream, and it looks so pretty with Cap'n Crunch on top."

"Umm. That sounds delicious. But I should probably be going."

She frowned. "Okay. But you're going to come again, right?"

I smiled. "Yes, definitely."

"When?"

"Why don't I work that out with your dad while you get washed up."

Birdie threw her arms around my waist in a hug. "Thank you for coming back."

This little girl truly made my heart melt. I bent down and gave her braid a tug. "Thank you for all the practice you did while I couldn't be here the last few weeks. I'm really proud of you."

After she skipped off to the bathroom, Sebastian had a funny look on his face.

"What?" I wiped at my cheek. "Do I have dirt on me again from Marmaduke?"

"No. I just . . . She really has a strong connection with you. Honestly, she hasn't bonded with any woman since her mom died."

"Are there . . . other women in her life?"

"She has an aunt who lives in Jersey. She comes to visit every few weeks and always brings her a thoughtful gift. But . . . I don't know . . . whatever you have together is just different."

I smiled. "I feel connected to her, too. I hope that's okay?"

Sebastian put his hands in his pockets and looked down. "Yeah, it's great, actually. I guess I didn't realize how much she missed a woman in her life until recently."

A woman in her life . . . That reminded me. I nodded toward the front door. "Do you think we can speak outside for a minute or two?"

His brows drew together, but he said, "Yeah, of course."

Once we were out front with the door closed, I wasn't quite sure how to say what I wanted to say.

Sebastian looked troubled as he waited for me to formulate my thoughts. "Is everything okay?"

"Yeah. Everything is fine. It's just . . . Birdie said something to me that I thought I should make you aware of."

"What's that?"

"Well, apparently she knows you talk to a woman online at night."

Sebastian's face fell. "*Shit.* What exactly did she say?"

"She thinks you're trying to buy a bride . . . a new mom for her."

"What?" His eyes widened. "Why the heck would she think that?"

"Sometimes at night she eavesdrops on your conversations from outside your bedroom door. She overheard you tell a woman that you didn't want to date her. So she assumed that meant you were looking for a wife and not a date."

Sebastian's eyes shut, and he shook his head. "I meant that I was looking for . . ." He opened his eyes, and our gazes met. "I occasionally will meet a woman online. I try to be up-front about . . . Well, when I said I didn't want to date, I meant I didn't want an emotional relationship." He frowned. "I don't want more than the physical part. If you know what I mean."

"Sure. Of course. I sort of figured that's what you'd meant. But I didn't explain it to Birdie because obviously it wasn't my place to tell her that her father was just cruising for a hookup."

Sebastian dragged a hand through his hair. "There haven't been too many. I don't want you to think . . ."

I put my hands up. "No explanation needed. We're adults. With needs. Trust me, I get it." I laughed nervously. "Or maybe I understand since I *don't get it* enough."

Sebastian cracked a smile. "Dry spell?"

"The profiles of the people who like my online dating profile look like a sex-offender registry."

We both laughed.

"Yeah, it's not easy," he said. Sebastian's eyes dropped to do a quick sweep over my body and then rose to meet mine again. Finding that I'd just watched him check me out, he cleared his throat. "So . . . when can you come again?"

Interesting choice of words.

"How about the same time next week?"

"That'd be great. And thanks for letting me know about Birdie's snooping. I really appreciate it."

"Of course. See you next week."

I walked down the front stairs and toward the corner. With every step, I had the strongest urge to look back and see if Sebastian was watching me. When I reached the end of the block, before I turned, I gave in and looked back. Sebastian hadn't moved from the spot I'd left him.

I sighed to myself. *Yeah. It's not easy out there. But I wouldn't mind climbing that man like a tree.*

CHAPTER 13

SEBASTIAN

"She's pretty, isn't she?"

"Hmm?" I pretended not to hear the question that Magdalene had just hit me with. We were alone in the kitchen right after Sadie and Birdie had left to head to the park with Marmaduke.

Sadie didn't really have a set day here. She basically agreed to come whenever her schedule allowed. Today happened to be a Sunday and was Sadie's second visit since her return. We hadn't discussed an actual end date, but she didn't seem anxious to stop the visits. As long as Birdie was happy, I wasn't going to be the one to initiate ending the arrangement.

"Sadie. She's very pretty," she repeated.

As if I hadn't heard her the first time.

I took one last sip of coffee and said, "I'm actually late for a meeting with an imported-olive-oil vendor at the restaurant, so . . ."

"You're trying to avoid the topic. I understand."

I froze just as I was exiting the kitchen, then turned. "What do you expect me to say? Of course she's a beautiful girl."

She wiped the counters. "And sweet . . . and seems like a good person."

"What are you getting at, Magdalene?"

"Nothing . . . I just noticed you . . . looking at her, and—"

"Goodbye, Magdalene." I smiled so she didn't think I was mad. But I needed to completely dismiss this topic of conversation.

The fact that she'd noticed me checking Sadie out was not good. I'd actually been making a concerted effort *not* to do that. But it wasn't easy. It was hard not to look at her, to admire her natural beauty whenever we were in the same room. Sadie was attractive in a clean and effortless way. She didn't need a drop of makeup. And let's not get started on her body. It was perfect. So I noticed. *Sue me, Magdalene.*

After I'd gone to my office to grab my keys and wallet, I was just about to head out the front door when she stopped me one more time.

"Mr. Maxwell . . ."

I turned. "Yes?"

She looked down at her feet. "It's just . . . it's been four years, and I wonder if—"

"I understand that your intentions are good. But I'm not interested in a relationship or a . . . replacement. No one will ever replace Amanda. Is that what you're hinting at?"

"Of course not. But you deserve to be happy . . . and Mrs. Maxwell would have wanted you to be."

I laughed. "Mrs. Maxwell would not have been happy that I was ogling the cute blonde dog trainer, Mags. If you think otherwise, then you didn't know my wife very well."

"I'm sorry." She shook her head. "I shouldn't have pried."

"I know you mean well. But I've finally developed a groove. And that doesn't include anything serious when it comes to dating or relationships. I barely have time for my daughter."

She shut her eyes and nodded. "Understood. As long as you're happy."

I wasn't gonna touch that comment. "Happy" wasn't exactly the right word. Stable, maybe. Holding things together, maybe. Not burning down the house, maybe. But happy? There wasn't any time for happy. Happy didn't live here anymore.

Magdalene had been around our family for a very long time. When she wasn't watching Birdie, she cleaned and cooked for us. At this point, she was the one constant in our lives. She also knew way too much. I knew she'd found the condoms in my underwear drawer once because she'd neatly placed the strip back into the box and closed it. She clearly knew I hadn't been celibate. Maybe that gave her the wrong idea—like just because my dick was functioning again, maybe there was hope for my heart. But it didn't work that way. Evidently, Birdie wasn't the only one wishing for a "special friend" around here.

Later that night, my daughter ran into the study, where I'd been doing some inventory work for Bianco's.

She seemed frantic when she said, "Daddy . . . you have to call Sadie."

"Why?"

She lifted a tablet she was holding. "She forgot her iPad mini here."

I took the device from her and looked down at it. "Oh. Well, I'm sure she can do without it until she sees us again."

"No! She told me she uses it for work. She puts all her notes on it. You know, from her dates and stuff. She let me borrow it to watch something with her Hulu account while she was talking with Magdalene. I put it down to go steal cookies from the pantry while they weren't paying attention. Then I started talking to them in the kitchen, and she left without taking it. I forgot I had it in my room until now."

I blew out an exasperated breath. "Alright. I've got her number. I'll give her a call. I can let her know it's here if she wants to come get it."

"Thanks, Daddy."

She placed her arms around my neck, and I gently squeezed her little frame.

Rubbing her back, I said, "Go get some sleep. It's late."

Birdie ran out of the room, and I listened to her footsteps as she headed down the hall.

I stared at the phone in my hands for several seconds before scrolling down to Sadie's name.

When she picked up, I heard a ton of background noise before she finally said, "Hello?"

"Hey . . . it's Sebastian Maxwell."

She spoke over the muffled sounds. "Oh. Hey. How are you?" It sounded like she might have been inside a crowded restaurant or bar.

"I'm calling because you left your iPad here. Sadie was adamant that I let you know."

"Oh crap. That's right. I'd let her borrow it and completely forgot to take it back before I left."

"Anyway, we can hang on to it. I just wanted to let you know it was here, in case you were looking for it."

"Do you mind if I stop by tonight and get it?"

Not expecting that, I hesitated. "Sure."

"Thank you. I'm sorry for the bother. I can be there in about a half hour."

I ran a hand through my hair. "Okay."

"Great. Thanks. See you in a bit."

After we hung up, I stayed at my desk, bouncing my legs up and down, swiveling in my seat, tapping my pen, crumpling up paper. Anything but concentrating on work. I finally gave up and took the iPad out into the living room while I anticipated her arrival any minute.

When that knock finally came, nothing could have prepared me for the sight on the other side of the door. When I opened it, I found Sadie standing there in a tiny black dress, only a fur cape covering her shoulders. She wore leather boots that went all the way up to her knees.

Her long blonde hair was wavier than normal. She looked sexy as all hell, and it honestly made me have to catch my breath for a second. My gaze lingered on hers. A streetlight caught her eyes just enough for the blue of her irises to glow in the dark. Fuck, she was beautiful. A thought of what those eyes would look like staring up from under me crossed my mind. *Really, Sebastian?*

She took a few steps inside the doorway, even though I hadn't exactly invited her in yet. Although it was cold out, and I would've anyway.

"You're awfully dressed up. Hot date tonight?"

She looked down at herself, seeming almost embarrassed by her attire. "Oh God. No. I *was* on a date. Or rather . . . an assignment for work. Not a real date."

"Ah. I should've known."

"That's where I was when you called. This was the perfect excuse to get out of it, let me tell ya."

"No wonder you were so eager to come get your iPad so late. Another bomb, huh?"

"Let's put it this way: he went to the bathroom more times than I could count. Either he had a bad case of diarrhea or he's a drug addict. Either way, I'm all set."

I broke out into a laugh. "Ouch."

"Yeah. Let's just hope he washed his hands each time before digging through the breadbasket." She sighed. "Anyway . . . I'll take my iPad and be on my merry way."

"Oh. Yeah. I have it right here." I scratched my head, momentarily having forgotten where I put it.

After I spotted it on the end table, I grabbed it. But not before tripping on the damn end table. Having her here was making me tense. I finally handed it to her.

"Thanks again," she said as she took it. "I can't believe I left this here. If it didn't have all my notes on it from earlier this week, I might have been able to wait until the next time I came, but I have a deadline." She looked beyond my shoulder. "I assume Birdie is asleep?"

"Yeah. Or possibly pretending to be asleep until she decides to sneak out of her room and steal a few cookies."

She smiled, and it lit up her whole face. "Of course." Her smile faded, and she backed up a few feet toward the door. "Well, I'll get out of your hair. Thanks again." She lingered as if she wasn't quite ready to leave.

The second she turned around, I felt this odd feeling, like the house went from warm to cold. And fuck. I wanted the warmth back.

Don't do it.

Don't do it.

"Sadie . . . ," I called out.

She turned back around in an instant. "Yes?"

"It's cold out. I usually put on some tea around this time . . . try to relax and unwind. Would you want to stay and have a cup with me before you hit the road?"

There was that smile again. "After the night I've had . . . a hot cup of tea sounds really good."

"Great. I, uh, promise not to run to the bathroom every two minutes."

She cackled. "Seriously. Who does that?"

Sadie followed me to the kitchen and sat down at the table. I grabbed the kettle and filled it with filtered water from the tap before setting two ceramic teacups down on the counter.

"Black tea okay?" I asked.

"Yes. I can have caffeine any time of night and still fall asleep."

"Me too. Even coffee."

"Same." She grinned.

"You take milk . . . sugar? Or I have honey."

"Just a little milk. Thank you."

As I waited for the water to boil, I leaned back against the granite and crossed my arms.

"So, how often do you do your *research* per week?"

"You mean how many disastrous dates do I endure?" She laughed. "A few at most. That's enough. It's seriously scary out there."

I felt oddly protective of her. "You always meet them in public, right?"

"Always."

It honestly surprised me that she didn't have her choice of any man she wanted.

"You know . . . I'm actually shocked that you don't have better luck. You're clearly attractive, smart . . . why all the losers?"

"New York is the problem, honestly. There are more women than men here. It makes the dating game tricky. You have to work much harder to find the good ones. And the good ones have their pick of many. I honestly avoid going out altogether when I'm not working."

"I met my wife in college and never had to do the online dating thing. It's one of the things I loved about being married, not having to worry about the logistics of all that."

"It's a huge time suck."

The kettle started whistling, so I prepared her tea, adding a splash of milk, then the boiling water before steeping the teabag.

I placed the cups on the table and sat down.

"Thank you," she said before blowing on the steam.

"So, today went well with the dog?" I asked.

"You're clearly referring to the actual dog and not the dog I met tonight . . ."

"Yes, I was referring to the Duke."

"The Duke." She nearly spit out her tea. "I love that nickname for him." She looked around. "Where the heck is the Duke anyway?"

"He sleeps when Birdie sleeps. Does that surprise you?"

"Not a bit. That's so cute." She beamed. "And yeah. Today was actually one of the better days we've had. He listens to Birdie so well now, which was the point of all this, right?"

"*Was* that the point? I thought the point of this was initially . . . a butterfly barrette, wasn't it?" I teased.

Her face actually turned pink, and it was fucking adorable. She looked down into her cup, shaking her head. "I deserved that."

"I'm kidding. You know that, right?"

"At least you're laughing about it and not calling the police on me."

"I wouldn't have called the police on you. That was an empty threat."

"Well, that's good at least."

"You'll be happy to know, I sometimes think back and laugh at the ridiculousness of what happened," I said, starting to crack up unexpectedly. "When you found out he was supposed to be trained in German . . . you must have inwardly freaked."

She was laughing now, too. "You have no idea."

"I've got to give you credit for even attempting to tackle it. That took some serious balls."

"Balls and a dash of lunacy."

Our eyes locked for a moment. There was something so comfortable about being around her. She always seemed familiar, even though I knew we'd never met before this whole thing with Birdie. Speaking of my daughter, there was so much I wanted to ask Sadie while I had her attention. But I didn't know if it would be too intrusive. I took a chance.

"Do you mind if I pick your brain about something?"

"Sure. I think I managed to salvage some of my brain that didn't get fried during my date tonight. I'll be happy to offer up what's left."

I chuckled. "Okay. I appreciate that."

She took a sip of her tea, then said, "What's up?"

I rested my chin on my wrist. "I know you said your mother died when you were six and a half, just like Birdie. Looking back at your childhood with just a father and no mother, what, if anything, do you wish your dad had done differently?"

She nodded a few times and pondered that. "That's an interesting question. I can see why you'd be curious about that, given you're in the same situation."

"Well, you have the rare gift of hindsight. I'm just trying to prevent making any mistakes along the way that might be avoidable. Birdie is still so young. I can't imagine what things will be like when she gets into her teen years. If there's a way to plan ahead . . ."

Her eyes moved from side to side. She looked like she was struggling to come up with an answer that would satisfy me. "There's really nothing specific I can say I'd change when it comes to how my dad handled anything with me. I was always very conscious of the fact that my dad was doing the very best he could. What more could I have asked for? But what parents fail to understand sometimes . . . is just how much kids can see through them. I could always tell if my dad was depressed, even if he was trying to hide it from me. I really wish he had taken more time for himself and not worried so much about how things might affect me. Us daughters . . . we're tougher than you think. And in the end, we really want to see our dads happy. Because that makes us happy."

"Yeah," I whispered. "Okay. Fair enough."

They say people come into your life for a reason. Maybe Sadie and I were meant to meet because her personal experience mirrored ours. I'd never encountered anyone who quite understood our situation like she did. Talking to her definitely brought me a lot of comfort, made me feel less alone. That was a first since Amanda died.

"Birdie knows how hard you try and how much you love her. And she can also sense when you're down."

"I'm starting to realize that more and more."

Sadie flashed a sympathetic smile. "When my dad was diagnosed with cancer, I—"

"Wait . . . your father had cancer, too?" I hadn't meant to interrupt her. But that was pretty shocking to hear.

"Yeah. My dad was diagnosed with colon cancer when I was a teenager. Can you believe that? He's in remission now, thank God."

I shook my head in disbelief. "I can't imagine how scary that must have been for you . . . and for him."

"It really was. It tested my faith big-time. I didn't understand how that could be happening to me twice. But I tried my best not to dwell on the *woe is me* aspect. He needed every bit of strength I had to help him get through it, not only mentally but physically. So the self-pity had to wait. It was a few years of touch and go. When he finally did make it through, I, of course, felt like I dodged a bullet. And it's made me even more grateful for him."

Her attitude blew me away. "Wow. You were really surrounded by cancer growing up."

"I was. So much so that at one point, I went and got genetic testing done because I was certain I was destined to have it, too. Which is absurd."

"I don't think it's so strange. A lot of cancers are genetic. Sounds like you made a mature decision to get tested."

"Umm. Did I mention that I'm adopted?" She laughed. "I understood that I didn't have the same genes as my mom and dad. Yet I was convinced that I had it, too. Still think it's not so strange?"

I smiled. "Alright. So I guess that does change things a bit."

"Yeah. My mom couldn't have children. She was diagnosed with ovarian cancer the first time at twenty-three. They tried for years after she went into remission, but the chemo did a lot of damage."

"It's amazing . . . how your situation mirrors ours. My wife and I struggled to get pregnant as well and went the route of getting fertility help."

"Oh wow. That's crazy. But I guess that's another reason why Birdie and I connected so easily. We're both extra special because our parents had to work that much harder to have us."

I smiled. "Anyway, I'm sorry if I got us off on a depressing tangent there for a little while. But I really appreciate the insight. It's been four years since Amanda died, but the solo-parenting thing still feels like uncharted territory every single day."

I closed my eyes for a moment, contemplating what my life had become. Then I opened them and spoke in somewhat of a daze. "You spend your youth trying to make something of yourself, feeling invincible, running on adrenaline. Finally fall into a career, have a family . . . everything's perfect, right? Then, when something like cancer enters the picture when your life has barely even started, it knocks the wind out of you. But it's too much to fathom. The only way I handled her being sick was to pretend it wasn't happening. Telling myself and her that everything was going to be fine. You go through the motions of each day, trying to be strong for everyone. It's like a constant state of numbness. And it has to be. Because feeling what was happening wasn't an option. Even when she died, I was still numb. It doesn't hit you, really, until some random time. You know, long after the people stop coming over and bringing food. I woke up one random morning. The *TODAY* show was on. It was just a regular morning for most. But that was the day it just hit me that my life as I knew it was really over. Or at least it felt that way. But it really couldn't be over, right? Because I had to keep going somehow . . . for Birdie. So you start to push again, building a new life from the ground up, still trying not to really *feel* anything too much, because that might throw your progress off track." I rubbed my eyes and sighed. "Anyway, it's a strange existence sometimes."

Jesus. I really had taken us somewhere depressing.

Her eyes were piercing. She looked like she might cry. I hoped to hell she wouldn't. I couldn't have handled that.

"I felt every word you just said, Sebastian. Every word. I've obviously never lost a spouse, but I watched my dad go through it. And I understand firsthand that feeling of going through the motions. I really do."

I downed the last of my lukewarm tea, wishing it were scotch, and placed the empty cup down. "What a fucking downer this tea turned out to be. I bet you're wishing you were back with Bathroom Boy right about now."

"God, no." She sighed. "Do you know how rare it is to have a deep, adult conversation that I can relate to?"

"I certainly didn't plan to ambush you with that."

"Anytime you want to talk. Honestly. I'm happy to listen." She winked. "But you might get an earful from me, too. That's the risk."

"Alright. Thanks."

Sadie tilted her head and studied me quietly. She seemed to be debating something she might want to say.

"Can I ask you something?" she eventually said.

"Pretty sure I owe you an answer to anything you want after what I just asked you to answer."

A giant grin spread across her face. "Good. If you were watching a naked woman dance, would you rather she danced to Sir Mix-a-Lot or Lewis Capaldi?"

I chuckled. "You're an interesting woman, Sadie. That is definitely *not* a question I could have anticipated you asking right now."

"Is that a bad or good thing?"

My eyes looked back and forth between her eyes. "It's a very good thing. And I really *like big butts*."

It took her a second to realize what I'd meant. I had no idea why she'd asked the question, but the smile on her face told me I'd picked the right answer, and I liked that a whole lot.

We ended up busting out Birdie's cookies and talking some more. She told me a little about her childhood upstate, about her dad's funny weather instruments, and asked me some questions about the restaurant business, which of course I could've talked about all night. We spoke about her career. Sadie told me while she didn't foresee leaving the magazine, she hoped to move away from the dating column eventually to try something new. The conversation with her was just . . . easy.

And it had felt good to unload, too. But now that I'd snapped out of my fleeting emotional stupor from earlier, I was back to staring at her lips while she spoke. That felt wrong for so many reasons. If it were just a physical attraction, maybe I could have justified it. But there was a pang in my chest right now that I didn't want to feel. That I *couldn't* feel.

And here comes closed-off Sebastian in three, two, one . . .

My chair skidded against the floor as I slid it back. "Well, I don't want to keep you."

She looked surprised by my sudden hint that it might be time for her to leave. She'd seemed so comfortable. Just like I'd felt before that realization hit. I *was* comfortable. *Too comfortable.*

She looked down at her phone. "Yeah. I, uh, better get going."

I ended up calling her an Uber.

After she left that night, I took our dirty teacups to the sink and noticed the red lipstick mark on hers. And my dick twitched.

Now I'd resorted to getting turned on by a lipstick mark? It was definitely time to get laid again. Just not with Sadie.

I repeat. Not with Sadie.

CHAPTER 14

Sadie

"So what's going on in Birdie Land? I feel like you've clammed up ever since you started going back to the Maxwell household again." Devin plopped down in a guest chair on the other side of my desk with her coffee in hand. She wiggled her eyebrows. "Better yet, what's going on with Hot Dad?"

I had been pretty quiet on that front lately. While I'd shared all the crazy antics with her since the very first letter, something changed after I'd come clean and Sebastian let me resume my visits. I wasn't pretending to be someone I wasn't anymore, so things sort of became . . . I don't know . . . real. And that made it feel private, like something I shouldn't be gossiping about.

But after the other night when I went to pick up my iPad, and Sebastian and I spent some time talking, I did feel the need to talk about things right now. God knows I'd overanalyzed that evening enough already and still couldn't make heads or tails of what had gone wrong.

"Actually . . . I spent some time alone with Sebastian a few nights ago."

Devin's eyes widened. "Oh my God! And you are telling me this *now*? Why didn't I get the play-by-play the day after it happened?"

I smiled. "It's not what you think. I forgot my iPad, and Sebastian called me to tell me. I was in the middle of a bad date, so I used his call as an excuse to end it early and went over there to pick it up. We wound up having tea and talking for a long time. I thought we were having a great conversation, very heartfelt, yet we were still able to poke fun and share a few laughs. At one point, I could've sworn I noticed him watching my lips with *that look* . . . you know the one . . . where you're paying attention to the conversation and then all of a sudden your body takes over for the brain and starts to focus on what that mouth might feel like if you pressed your lips up against it."

"Oh wow. That kind of a look. Yeah, I totally get it."

"Right. Well, shortly after what I thought might've been him giving me that look, he got up and abruptly ended the conversation. Next thing I knew, I was suddenly in the back of a smelly Uber with a driver eating curried goat as he drove."

"Mm . . . did you find out where he got the curry? I love it, and the place I used to go to closed down."

"Uhh. No, sorry."

Devin shrugged. "Anywho . . . back to Hot Dad. It's obvious he's into you and that freaked him out a bit."

"But why? He's been with women before. He as much as admitted that to me when I told him his daughter was listening to him talk to women at night. So his problem isn't celibacy."

Devin frowned. "You're looking for Mr. Right, Sadie. Anyone can see that pretty quickly. It's why you haven't really had a long-term relationship of more than a few months. You don't want Mr. Right Now or just some random guy to take care of business. I'm sure Sebastian senses that about you."

I sighed. "I wouldn't mind Sebastian taking care of my business."

My friend's eyes sparkled. "Now you're talking. So why not put that out there? You're both adults. He's attracted to you, we're attracted to him."

I laughed at how she'd said *we're* attracted to him. But I wasn't so sure about proposing to Sebastian that we get it on. "What if I misread the entire situation, and I had a piece of salad from dinner between my teeth that he was staring at?"

"Do some testing. Bend to tie your shoe when he's behind you, and see if you find his eyes glued to your ass. Better yet, show him that red-and-black lacy bra and underwear set you bought at that Victoria's Secret sale we went to last month."

"Sure . . . I'll just whip off my top and jeans while I'm training a Great Dane. That's a great plan."

Devin stood. "You'll figure out something. I'm pretty sure you can easily get the reassurance you're looking for to feel certain that Sebastian is attracted to you. That's not the issue."

My brows drew together. "It's not?"

"Nope. The issue is you'll be too chicken to act on it even once you're sure he wants to bang your brains out. You don't do that type of thing."

"I've had casual sex before. You know that."

She sipped her coffee. "Yes, but that's when you knew the guy was all wrong for you. In your mind, it could only ever be casual sex. But with Sebastian, I think you see him as real potential. You'll be too chicken to jump into the fire—no matter how hot and sweaty that fire might be—because you'll be too concerned about getting burned."

"That's ridiculous."

Devin walked to the door of my office. "Prove me wrong. I'd love to see it."

Friday night, I had a forty-five-minute yoga class at five thirty in the evening and then I was scheduled to go train Marmaduke at seven thirty. I figured I'd have time to run home, take a quick shower, and throw my hair into a ponytail before heading uptown. But I considered altering those plans after walking out of the studio. I hadn't changed out of my yoga outfit, and a really cute guy looked my way while I stood out front checking my cell phone messages. His eyes were so glued to me that he actually tripped over his own two feet.

I looked at him on the ground. "Are you okay?"

The man looked embarrassed. He stood, wiped dirt from his pants, and offered a crooked smile. "Yeah. Though you really shouldn't walk around the streets in that. People could get hurt."

I blushed a little, and after he walked away, I looked down to check out my outfit. I had on a deep-purple Lululemon cropped top and a pair of matching leggings with a swirl of mesh cutouts running down each leg. It fit like a second skin, which was why it was perfect for yoga. I had a matching zip-up sweatshirt, but it was stuffed into my gym bag, since it was almost seventy degrees out still, even though it was late October. The last two days had been a real Indian summer. But the man's reaction gave me an idea. Or rather it was Devin's idea. Perhaps I should skip going home to change and head over to the Maxwell house dressed like this.

I picked up my phone and debated texting Sebastian to see if I could come a little early, but after a minute, I rolled my eyes at what I'd been considering. *What the hell is wrong with me?* I didn't need to resort to tactics like this to get a man's attention. Any man who wasn't interested in me without me being half-naked wasn't really interested in me. Wow . . . I *really* just sounded like my dad.

Blowing out a stream of hot air, I headed for the subway. Once I got on my train, I noticed another man looking my way. This outfit definitely caught attention. It made me wonder about what Sebastian would do if I actually showed up wearing it. Would I be disappointed that he didn't even notice, or would he trip over his own two feet?

Oh my God.

Sebastian *had* tripped the other day! I'd forgotten all about that. It was right after he'd opened the door and went to go get my iPad. But that had to be a coincidence. I'd only ever noticed him ogling my body once before that. Though that night, I had been all dressed up for my date. But then again, the Maxwell house had an area rug in the living room. I bet the end was rolled up from Marmaduke's running around like a madman, and Sebastian hadn't noticed. Yeah . . . that had to be it.

I took out my phone to scroll through emails and occupy my six-stop train ride with something other than thoughts of Sebastian Maxwell. It worked for the first two stops, but then the train came to an abrupt halt. A few minutes later, we were still not moving when a muffled voice came overhead.

"Ladies and gentlemen. We have another train on the track up ahead that seems to have run into some mechanical problems. We're going to stick it out here for the time being. I'll update you as soon as I know more."

The occupants of the train let out a collective sigh and mumbled bitching echoed all around. After ten more minutes, the conductor's voice came overhead again.

"Alright, so it looks like they're going to need some time to work on that disabled train up ahead. We're going to have to back it up to the 23rd Street Station and let you out to jump on another line. But there's a train behind us, and they need to be relocated first. Service employees will be on hand for those of you not familiar with our lovely subway system. Hope you enjoyed this fun start to your weekend."

Everyone groaned. It took almost another half hour of waiting, but eventually we started to back up slowly. By the time we made it to the 23rd Street Station, it was twenty after seven already. As soon as I got up to street level, I dialed the Maxwell house. Birdie answered.

"Hello."

"Hey, Birdie. It's Sadie. Is your dad home?"

"No. He's at work. Are you still coming?"

I smiled hearing the concern in her voice. "Yes, of course. I'm just running late because my train got stuck. Could I maybe talk to Magdalene to see if it's okay if I come later than planned?"

"Sure!"

Magdalene got on the line. "Hi, Sadie."

"Hi, Magdalene. I'm running a little late. Would it be alright if I came at maybe eight thirty? Is that too late for Birdie?"

"Umm. Well, she actually has a sleepover tonight. Her friend down the block is having a slumber party for her birthday. Six girls are going. It starts at eight, but I was just going to run her down when you guys were done. But I guess she could go at nine thirty. She just went into the bathroom. Want me to ask her if that's okay with her?"

I sighed. "No. I don't want her to miss even more of her party. I can jump back on the train and head uptown now. I'll probably still be, like, ten minutes late."

"Okay. No problem."

"Thanks, Magdalene."

I speed walked the two blocks to cross over to the uptown line that stopped closest to their house and then slipped inside a waiting train just as the doors were beginning to slide closed. The car was packed and standing room only. So I jockeyed for a spot next to a pole so I could hold on as the train jerked to start moving.

Unlike my earlier commute, the express train uptown proved uneventful, and I arrived at the Maxwell house only seven minutes late. I knocked and waited, expecting Magdalene to let me in.

Only it wasn't Magdalene staring at me once the door swung open.

CHAPTER 15

Sebastian

Jesus Christ.

I swallowed. What the hell was she wearing?

"Uhh. Hi. I didn't expect you to be home. Birdie said you were at work."

My uncontrollable attraction to Sadie pissed me off, and I took my frustration out on her. "Is that why you're late? When the cat's away, the mouse will play?"

"*No.* I called Magdalene and told her that my train got stuck. I was planning on going home to shower after my yoga class. But since the train delayed me an hour, I rushed straight here so I wouldn't make Birdie even later for the birthday party she has tonight."

She has a belly-button ring. So sparkly . . .

Fuck. I forced my eyes up to meet Sadie's and found her staring at me expectantly. Had she just said something? Trying to rewind the last ten seconds in my head, I thought she might've . . . something about a train?

Whatever.

I stepped aside. "Come in. Magdalene just brought Marmaduke back from a long walk, so he's sprawled out on the living room floor."

We walked into the house, and Marmaduke looked up. He spotted Sadie, and his tongue started to wag out of his mouth.

Yeah, I know the feeling, buddy.

Birdie ran out from her room and hugged Sadie, who bent as they embraced, giving me a front-row view of her ass. *Christ.* She looked as good going as she did coming. My eyes were still glued to that ass when she turned around to speak to me, and I almost got caught.

"Were you able to get the training clicker I mentioned last week?" she asked.

My daughter ran to the coffee table and got the contraption from hell and started to click it.

Click-click. Click-click. Click-click.

That sound had been grating on my nerves for the better part of a week since I'd brought it home from the pet store. I looked at Sadie, still feeling irritated, though I was bullshitting myself if I thought my current mood had anything to do with that training clicker.

"Maybe next time you can pick something a little less annoying to use to train."

Sadie's hands flew to her hips. *Her very shapely hips.* "Is there something wrong?"

I raked a hand through my hair and grumbled. "I'll be in my office if you need me."

Luckily, my office had alcohol. Today had been a long day to begin with. My manager had given me two weeks' notice, which meant I was going to have to find a replacement and spend a lot more time at the restaurant until I got a new one trained. Then a small grease fire had broken out in the kitchen, rendering one of our deep fryers unusable, and finally our vegetable shipment had been switched with another restaurant that apparently planned to make corn a side dish with every meal. I'd come home early, figuring that I wouldn't get many chances to do that again in two weeks. Plus, I hadn't been sleeping well the last few days for some reason. So I opened a bottle of wine from where I kept the liquor locked up in a credenza and poured myself a very full glass of cabernet as I sat down in my chair.

God, she is fucking sexy.

I slurped a mouthful of the purple liquid down.

I had the craziest urge to clasp my teeth around that diamond in her navel and give it a good strong tug.

I swallowed another mouthful.

And that ass. Maybe she could teach Duke to jump again. I bet it would be some view of her down on all fours in the getup she had on today.

Another mouthful.

What had she called it again? *"Flunk shit." "Flukerbutt." "Flunkerbsht."* That was it. "Jump" was *"flunkerbsht."* I started to laugh. The sound was almost maniacal.

Flunkerbsht.

I want to flunkerbsht *the pretend dog trainer.*

I shook my head and took another swig.

For the last week, I hadn't been able to stop thinking about her. The night she picked up her iPad, she'd been so vulnerable and open when I'd asked about her father. Her big blue eyes had been filled with emotion and sincerity. It had been a long time since I met a woman who put her heart out there for the world to see. Not to mention, there were a lot of other parts of her worth seeing. The little workout outfit she wore today nailed that point home, that was for sure.

God, that outfit.

I knocked back the last of my wine.

Over the next hour, I polished off half the bottle. The sound of Sadie and Birdie laughing in the other room had become so distracting that I'd cranked up music and shut my eyes. So I hadn't heard the knock at the door when they finished up.

"Hey." Sadie cracked the door open enough to stick her head in. "Sorry. You weren't answering. We're all done. Birdie just went to grab her backpack for the slumber party. Would you want me to walk her down to the house where the sleepover is?" Her eyes zoned in on the wine bottle and my empty glass. She smirked. "I can see you're very busy."

My lips pursed. "No, it's fine. I'm perfectly capable of taking my daughter. Thank you."

Sadie's eyes narrowed. We stared at each other for a solid thirty seconds, and then she opened the door and stepped inside. Closing the door behind her, she asked, "Is everything okay? You seem . . . upset."

Don't check her out.

Keep your eyes on her face.

"Everything's fine."

She tilted her head and assessed me.

"Are you sure?"

My eyes dropped to her stomach. I just couldn't help myself.

God, you're such a dick, Maxwell.

Eyes back up.

Raise 'em up.

Come on. You can do it.

Sadie stayed quiet. I couldn't even tell you if she was looking at me. Because my eyes were all over her . . . tracing the curve of her waist, salivating over her flat stomach . . . fantasizing about that sparkly diamond in her belly button.

She took a few steps and started to walk toward my desk.

Maybe it was the wine, but my heart started to beat out of my chest. I attempted to lift my eyes to her face, and this time it worked. Well, sort of. They raised, but unfortunately, they snagged on her chest.

What are those, C cups?

Nice.

Very nice.

I bet her cleavage gets really sweaty doing that yoga.

Hot sweat dripping down from between her luscious round tits to that belly button.

By the time I managed to drag my eyes up enough to meet hers, Sadie was standing right in front of my desk.

She rocked back and forth ever so slightly. "What are you doing, Sebastian?"

Our eyes locked, and the wicked hint of a smirk made me think she'd just heard all my thoughts. I swallowed. "Nothing."

"Nothing, huh? So you're just sitting there . . . looking around, then?" The corner of her lips tilted upward.

What a smart-ass.

She knew exactly what I was doing.

I straightened up in my chair and cleared my throat.

"If you're done. You can show yourself out."

"Is that what you're sitting there thinking about? How much you want me to . . . leave?"

A knock at my office door made me blink a few times.

I was thoroughly confused when I looked over and saw Sadie pop her head into my office.

What the . . . ?

Wasn't she . . . ?

I glanced to where I could've sworn she'd just been standing. It took a few seconds to snap out of it and realize that I must've dozed off from the wine and had been dreaming.

Jesus.

Sadie smiled. "We're all done. Why don't I walk Birdie down to her sleepover for you, since I'll be heading out anyway?"

"Umm. Yeah. That would be great. Thank you. Let me go say good night to her."

I walked out to the living room. Birdie was already standing there with her backpack on, a pillow and sleeping bag in her hands. "Looks like you're all ready." I squatted down to her level. "How about a hug for your old man."

My daughter threw her arms around my neck with a huge smile. "I love you, Daddy."

"I love you, too, sweetheart."

"Marmaduke did great today! When Sadie clicks the clicker, he sits now."

"Is that so?"

She nodded.

"Alright." I gave a gentle tug to her ponytail. "Why don't you get going to your party."

Birdie turned to start to walk away but then ran back to me. Her tiny hand cupped my cheek. "I'm right down the block if you need me."

My heart squeezed and I smiled. "Thanks. I'll remember that."

She kissed me one more time and then skipped off toward the door.

"Anything you want me to tell the parents?" Sadie asked.

"No. I'll text Renee and check in later."

"Okay." Apparently that nap and my ensuing fantasy had done me some good. I managed to have a civil conversation with Sadie and didn't eye fuck her like I'd done in that dream. Though when she turned around to follow Birdie to the front door, I just couldn't help checking out her ass in those yoga pants again. I mean, it was right there, so in my face. What man in his right mind *wouldn't* take a peek?

"Oh, I almost forgot . . ." Sadie turned around, and my eyes jumped to meet hers.

Fuck.

She caught me.

If I hadn't been sure I'd just gotten busted, the knowing smirk Sadie flashed would have confirmed she knew what I'd done.

She didn't even bother to try to hide it. Extending her hand, she held out the clicker. "This is yours."

I looked away as I took it from her hand. "Great. Thanks."

After she walked out, I hung my head behind the closed door.

God, you're a jackass, Maxwell. You need to get laid.

Since I had the night all to myself, maybe that's exactly what I should do. I'd been talking to this woman Irina for a while, a busy advertising executive who I'd met online and who was seeking the exact same type of arrangement as I was. But I had blown her off for the last few weeks. Maybe it was time to get back in touch.

As I walked back to my office where I kept my laptop, I tried to psych myself up.

Irina.

She was sexy.

Long red hair.

A woman who knew what she wanted.

That's exactly what I needed.

Yeah, that's it.

I'm definitely going to see what Sadie's doing tonight.

Irina. I mean Irina.

Reaching my desk, I decided to pour another glass of wine before jumping online to see if *Irina* might be available.

I sat down and sipped but decided to shut my eyes once again. I needed a moment to clear my head.

But instead of gaining clarity, visions of Sadie flooded my mind.

Again.

She was so damn sexy.

That ass.

That flat stomach.

That sparkly freaking diamond.

Her big, beautiful eyes.

And that mouth. The way the corners turned up when she'd caught me checking out her ass . . . Jesus . . . what I wouldn't give to fuck that mouth.

I laughed at myself and opened my eyes.

Good thing she was gone. Because God knows what dumb thing I would've done tonight. The woman had me losing my mind.

I took another big swig of my wine and opened my laptop.

Just as the doorbell rang . . .

CHAPTER 16

Sadie

He opened the door, and my mind went blank. Turning around and ringing the bell had been a split-second decision. I just hadn't wanted to leave. The problem was, I probably should've thought up an excuse as to why I came back *before* I did it.

Sebastian's breathing quickened with every second that he took me in. "Everything okay?"

I swallowed but continued to blank out.

What was I supposed to say? I couldn't tell him the truth: *I saw you checking me out and thought you might be interested in touching me, too?*

He broke the ice. "Is this the part where I assume you're the dog trainer and scold you for being late? Feels like déjà vu right now. Me opening the door and you looking stunned." He flashed a crooked smile, which calmed me down a bit.

I laughed nervously.

He gestured with his head. "While you're figuring it out, why don't you come in? It was so warm today, but it's getting chilly now."

I brushed my hands over my arms. "Thanks."

Marmaduke ran to the door and began to jump all over me. Not exactly the man I wanted on me right now.

Thankfully, he calmed down pretty quickly before heading to the corner of the room to hump a stuffed toy.

Yeah. You're not the only one all worked up tonight, buddy.

Sebastian just stared at me, still in need of an explanation as to why I'd suddenly returned.

Jesus Christ. Grow some balls, Sadie. You're a dating-advice columnist, for Christ's sake, and you can't seem to remember how to act around a man you're attracted to.

"I came back because I wondered if you might want some company tonight," I blurted.

Sebastian placed his hands in his pockets, looking less than comfortable with my proclamation.

His reaction made me panic a little, so I tried to laugh it off. "That's stupid, right? You probably have plans. If so, I can just lea—"

"Do you like white or red?" he suddenly said.

It took a few seconds for his question to sink in. He was referring to wine.

I'm in?

"Actually, the red you were drinking looked really good."

"Be right back," he said.

I fidgeted as Sebastian went back into his study, returning to the living room with the bottle and his glass. He placed them on the coffee table before venturing into the kitchen.

After he returned, I watched as he poured me a large glass before emptying the remainder of the bottle into his own.

"Thank you," I said.

I sat down on one end of the sofa. Then he proceeded to sit all the way at the other end at the farthest spot away from me.

I took a sip of my drink and said, "So, what were your plans tonight if I hadn't weaseled my way into your evening?"

His lips twitched. "I hadn't quite figured it out."

"It's probably rare that Birdie's not home."

"Yeah. I think she's only had one other sleepover before this."

Sebastian looked exceptionally good tonight. He was dressed more casually than normal. A navy T-shirt clung to his broad chest. He wore jeans, and his feet were bare. He had large, beautiful feet—if a man's feet could even be considered beautiful. Well, he and his feet were totally beautiful in every way.

"Did I step in something?" he asked.

Shit. He'd caught me.

"Oh, no. I was just . . . admiring your feet."

I cringed. *Maybe I shouldn't have admitted that.*

"Thank you." He wrinkled his forehead. "I think?" Sebastian rested his arm on the back of the sofa and continued to stay in his corner of the couch. "So where exactly do you go to work out, Sadie?"

"I do a forty-five-minute yoga class a few times a week. It's near my place."

"Nice. I probably should be taking up something like that for stress relief."

"It's excellent for stress relief . . . but I do it for flexibility."

He cleared his throat. "So you're . . . flexible?"

"Very." I'd been intentionally self-assured in my answer on that one. "Today she had us practice this pose where your legs go back over your head."

He looked like he almost wanted to spit out his wine. "That sounds very . . . adventurous. What's that called . . . downward dog? Dogs are your thing." He winked.

I chuckled. "No. Downward dog is a front-facing exercise. She had us bend our legs back and over our head. It's called plow pose."

His eyes widened. "You're bending your legs over your head and it's called *plow* pose?"

The irony in that terminology only now just hit me.

He has a dirty mind. I love it.

"I guess it's a waste of a skill, considering nothing has been happening in that arena."

Sebastian said nothing as he downed the last of his wine. Then he lifted the bottle. "More wine?"

"I'll have a refill, yeah. Thanks."

"This bottle is empty. Want to try something else, or shall I open another bottle of cab?"

"I really liked that one. What's it called?"

He went to check the label, and I could've sworn I saw his face turn red. Apparently he hadn't realized the name until now.

He wouldn't say.

"Well?" I prodded.

"It's called . . . Pornfelder." He laughed awkwardly as he opened the bottle and refilled our glasses.

I couldn't help but laugh myself. "What a name."

"Sounds like someone made it up. Sort of like *flunkerbsht*."

My face felt numb from embarrassment. "Ah, yes."

He raised his glass. "You should trademark that, by the way."

He drank some more of his wine, and when the glass left his mouth, I noticed his eyes travel down to my navel and back up again. I loved noticing him looking at me. He immediately started a new topic of conversation to divert from the fact that I'd caught him staring at my belly ring.

"So you never told me how you got into writing."

I repositioned myself in my seat, making myself a bit more comfortable. "Well, I was a journalism major in college, but for many years, I never did anything with my degree, just worked odd jobs. At one point, I took an internship with the company that owns my magazine, and the reporter I worked under let me dabble in writing some of the articles. Eventually, I was hired as a general staff writer, and I've bounced around various departments ever since. The *Holiday Wishes* column has stuck with me for years, but my main writing assignments have changed a few times. I did articles on business etiquette for a few years and then switched to writing the *Beauty Basics* column. Writing about makeup got boring pretty fast."

"But you've been doing the dating column for a while, right?"

"Yeah." I smiled. "For a few years. That one stuck. They seem to think I'm the right fit for it, and it's become pretty popular."

"Well, I can see why. Women must love to live vicariously through a beautiful, successful woman living in the city. It's like that show my mother used to watch . . . the one with the girl from *Hocus Pocus*."

That made me crack up. "Sarah Jessica Parker, yeah. *Sex and the City*. Although I'm more like the poor girl's Carrie Bradshaw."

He seemed to be almost looking through me when he said, "You blow all those chicks out of the water."

My entire body filled with heat. He'd just complimented me, and I had no clue how to handle it. I basically just wanted to jump him—but didn't think that would go off too well.

"Do you see yourself staying at that job?" he asked.

"As much as I might complain, I really do enjoy it. Couldn't really imagine myself with a typical nine-to-five."

"What happens if you find someone you want to spend your life with? Do you still do the dating column?"

His question made my heart flutter a little. "I'm not betting on that with my luck . . . but if it were to happen, then I wouldn't do the dating column. It has to be organic. If my heart belonged to someone else, what would be the point in faking it out there? It wouldn't work, and it wouldn't be fair to my partner, either."

"So you'd ask for a reassignment?"

His curiosity on the topic gave me what was probably a delusional sense of hope. "Yes. I'd probably just write in one of the other departments if they'd have me."

"Like the Santa column . . ." He smiled. For the first time, I noticed he had subtle dimples.

"That's seasonal, so it wouldn't cover me for the whole year . . . but that one I'll stick with regardless, as long as they'll have me. It's so gratifying."

"I'm happy you love your job," he said.

"Yeah, you know, because the dog-training thing . . . well, that's not going anywhere."

He chuckled. "Exactly."

I finished off my wine and sighed. "Things could always be worse, you know? I'm not exactly where I thought I'd be at almost thirty. But I'm fortunate to be happy overall, healthy, and to have one part of my life right—my career."

"And the other parts?"

"Well, I always thought I'd be settled by this age, maybe have a child. I'm not sure if that's in the cards for me."

He stared at me for a few moments, then said, "But you want it? You want the family, the house, the dog . . ."

Without hesitation, I said, "I do . . . but only if it's with the right person."

He nodded and seemed to be deep in thought. I wondered if he was thinking about Amanda, how he *had* had all those things at one time . . . the house, the family, the beautiful wife. But now she was gone. None of it really came together without your significant other, the one you love. And not having her around meant that he had to be both the mother and father to Birdie, which couldn't have been easy, given his demanding job.

"Are you okay, Sebastian?" I felt compelled to ask. "I'm not referring to this moment, but I mean . . . in a general sense, handling the single-dad thing?"

"You mean, am I just pretending to hold it all together while really being depressed inside?" He stared off. "Honestly? Sometimes. But I make sure I keep going so fast that I don't get swallowed up by the depression part. It's just there in the background."

I gulped, not sure what to say. "It must be hard to move on when you had such a great marriage. I know it was hard for my dad."

He closed his eyes and shook his head. "Birdie thinks her mom and dad had the perfect marriage. But my wife and I had our fair share of struggles. When my daughter was two, we actually separated for a while."

My eyes widened. That was the last thing I'd expected him to say. I'd thought he had the perfect little family. "Wow. I had no idea."

"Obviously, my daughter doesn't know. And I'd really like to keep it that way."

"Of course. I'd never say anything to her." I shook my head. "Can I ask what happened?"

"I'm going to need more wine for this." Sebastian refilled his glass and poured me another. Sighing, he said, "The restaurant took a while to become what it is today. We both worked a lot of hours, had a new baby. We put all our energy into the business and our daughter, and I guess at the end of the day, we didn't have enough left to give our relationship the focus it needed. I'm partly to blame for that. But . . ." Sebastian sipped his wine. "I guess my wife needed someone to talk to about something other than money problems or diapers. And, well, she got close to a waiter at the restaurant. One night, they had a little too much to drink, and they got a little *too close*."

"Oh God. I'm sorry."

He nodded. "We tried to go to counseling, but I couldn't seem to get past it. So after a few months, we separated. I moved out and got a small apartment nearby so I could still be near my daughter. We were just starting to adjust to living on our own when Amanda found out during a routine exam that her ovarian cancer was back. It put things into perspective. I'd never stopped loving my wife, and she needed me."

"So you got back together?"

He nodded. "We had good years after that. But Amanda always thought the only reason that I made things work was because of her cancer diagnosis."

"But it wasn't?"

Sebastian smiled sadly. "I don't know how things would have worked out had she not gotten sick. But it doesn't matter. Sometimes in life you need a little push to get where you should be. Her illness was my push. We made it work, and I was in awe of the strength she had, watching her fight every day. I have a lot of guilt that she died thinking I only stuck around because she was sick." He shook his head. "I did love her. I really did."

I didn't want to cry, but I had no control over the tears that seeped out.

When he noticed, a look of alarm crossed his face. "Oh shit. What have I done? I didn't mean to make you cry."

Wiping my nose with my arm, I sniffled. "No. I'm sorry. It's just . . . it's sad but it's beautiful, Sebastian. To have had someone you love in your life even for a short time is beautiful. It's amazing that you found forgiveness for her and rekindled that love. And she'll always live on through Birdie."

"I don't know what it is about you that makes me want to open up." He rubbed his eyes. "Let's move on to something lighter . . . okay?"

I searched my brain for something "lighter." "Birdie swears that Marmaduke can say 'hi.'"

His mouth transformed into a slight smile. "Oh yeah?"

"Yeah. We actually recorded it. Hang on."

Taking out my phone, I pressed "Play" on a video I'd taken displaying Marmaduke making a noise that did sound suspiciously like "Hiiiiiiiii."

He chuckled. "I asked to move on to something lighter, not utterly ridiculous."

We were both cracking up now, and thank God the sadness in the air seemed to have eased up a bit.

"Can I use your restroom?" I asked.

"Of course."

My legs felt wobbly as I stood up and made my way to the bathroom. Splashing some water on my face, I looked at myself in the mirror. The wine was starting to hit me, and the physical and emotional toll of the night was as well. My attraction to Sebastian was almost painful. I just wanted to make him forget about everything for one night, but more than that, I also wanted him to want me. I was pretty sure he was attracted to me, but I was also pretty sure he respected me. And that meant he wouldn't look at me as a one-night conquest. The latter very well may have been all he had the mental space for right now, which meant there would likely not be any room for someone like me in his life.

When I reemerged from the bathroom, Sebastian was still sitting on the couch waiting for me. I was starting to feel like if anything were going to happen between us, I was going to have to give him a little push, test the waters. At least then, based on his reaction, I might know if I even stood a chance for something more with him. I sat down, but this time, in a brazen move, I sat down right next to him. The heat of his body was palpable. His jaw tightened as he just looked at me. His breathing became labored as he very blatantly allowed his eyes to wander down to my cleavage, then back up at my face. Unlike the other times he'd snuck glances at me, it almost seemed like he wanted me to notice. I wanted his mouth on me, but I'd made enough of a move by just sitting this close. The wine was definitely going to my head, amplifying the physical need I was experiencing.

He was looking at my lips now.

"Are you okay with my sitting close to you like this?" I asked.

He nodded, still breathing heavier than he had all night. There was no way he wasn't affected by me. I knew that for certain now.

"I think you're amazing, Sadie. Both inside and out," he whispered gruffly.

I bit my lip, then continued his sentence. "But . . ."

"Don't take this the wrong way . . . but I'm almost *too attracted* to you. I feel very out of control around you, like there's the potential to get addicted. And—"

"And you've made the decision not to let that happen with anyone."

"It's what's best for many reasons . . ."

My heart sank upon finally hearing confirmation of what I already feared.

"I just thought that maybe . . . there could be something there."

His eyes were piercing. "There *is* something. I just don't want to act on it."

"Okay." I looked down at his bare feet. A few moments later, I looked up at him. "What would you be doing tonight if I wasn't here?"

"Why does that matter?"

"It doesn't. I'm just curious." I leaned in a little. "Don't lie to me, either. Tell me what you really would have done."

He nodded. "Alright." After taking a long sip of wine, he finally said, "I was going to call a woman I knew wanted nothing more than to sleep with me. I was going to go to her place—because I don't bring women into this house. I was going to fuck her—safely—and then leave and come back here, feeling no more fulfilled than I had before I left. Which is exactly the way I need it to be."

His admission left me speechless for a bit.

"When was the last time you were . . . with someone?" I asked.

"It's been a while. A couple of months, maybe." He exhaled. "What about you?"

"Way longer than that."

Sebastian swallowed hard. "Why?"

"Because I can't just be with someone to fuck them. I need something more. I need a connection. I need to be able to look into their eyes and love what I see within them just as much as what's on the outside. A mental connection is very important to me." My feelings seemed to be bursting from me. Somehow I felt like this could have been my one opportunity to express them. I shocked myself when I said, "I'm very attracted to you . . . in every way. But I totally get why you need to compartmentalize. I get why it would be scary for you to let someone in . . . not only into your heart but into your life. I think I'd be the same way in your shoes."

He sat there in silence as I went on.

"I'm sorry, Sebastian. I'm sorry that things aren't easier. I'm sorry you lost your wife and that you go to sleep alone. I hope that someday you can be happy again. As much as I wish that I could have a chance at getting to know you on a deeper level, I also understand that the space for that in your heart is still taken."

He was back to staring at my mouth when he said, "You make it *very* difficult to want to compartmentalize, Sadie."

My heart raced.

"Do you want me to go?" I whispered.

He reached for my hand. "No."

The feel of his big, warm hand intertwined with mine was just about the best damn thing I'd felt in a very long time.

"Then I'll stay. *As a friend.* As long as you want me to say, I'll stay. And when you're ready to be alone again, I'll leave."

He looked down at our hands. "I really don't like being alone. I hate it. I hate being here when Birdie's not home. Because then I have to face what I'm left with. Which is nothing without my daughter. I don't want my life to be like this. I want to be happy again. I just haven't figured out how to achieve that."

"I think it just happens on its own. Being happy is not really something people can make happen. It just occurs randomly while we're living and not trying."

What he said next broke my heart.

"Amanda never told me whether she would be okay if I moved on. And I think that's part of what holds me back. I would never want her to look down and feel like she'd been replaced. And that haunts me."

His eyes watered as he let go of my hand and said, "God, this is not what you signed up for tonight. Fucking hell."

"Please," I pleaded. "Please don't apologize. Your honesty is breathing life into me. You have no idea how amazing it is to experience, through your love and respect for your wife, what true love is like. You've given me so much hope, Sebastian. Truly."

He stared deeply into my eyes. "Wanna know the fucked-up thing?"

"Yeah."

"As I sit here talking about my wife, I still can't help wanting to kiss you."

His words ignited what felt like a fire inside me. Talk about a roller coaster of emotions. "No one says feelings have to make sense," I said, my chest heaving with need.

"You asked me what I was really planning to do tonight . . . ," he said. "I told you half of the story. But what I didn't tell you is that after you left, I couldn't stop thinking about you, your infectious smile, and how sexy you looked. No woman in the world was going to stand a chance to get you out of my head tonight. And when you came to the door again, I nearly shit a brick. It was like you'd read my mind."

I moved closer to him so that my face was only inches from his. The physical pull felt really intense. I normally wasn't this assertive, but maybe it had to do with the fact that I'd never been into anyone like this. Yes, I would've loved more than a sexual relationship with Sebastian. But if he wasn't ready for more, would I still want to experience being with him? The answer was yes.

Barely able to breathe, I said what I was feeling in that moment. "If you want me, you can have me. No questions asked. I need it as much as you do. We can just take out our frustrations on each other."

He swallowed and let out a groan before he shook his head. "You're intoxicated, Sadie, and so am I. We can't go there."

I nodded silently. I totally understood his point.

Therefore, given what he'd just said, you could imagine I was completely shocked when he seemed to lose control, wrapping his hand around my face and pulling me into him just seconds later. The heat of his mouth on mine sent shock waves throughout my entire body. Sebastian groaned into my mouth, and it vibrated deep in the back of my throat. He tasted like wine and the most amazing flavor I'd ever tasted. It was all man, all him, and I needed more. I didn't care how buzzed I was, I didn't care about anything other than experiencing every second of this. He pulled me onto him and I grinded down. I felt like I could come from merely the friction of his erection rubbing against me through his pants. Not to mention, it was clear from that limited contact that he was massive. My legs were quivering as his fingers raked my back.

"Fuck," he muttered into my mouth. "You're so sexy. I want to eat you alive."

Those words literally made the muscles between my legs contract. Someone could have told me I'd have to risk my life to have him inside me right now and I might have considered it.

Right when I'd felt like I was going to reach my breaking point, Sebastian seemed to fall out of his trance as he pulled back.

He covered his mouth and stood up. "I can't, Sadie. I just can't. I want you, but I can't take you like this. You've had too much to drink, and so have I."

My lips were swollen, my nipples hard. My body was so ready. So naturally, this was a disappointment but one that was for the best.

Panting, I asked, "You want me to leave?"

He shook his head vehemently while keeping his distance. "No. I wouldn't feel right sending you home right now. Please stay. You can have my bed, and I'll sleep in Birdie's room."

I filled with hope. "Are you sure?"

"I insist. No way I'm letting you get in a car with a stranger while drunk, not even if it's an Uber."

His concern made me feel warm, protected. "Thank you."

He nudged his head. "Come on. I'll show you to the room." Sebastian led me down the hall to his bedroom.

A massive king bed with a dark-wood headboard took up the center of the space. A satin gray comforter lay atop it. A gorgeous view of the moonlight outside could be seen from the window. As inviting a space as this was, it felt intrusive and forbidden to be in here.

"Make yourself at home. Take a hot shower in the master bath, anything you want."

"Okay . . ." I smiled. "Thank you."

After he left the room, I somehow suspected I wouldn't see him for the rest of the night. He'd made the mature decision. I respected him for that, but it in no way extinguished the fire burning inside me right now.

That night, I took a shower in his fancy bathroom and lay in his massive marital bed. It felt a bit strange to be lying in the same bed that Sebastian had slept in with his wife. I could completely understand the emptiness he described feeling. And I longed for him. My feelings for this man went way back to before I'd ever even met him. But now that I'd experienced how passionate he was firsthand, it made me fall for him even more.

CHAPTER 17

Sebastian

I'd come *very* close to fucking up last night. So close, I could smell it. Smell her. I sighed. She smelled phenomenal. Even though I knew I wasn't still drunk, I somehow still felt drunk off her.

It was a miracle I'd gotten any sleep at all, but the wine must have knocked me out, because sometime after 2:00 am, I'd totally passed out in Birdie's bed. But not before I'd retreated to the bathroom off the hallway to jerk off to thoughts of ramming into Sadie while she was in that yoga plow pose with her legs backed over her head. It took me all of thirty seconds to come harder than I had in months all over the shower door. Better there than inside her last night, and believe me, if she hadn't been intoxicated, that might have very well happened.

I threw on a white T-shirt and some jeans and made my way to the kitchen. The smell of coffee infiltrated my senses.

The sight of her in my kitchen made my heart nearly stop. I hadn't realized how much I missed having a woman to wake up to. Perhaps it wasn't until this moment that I realized just how fucking lonely I'd been. But it wasn't even that. She was wearing my shirt. My white dress shirt. And no fucking pants. And she was bopping her ass a little, even though there was no music on.

"Hey," I called out.

Sadie jumped. "Hey." She smiled. "I took it upon myself to make breakfast." She looked down at herself. "I stole one of your longest shirts. I just didn't feel like putting on my dirty workout clothes after the shower I took last night. I hope that's okay."

What could I say to that? It was apparently fine with my dick, because I was getting hard just looking at her in my shirt. In fact, I was starting to feel like a goddamn caveman. Sleep had done nothing to curb my appetite.

I never answered her. I was too busy staring.

"I figured the least I could do after you let me have your room last night was to make you a nice breakfast."

She was being more than gracious, considering I'd mauled her mouth, then sent her off to bed alone last night.

The smells of eggs, coffee, and a hint of cinnamon filled the air. And for some reason, instead of feeling guilty or conflicted this morning, I continued to feel fucking high.

"This is amazing. Thank you," I said as I came up next to her.

Just then, the doorbell rang.

I looked out toward the door. "What the hell?"

"Are you expecting someone?" she asked.

"No."

When I opened it, Birdie stood there with a woman I recognized as her friend's mother. My daughter wasn't supposed to be back until this afternoon.

"Hey! What happened?"

Birdie looked up at me. "I have pink eye."

"I'm sorry, Mr. Maxwell," the woman said. "It's contagious, so I thought it best to bring her home."

Shit.

Renee noticed the frazzled look on my face.

"Is this . . . a bad time? I tried to call first, but your cell went right to voice mail."

That's because charging my cell phone was the last thing on my mind when I went to bed last night.

I shook my head. "No. It's fine. Of course it's fine. I totally understand."

While I'd gotten the words out, my body was still physically blocking the door.

What the hell am I going to do? The last thing Birdie should see was a half-naked Sadie standing in our kitchen. It was inappropriate on so many levels. How would I explain it to her?

"Apparently pink eye is going around in their class. It's usually nothing more than a little bit of eye drops to clear it up. Birdie said she didn't even notice it, right, sweetheart?"

My daughter shrugged. "It doesn't hurt at all."

At that moment, Marmaduke came to the door. He forced his way past me and practically knocked Birdie over on the front step.

"Hey, Marmaduke. Did you miss me?" She bent down and started to pet him, even though he was as tall as she was.

Renee smiled. "I left my husband alone with seven girls. So I better run back."

"Okay. Yeah. Umm. Thanks a lot for bringing her home."

She turned to walk down the stairs, and I looked back over my shoulder while Birdie was distracted with the dog. *No sign of Sadie.*

"Uh. You know what, honey. I was just about to take Marmaduke for a walk. Why don't I grab his leash, and we'll go together. I'll call the doctor and get you an appointment when we get back."

"Okay, Daddy."

"I'll be back in a minute. You can stay here while I get the leash from the kitchen."

Birdie laughed and pointed. "It's right there, next to your head, Daddy."

Shit. Yeah . . . the damn leash was hanging right on the key hook in the vestibule next to the front door, wasn't it?

Birdie stood and wiped off her knees. "I'm going to put my pillow and sleeping bag in my room."

"*No!* Don't do that."

Her little face wrinkled. "Why can't I put them in my room?"

"Umm." *Think. Think. Oh wait!* "Because they might have some bacteria on them. From your eye infection." I smiled coming up with that excuse. Though my daughter looked at me funny. Like . . . *why the hell are you smiling because my eye infection might be on my blanket, you weirdo?* Nevertheless, I took the pillow and sleeping bag and tossed them behind me, into the living room.

Then I stepped outside and pulled the front door shut as fast as I could. "Ready?"

"Uh . . . Dad . . . you forgot the leash?" She looked down. "And your shoes!"

Jesus Christ. "Shoot. Okay . . . give me one second." I opened the door back up, only enough to reach in and grab the leash off the wall and a pair of shoes, and then pulled it shut again.

"Let's go."

Birdie walked down the stairs. I looked back over my shoulder a few times, but there was still no sign of Sadie. Hopefully she'd figure out what had happened and at least be dressed when we got back.

I stalled for a good half an hour, taking Marmaduke on a long-ass walk, until Birdie said she needed to go to the bathroom. Arriving back at the house, I hesitantly opened the front door. Birdie's sleeping bag and pillow were exactly where I'd left them. I glanced around—the house seemed quiet. While Birdie ran off to the bathroom, I peeked into the kitchen. No sign of Sadie. So I went to the bedroom and the master bath. Both empty. On my way back out to the living room, I noticed my dress shirt folded in the middle of my bed—the one she'd been wearing this morning, the one she'd worn to sleep last night.

She was gone. I blew out a sigh of relief, and my shoulders relaxed. Though while I was glad to protect my daughter, a part of me felt like shit for letting Sadie leave without having said anything to her. Especially after what had gone down last night. She deserved better than that.

So after I called Birdie's doctor to make an appointment to get her eye checked, I let my phone charge for a little while and then decided to send a text to Sadie.

Sebastian: Sorry about the abrupt departure. Birdie came home early with pink eye. I'm taking her to the doctor now.

A few minutes later, my phone dinged with a response.

Sadie: No problem. I completely understand. Good luck at the doc!

I debated addressing what had transpired between us last night, but what the hell would I say?

Thanks for letting my drunk ass grind against you.

I don't want to shower so I can keep your smell all over me.

Figuring sometimes it's just better to leave well enough alone, I typed something innocuous.

Sebastian: Thank you. Talk soon.

Then I set my phone back on the charger.

I forced myself to take a quick shower and shave before getting ready to take Birdie to the doctor. Inside my closet, I grabbed the first shirt on a hanger that my hands touched, then went to my dresser to get a T-shirt for underneath. But the folded shirt on the bed caught my eye again.

I shouldn't.

That would be fucked up.

Looking at my closed bedroom door, I stood five feet away, staring at the goddamn thing as if I went too close, it might bite me.

But the damn thing taunted me even from a distance.

Touch me.

Smell me.

Wear me.

Just once won't hurt.

I tried to ignore it, but then I started to reason with myself.

I should probably just smell it once. See if it needs to be washed.

Yeah . . . that's what I should do.

Of course that made sense.

One sniff.

Just one sniff.

I walked over to the bed and picked up the shirt and brought it to my nose. Inhaling deeply, the smell of Sadie permeated my senses. It smelled exactly like her.

Fuck.

Fuck me.

I inhaled a second time.

Though I should've listened to myself . . . *Just one sniff* . . . because the second time . . . Birdie busted through the door, catching me red-handed with my face nuzzling the shirt.

Her brows drew together. "What are you doing, Daddy?"

"I . . . uh. I was just making sure my shirt was clean."

She giggled. "Is it?"

"Umm. Yeah. I guess so." I stood there staring at her.

"Do you feel okay, Daddy? You're acting really weird today."

"Yeah. I'm fine, sweetheart. Sorry."

"Come on." She held out her hand. "It's time to go to the doctor."

"Okay . . . just let me grab a shirt."

"What's wrong with that one?"

"It's dirty."

She laughed. "You just said it was clean."

"Oh. Yeah . . . it is clean. It just . . . has a stain on it." I wadded up the shirt in my hand and tossed it on the bed, picking up the one I'd taken out from the closet. "I'll just wear this one."

Later that evening, I was glad when Birdie said she was tired and going to turn in early. We were both wiped out from our slumber parties last night. I really needed to unwind, and I looked forward to going into my room, kicking my feet up, and watching some TV maybe. But after flicking through the channels and finding nothing, I decided what I really needed to relax was more than some stupid show. I needed a release.

So I got up and locked my bedroom door and slid open my end table drawer, where I hid lotion. Only when I went to grab it, there was a folded piece of paper sitting on top of the bottle. Thinking nothing of it, I took it out and unfolded it.

Dear Sebastian,

I had a great time last night. If you're reaching into the drawer for what's underneath this note, I hope you think of me while using it.

God knows I thought of you while I did my thing last night in your bed.

Love,
Sadie

P.S. You might want to wash the sheets ;)

CHAPTER 18

Sadie

Talk soon.

That's what his last text had said. But apparently the two of us had different definitions of *soon.*

Five days and still no contact.

As if I'd suffered a loss, I'd gone through the stages of grief. At first I was in denial that Sebastian wasn't going to contact me again. I'd checked my phone every twenty minutes, even though I had the volume set all the way up and my ringer also set to vibrate . . . you know, just in case he'd messaged or called when I fell asleep or something. I knew that Sebastian and I were looking for different things, but even a hookup deserved some gratuitous conversation after the fact.

After the first few days of silence, I'd gone on to anger. How dare he not call or message after that evening? I knew I'd been the one to initiate things, but he was more than a willing participant. The erection prodding at my hip was proof positive of that.

Then, on day six, contact had finally come. Sebastian's number had popped up on my cell phone, and I got so excited that I fumbled it in my hands and dropped it on the floor—which resulted in the screen cracking. But hey . . . at least he'd finally called.

Only the voice on the other end when I'd answered wasn't Sebastian's at all. It was Magdalene's. She'd called to make arrangements for my next training session because Birdie had been asking when I was coming. Apparently the man of the house was too damn busy to call himself.

After that, I'd moved on to the next stages . . . the ones that are supposed to come after denial and anger. I think those are bargaining, depression, and acceptance. But I'm not positive, because who am I kidding? I didn't go to any next stage. Well, unless *even more pissed off* was the stage that came after anger.

Now here it was, Saturday morning, and I stood in front of the Maxwells' brownstone ready to toss around a big attitude as I knocked for my weekly training.

Except when the door opened, it wasn't Sebastian.

Or Birdie.

Or Magdalene, even.

It was a woman wearing a bathrobe who had her hair wrapped up in a towel.

She smiled at me and extended her hand. "You must be Sadie. I'm Macie. Seb told me you'd be here at eleven, but I seem to have lost track of time in the shower. His water pressure is incredible."

Seb? Shower? I felt like I got kicked in the gut. All my anger suddenly vanished and I skipped stage three and went right to stage four: depression.

"Uh. Hi."

The woman opened the door wide. "Come on in. Make yourself at home while I run and throw on some clothes."

I nodded and followed her inside, even though all I wanted to do was turn around and leave. The woman walked down the hall . . . toward *Sebastian's bedroom*. In a state of shock, I stood there staring after the door closed and couldn't seem to move until she came back out.

"There, that's better." She walked out wearing a pair of tight jeans with a T-shirt and pulled the towel from her hair. Long red locks cascaded around her pretty face.

"Birdie and Magdalene should be back any second."

I blinked a few times, realizing I hadn't even noticed that they weren't here. "Oh. Okay. Are you . . . staying here?"

"Just until tomorrow. I hadn't planned on coming. But it was such a nice surprise when Seb called and invited me that I just couldn't say no." She smiled. "I'm usually the one pushing myself on him."

Jealousy pulsed through my veins, and I clenched my teeth. This woman obviously had no clue that just one week ago, I was the one sleeping in that same exact bedroom she'd just gotten dressed in. I couldn't help but let her know that little fact.

"I hope he washed the sheets before you two . . ." I motioned with my hand toward Sebastian's bedroom. "Before you two did whatever you did in there. Because my naked ass was all over them less than a week ago."

The woman's brows shot up. She started to say something when the front door flew open. Birdie and Marmaduke came racing in, making a giant ruckus. Magdalene walked in a few seconds afterward, out of breath. She smiled. "They raced for the last block. I'm no match for a ten-year-old and a four-legged runner."

The redhead from Sebastian's bed walked over and helped Birdie with her jacket. As soon as it was off her shoulders, she ran to hug me. I felt an ounce of vindication. At least Birdie liked me better.

"Sadie, can we work on *roll over* today?"

"Sure. Whatever you want."

"Can Aunt Macie help?"

My brow furrowed. "Who?"

"Aunt Macie."

A feeling of dread washed over me. The redhead walked over and put her hands on Birdie's shoulders, looking down at her. "I didn't get a chance to explain who I was yet, sweetheart." The woman looked up at me. "Like my niece said, I'm her aunt."

I closed my eyes. *God, this can't be happening. Please, please tell me she's Sebastian's sister. That's the least you could give me, here.*

Swallowing, I opened my eyes. "Sebastian's sister?"

The woman shook her head back and forth. "No. His wife's."

I wanted to crawl into a hole.

After my training session with Birdie ended, Magdalene said she was taking her to a playdate at a friend's house. I figured I'd slink out with them, even though I knew that I owed Macie an apology. But apparently I wouldn't be getting off that easy.

"Sadie . . . do you have a minute?"

Damn . . . I'd been so close to the door. I sighed and nodded, then bent to hug Birdie goodbye and told Magdalene I'd see her next week.

When the door closed, I took a deep breath and turned around to face Macie.

"I'm so sorry about earlier."

She smiled warmly. "How would you like a cup of tea or maybe some coffee?"

"Is it too early for wine?"

Macie laughed. "A girl after my own heart. Come, let's raid Sebastian's liquor cabinet. I'm pretty sure he has some Baileys that we can spike our coffees with."

I'd been joking, but apparently Macie wasn't. She went into Sebastian's office, pulled out a bottle, and then headed to the kitchen to make two coffees and stirred in the creamy liquor.

Back out in the living room, we sat together on the couch.

"I'm mortified by what I said." I shook my head. "I honestly don't know what came over me. Obviously, I didn't know you were his sister-in-law. I just saw you going into his bedroom to change, and you'd said you were usually the one *pushing yourself* on him and . . . I just . . . I'm so sorry."

She waved me off. "No big deal. I get it. If I were in your shoes, I'd probably have done the same thing. Maybe worse. I once caught my ex-boyfriend cheating on me and yanked off his plaything's bad extensions."

I laughed yet still felt nervous. "Thank you."

Macie sipped her coffee. "So . . . how long have you two been seeing each other?"

I shook my head. "We aren't. Well, not really. We just . . . The other night we . . . And then . . ."

Macie put her hand up. "No explanation needed. My brother-in-law is a complicated man. I miss my sister something fierce, and I know she and Sebastian loved each other. But I know she'd want him to move on. He's grieved long enough. I couldn't help but notice that you and Birdie really seem to have a strong bond."

I smiled. "Yeah, I think we do. I lost my mom when I was little, about her age actually. So I feel like I can relate to a lot of what she's going through . . . the simple things . . . not having a woman to go clothes shopping with her, do her hair, just have those moments a girl and her mom have."

Macie frowned. "I should've come down more often the last few years."

"Oh my God. I'm so sorry. I didn't mean to imply she didn't have you." I felt my face flush with embarrassment. "I just keep putting my foot in my mouth with you today."

She smiled sadly. "It's fine. I just feel bad because you're a hundred percent right. Sometimes the truth hurts to hear, but that's not your fault. My niece is missing out on those moments with her mother and should have a woman role model." Her eyes searched my face. "I saw that in you today. She looks up to you."

"She's a great girl."

Macie caught my gaze. "She is. And I take it you like her dad?"

It felt really odd to be having this conversation with his dead wife's sister, but she was being so nice after I was a total jerk. So I was honest. I nodded. "He's a really great guy and a special dad."

"Can I offer you some advice?"

"Sure."

"If you think there's something there . . . don't be nervous to push a bit. A lot of men are afraid of commitment, but Sebastian isn't one of them. He's a *for better or for worse* kind of guy. Unfortunately, life gave him a few more *worse*s than *better*s lately. The problem with him is, his decisions don't just affect him, obviously. And he's afraid to make decisions that might hurt his daughter."

I smiled. "I did push a bit last week. And while we moved forward in that moment, he seems to have taken four steps away from me after it happened."

"So if he took four back . . . then you take two forward and make him take two forward. Have you two been out on a date yet?"

I shook my head.

"Try starting there. Baby steps."

I sighed. "I don't know."

Macie patted my hand. "You'll figure it out. In the meantime, thank you for being there for my niece."

"It's my pleasure."

We finished our coffees, and then Macie walked me to the door.

"Oh. One more thing . . . tomorrow I'm taking Birdie to brunch and a play in the city. It's a surprise, but we're seeing *The Lion King*. Just the two of us."

I smiled. "That's great. I'm sure she'll love that."

"Yes. We're leaving about ten. We won't be back until at least seven. Sebastian goes into the restaurant about three on Sundays. So he'll be home all alone from ten to three." She winked. "I thought maybe you might want to know that."

The next morning, I kept going back through my conversation with Macie over and over again. Maybe she was right. In hindsight, my dad could have used a little push. He'd spent so many years worrying about doing the right thing for me and feeling guilty over moving on. I wish a woman who cared about him had pushed him a bit to find some happiness for himself.

So I took a deep breath and picked up my phone. Without allowing any further debate, I shot off a text and immediately hit "Send." Except in my haste to get the message out before I changed my mind, I hadn't noticed the typo.

What I'd meant to type was:

Sadie: Hey. Are you free? I was wondering if you could meet me this morning?

But what I'd actually typed was:

Sadie: Hey. Are you free? I was wondering if you could eat me this morning?

I shut my eyes and shook my head. I watched the message go from *Sent* to *Delivered* to *Read* and started to laugh out loud. I'd been so grumpy this week that it felt good to not take myself so seriously. The little dots began to jump around and then stopped, then started to jump around again. I imagined what Sebastian's face might look like after reading that text, and it amused the hell out of me. While I waited to see how he might respond, the ridiculousness of the last week just hit me and I cackled like a loon.

Though my laughter came to an abrupt halt seeing the response pop up on my screen. My eyes nearly bulged from my head, and I had to blink twice to read the text a second time.

Sebastian: Be here at eleven.

Oh. My. Freaking. God.

Did I just invite myself over for oral sex and he accepted?

I think I might have.

Is it possible he could have read my text as it was originally intended and not how it had been delivered with the typo?

I reread the short exchange one more time.

Sadie: Hey. Are you free? I was wondering if you could eat me this morning?

Sebastian: Be here at eleven.

It seemed pretty clear to me.

Though what the hell was I going to do now?

CHAPTER 19

Sebastian

I kept staring at the text. She didn't mean "eat," did she? I laughed at the fact that I truly didn't know. After that little note she'd left by my bed, I honestly couldn't be certain if Sadie was being sexually blunt or not. I also couldn't seem to decide whether I *wanted* her to have meant "eat." What I was sure of? The thought of eating her made me hard as all hell.

The doorbell rang almost as soon as the clock struck eleven. I went to the door to greet her, feeling somewhat tense, especially given the thoughts that had just been running around in my mind.

Sadie looked gorgeous, dressed in a white wool peacoat. It was finally starting to feel like fall now. Her cheeks were flushed from the cold. Her hair was down in long, loose tendrils.

"Come in."

Before I had a chance to say anything, Sadie just started talking—fast.

She looked down at her feet, then up at me. "I, uh, realized my message said 'eat me.' I meant 'meet me.' I didn't want you to think I meant *eat* me. I mean . . . if you wanted to do that . . . I wouldn't complain, but I didn't want you to think I was suggesting anything. You know . . . stupid voice to text. I can't even tell you how much trouble it's gotten me into in the past. I—"

"Sadie, relax. I figured it out. I was eighty percent sure you meant *meet* me."

She blew a breath up into her hair. "Oh great. And the other twenty percent?"

"Well, that's sort of what I like about you . . . that there *could* be a doubt. You have bold tendencies. You're not afraid to say what you want. It would have been an *interesting* request."

Thoughts of ripping that coat off, carrying her to the couch, before spreading her legs apart and burying my face between them came to mind. That certainly wasn't the worst thought in the world right now at all. And if she'd meant "eat me"? God knows what I would have allowed myself to do right now.

Getting out of here for a bit would be a good idea.

"Speaking of eating, Sadie, it's almost lunchtime. Do you happen to like Italian?"

She smiled. "I happen to love Italian."

"How about we head to my restaurant? It's rare I actually get to enjoy it from a visitor's perspective. I normally go there in the afternoons on Sundays to do business and take inventory. We could grab some lunch together first?"

She beamed. "That sounds amazing."

"Let me grab my crotch," I said.

Her forehead crinkled. "Excuse me?"

"I meant coat." I winked. "Let me grab my coat. I just wanted to show you how easy it is to misspeak."

The laughter she let out after that made the risky joke totally worth it.

That afternoon at Bianco's, my employees seriously were a little too interested in my guest. Every time I would make eye contact with the hostess or the waiters, they would be looking over at us, smiling.

It was true that my staff had never seen me bring anyone but my daughter to the restaurant since Amanda's passing. Of course, as soon as they spotted Sadie, each and every one of them drew a certain conclusion. I suppose I still didn't really know if their assumptions were correct. Was I dating Sadie at the moment? Was this an official date? I had no idea. It sure as hell felt like dating: the adrenaline, that excitement you feel when you first start seeing someone. It was all there. I supposed the only thing stopping me from truly experiencing all those things without any hesitation was my own conscience.

My head waiter, Lorenzo, returned to the table to take our order.

His goofy smile totally gave away what he was thinking.

He turned to her. "What can I get you, madam?"

Sadie closed her menu. "I think I'm going to try Birdie's Pasta Bolognese."

"Birdie will be tickled you chose that." I smiled.

Lorenzo nodded. "Wonderful choice." He looked over at me. "And you, Mr. Maxwell?"

God it feels surreal to be ordering in my own restaurant.

"You know what, Lorenzo? I'll have the same."

He took the menus and walked away with the same grin on his face. He turned around where Sadie couldn't see him and gave me a huge thumbs-up. I grinned and shook my head. *Maybe bringing Sadie here was a mistake.* Everyone was just a little too excited about this.

Sadie looked around. "It's so beautiful here. You've done an amazing job with the decor."

We had fireplaces in various corners of the restaurant. Exposed brick and dimmed lighting made it a very relaxing atmosphere.

"Amanda had a lot to do with choosing the decor. So I can't take full credit for it."

Could you maybe learn not to mention your dead wife every time the opportunity arises?

"Well, she had remarkable taste."

My eyes wandered the space. "This place was our other baby. Continuing to run it has been challenging but also a blessing. It's the one thing that truly got me through the toughest times."

"Work can be good that way for sure."

"Restaurants are risky endeavors, especially in this city, where good meals are a dime a dozen. There's just so much competition. You have to really figure out a way to break the mold."

Sadie's eyes were filled with wonder. "It's amazing, really. I think love and passion go a long way. This place thrives because it started out with two people who loved and respected each other, putting their minds together. Couple that with the fact that most of the meals are old-school recipes from your grandmother? This is more than just a restaurant. It's history and love and spirit all rolled into one. Just sitting here, I can feel it."

Sadie looked like she was about to cry. She wasn't just saying all that to blow smoke up my ass. She'd truly meant it. *Her* passion was definitely remarkable.

"I always feel that, too, here. I'm glad you recognize it."

After our food arrived, we had an easy and enjoyable lunch. Add wine into the mix and it was probably a good idea that I planned not to get much work done this afternoon after all. We weren't drunk. Certainly not anywhere near the level we'd been when she'd spent the night. I would call it just . . . slightly buzzed and happy.

After lunch, I placed my hand on the small of her back as we left the table. Initiating even that amount of contact was huge for me. Deciding to do that hadn't even felt like a struggle. It had felt natural, almost a protective touch to ward off all the prying eyes that were upon us. I was tempted to be alone with her and just remembered something I wanted her to see before we left.

"Come on. I want to show you something," I said.

Walking her down to the basement, I used my key to unlock the door to our massive wine cellar.

Her mouth went agape. "Wow, this is like heaven."

"Yeah. Pretty proud of this. It's not something the patrons even know exists most of the time. Although our VIP guests often come down and choose their wine, but we don't let just anyone down here."

"It looks like something I'd imagine in Europe."

"Well, we actually built it out of stone and brick to mimic cellars found in Europe, so you're not that off base."

"It must have been quite the project putting this all together."

"It was. You have to make sure you have the right shelving for the bottles, and of course it has to be just the right temperature for the wines, to keep them preserved. So we had to put in a high-end temperature regulation system and a backup generator, too."

"Wow, so much to think about."

Her eye was on a bottle of cabernet.

"Would you like to pick something to take home?" I asked.

"Oh, no. That's not necessary."

"I insist."

She grinned, then began running her index finger along the bottles as she walked slowly down the cellar wall. I followed her and couldn't help breathing in her amazing scent. Finally, she turned to me.

"I've made my decision," she said.

Eager to see which bottle she'd selected, I waited for her answer.

Instead of taking one of the bottles off the shelf, she wrapped her hands around my face instead and said, "I pick this one."

Before I knew it, her lips were on mine, and my tongue had slipped inside her hot mouth. Any other thoughts I might have had evaporated. All I could think about was how good it felt to kiss her again.

She spoke over my lips. "I want to take *you* home. Not some bottle of wine."

I was hard as a rock as her soft breasts pressed against my chest.

Certainly, I wasn't thinking with my brain when I grabbed her by the hand and said, "Let's get out of here."

Leading her outside, I wasn't even sure where we were headed as I hailed the first cab that would stop, nearly getting run down in the process.

When the cabbie asked our destination, we just looked at each other. She must have seen the clear hunger in my eyes because she gave him what I assumed was her home address.

The ride to her apartment was a blur, a mix of being in a lustful haze along with continuing to question whether I was doing the right thing in going home with her.

After I paid the cab fare, I grabbed her hand as she led me up the stairs to her apartment. The door had hardly opened before she threw off her coat, and her purse fell to the ground when I pulled her in to me. My mind felt almost outside of my body. Lifting her up, I guided her legs to wrap around my waist. She sucked on my neck and grinded against my engorged cock. We were still standing as I carried her, desperate to find the bedroom.

"First door on the left," she rasped into my ear.

It felt like the longest walk of my life to get there.

I'd never been so hungry for anyone in my entire life. Lifting her shirt over her head, I marveled at her full yet perky tits busting out of her lavender lace bra. Lowering my head down, I sucked on her skin but needed to taste her nipple. I promptly undid her bra from the back and let it fall to the floor.

"Fuck, you have beautiful tits," I said as I devoured them one by one.

Sadie's head was bent back in ecstasy. I wanted nothing more than to see what noises she'd make if I lowered my mouth even farther south.

I whispered in her ear, "Still want me to *eat you* today?"

She laughed a little through her heavy breaths and nodded. "Fuck yes."

Sadie fell back onto the bed as I hovered over her. I worked to pull off her pants, then her panties. Spreading her legs apart, I did what I'd been dreaming about all damn day, bringing her pussy to my mouth. She tasted so fucking sweet. I hadn't done this to anyone since my wife. I'd stuck to quick vanilla sex with a condom. But feeling Sadie's warm flesh against my tongue, tasting her and consuming her arousal was just about the most intimate thing I'd done with anyone for as long as I could remember.

She moaned as I lashed my tongue over her clit, circling and sucking the sensitive flesh there. Her hands raked through my hair as I worked my face overtime to please her. My dick was so hard, I thought I might come in my trousers before this was even finished.

Sadie bucked her hips to meet my not-so-gentle tongue thrusts. I knew she was close to coming and needed to make a decision as to whether I wanted to let her come on my face—or whether I wanted to join in on the fun.

When it seemed like she was close, I pulled back suddenly. "Do you want to come on my mouth or with me inside you?"

"I want you inside me," she panted.

Those words were clear as day and they were all I needed to hear.

Thank fuck I always traveled with a condom in my wallet. I could honestly say I'd never had to use one so unexpectedly before. Reaching into my back pocket, I took the condom out and ripped it open with my teeth, so desperate to be inside her. I lowered my pants, causing my erect cock to spring forward. The tip was completely covered in precum. Sadie's eyes were fixed on my dick, and when she wet her lips, I couldn't sheath myself fast enough.

I should've been gentler with her, but my instinct was to just enter her in one rough movement. The sound of pleasure that exited her when I pushed balls-deep inside confirmed that she wanted it this way, too. Never had I been comfortable enough with anyone but my wife to let myself get completely lost in sex. There was no trepidation, no hesitancy on my part, just raw need.

"Sebastian . . . ," she whispered over and over. Every time Sadie said that, it made me thrust harder, wanting to earn every last utterance of my name.

"Fuck, Sadie. Just . . . fuck . . ." I could hardly speak, feeling like I'd totally lost my mind. "Pull my hair harder . . . ," I said, having no qualms about telling her what I wanted. "Spread your legs wider . . ."

She did as I asked and bucked her hips even faster. It seemed someone liked to be ordered around in bed, and I was happy to oblige.

"Tell me when you're ready, Sadie."

A few seconds later, her body quaked as she grabbed my ass. "I'm coming," she said. It was barely audible, but I'd heard it.

I let myself go, pushing so deep inside her as I emptied my endless load into the condom. Her hand was on my ass the entire time, guiding me as I came. The sounds she made along with her orgasm were something I would never forget. This girl had totally rocked my world in a matter of minutes.

As I collapsed over her, we panted almost in sync. It was seriously the craziest sex of my life. And while it was completely primal and raw, I knew that part of the reason I was able to let go to that level was because I trusted her. It was different from anything I'd experienced since Amanda. And if I were being honest, different from anything I'd experienced before Amanda. But I wouldn't let my mind go to thinking about my wife right now, because that was somewhat fucked up.

It took a few minutes before I could bear to pull out of her. If I'd had my way, I would've stayed inside her for a lot longer. But I wasn't exactly clear on the safety of doing that, considering the massive load I'd expelled into that rubber.

After I disposed of the condom, I returned to her and laid my head on her bare breasts. I could feel her heart beating against my ear a mile a minute. That was my first confirmation that what had just happened between us was far more than just the best fuck of my life.

CHAPTER 20

Sadie

I didn't know what was better, what had transpired this afternoon or the sight of Sebastian's tanned, muscular ass as he got up off the bed to put his pants back on. He turned to the side just enough for me to catch a glimpse of his erect cock bobbing up and down before it disappeared into his boxer briefs. Damn. His body was literally perfect. His legs so toned, his skin so bronze, and his abs looked carved from stone. I couldn't believe I'd just had sex with him. I couldn't believe we'd managed to resist doing it again. But he'd only had one condom, and though I was on the pill and mentioned that to him, the thought of doing it without one didn't even seem like an option to Sebastian. So instead, I'd lowered my head and taken him into my mouth until he came down my throat. The guttural sounds he made when I was going down on him were beyond sexy. It was the least I could do, considering I'd riled him up by rubbing my wetness against his leg. Not to mention the amazing oral sex he'd given me earlier.

"You're a beautiful man," I couldn't help but say as I continued to watch him get dressed.

He smiled back at me as he threw his shirt over his head.

After he finished getting dressed, he crawled back onto the bed and faced me as I remained naked under the covers.

He leaned in and kissed my nose. "I have to get home before Birdie gets back."

I looked over at the clock and couldn't help noticing that it was actually a bit early for him to have to leave so soon. She wasn't supposed to be home until seven. I'd hoped he'd want to stay and hang for a while longer. But I wasn't about to seem clingy, because that wasn't very attractive. Sebastian didn't seem like the kind of man who would appreciate that, especially since he already had one little girl to coddle; he didn't need another.

So I put my neediness and vulnerability aside and said, "Yeah, you'd better get back."

He lifted himself off the bed. I stood up, grabbing one of my robes to cover myself. But not before I caught Sebastian ogling me every second that my flesh had been exposed. Whatever hesitancy he might have been experiencing right now, I didn't think it had anything to do with a lack of physical compatibility with me.

He stood staring at me for a moment, like he wasn't sure what to say. "We'll talk soon, okay?"

I leaned in to plant a chaste kiss on his lips, then answered, "Yeah."

After he left, I'd be lying if I said I didn't feel a little empty. We'd gone from the most amazing sex I'd ever had to this odd feeling of detachment. Which was weird because I'd felt so extremely connected to him the entire day, not just sexually but in every way. Nevertheless, our having sex seemed to change something.

As if someone upstairs knew I needed the support, Devin sent me a text as I was ruminating.

Devin: Super bored and the guy is out with his friends. Want some company?

Sadie: Yes . . . but don't bring wine. I had my fill today.

Devin: Speak for yourself! More for me.

Sadie: LOL. Okay. See you soon.

She knocked in her usual upbeat rhythm. When I opened, Devin looked at my face, then down at my neck. "What the hell got into you? Or should I say . . . *who*?"

"What are you talking about?"

Admittedly, I wasn't necessarily going to tell her about Sebastian. I hadn't fully decided whether that was a good idea, regardless of how much I wanted to talk it out. So I wondered how she could be so sure that something had happened.

I tried to play dumb. "What are you talking about?"

"Have you looked at yourself in the mirror? You have bruises down your neck and chest."

I ran to the mirror in the hallway. *Shit.* Sebastian had given me multiple hickies.

"Spill. What happened?"

She figured it out before I had a chance to confess.

"Oh my God. Oh. My. God." She shook her head. "It was Sebastian Maxwell, wasn't it?"

When I continued to not say anything, that was all but an admission.

"Holy shit." She put the wine on the counter and proceeded to open it. "I'm grabbing a glass for this, and then you're gonna tell me everything."

After, we sat down in the living room, and I told Devin everything that had happened today while sparing some of the most intimate details (as much as she would have wanted and appreciated them). So I told her that we slept together but kept the specifics to myself.

"Holy shit. I can't believe it. Why don't you seem stoked? This is, like, the best thing ever to happen to us."

Us?

I frowned. "It really *was*. The best thing ever. No one's ever made me feel the way he did."

Drawing her own conclusion from my expression, she added, "But . . ."

"But something I couldn't quite figure out changed before he left. I think maybe what happened really hit him."

"What do you mean . . . like the fact he fucked you?"

"It's not the first time he's had sex since his wife died. But I get the impression it was the first time it was with someone he might have feelings for. I think maybe either he started to feel guilty or maybe he regretted it. I can't be sure."

She sighed. "Of course it can't be simple, right?"

"No. And in this case, I wouldn't expect it to be. To be honest, I'm still a little shocked that it actually happened. So I can imagine how he feels, all the emotions he might be going through once the reality of what we did sets in. I just hope he's okay."

She swirled her wine around in the glass and shook her head. "Wow."

"What?"

"Most women would feel neglected in your shoes. But you're actually thinking about *his* feelings? You really care about him, don't you?"

I didn't even have to think about it. "Yes. Yes, I really do, and it's scaring me because I stand a very real chance of getting hurt because of that."

The way our texts read, anyone picking up my phone might've thought this man was my brother. I sighed and scrolled back to reread our messages from the last couple of days.

Late Sunday night, after Devin had left, there had been:

Sebastian: Hey. Sorry I had to run this afternoon. I had a really nice time.

Nice?

That wouldn't be the word I'd use to describe earth-shattering sex. Phenomenal? Amazing? Incredible? "Nice" . . . was more like something your great-aunt said to you. *Thanks for stopping by the nursing home today, Sadie. It was so nice to see you.*

Yet . . . I'd followed his lead and typed back.

Sadie: No worries! I had a nice time, too.

Then on Monday evening, I just couldn't stop wondering what was going on in Sebastian's head. So I decided it was my turn to initiate contact this time. I figured I'd be funny. So I typed:

Sadie: Hey. How was your lay?

The dots had moved around a bit, then stopped, and then started again. Eventually, he'd typed back.

Sebastian: Busy. How about yours?

I'd been disappointed he didn't take the bait with my intentional typo, yet I replied back:

Sadie: Good!

Tuesday and Wednesday, we had no interaction, then last night I got my hopes up when my phone buzzed with an incoming text:

Sebastian: Are you busy Saturday evening?

I'd been thinking . . . dinner . . . a movie . . . sex maybe?

Sadie: I'm free after seven!

But my heart sank reading his response.

Sebastian: Think we can do training at 7:30 or 8:00? Birdie has been bugging me. Apparently she taught Duke a new trick, and she can't wait to show you. She won't even show it to me first.

I smiled at Birdie's being excited. Though again I felt disappointment that the text didn't mention anything about the two of us. Yet still, I said nothing. Instead, I'd answered:

Sadie: That sounds good. Can't wait!

Half an hour later it was still irking me how innocuous our texts had been. So I decided to see if maybe I could get a rise out of him. It was dumb, a spur-of-the-moment reaction to my feelings being hurt, and I regretted it right after I hit "Send."

Sadie: It might be closer to 8:00, but I'll come straight after my . . . work thingy.

I chewed on my nail, waiting to see how he'd respond. He knew what type of work things I often did after business hours. This time, I had a combination happy hour and *six minute dating with a friend* event. After everything that had transpired between Sebastian and me the last two weeks, the truth was, I felt weird about going at all. Eight six-minute dates with men consuming copious amounts of alcohol wouldn't have sounded appealing even if I'd never met Sebastian Maxwell. But I'd signed up two months ago because the *with a friend* part intrigued me, and I'd thought it would make for a fun article. In regular speed dating, you spent five to ten minutes talking to a stranger and then moved on to the next. At the end of a session of six or eight different mini dates, you wrote down if you were interested in an actual date with any of the men. If they also wrote your name down, then your contact information was given to each of you by the host. That was all true with this event, too. Only tomorrow night's event had a twist. Both the man and woman seeking the dates brought a friend, and it was the friends who did the talking on the six-minute dates. They each asked questions about the prospective date to the prospective date's friend. It sounded a little nutty, but I knew bringing Devin would make it interesting. Plus, months ago, I'd had no idea the Maxwells would be in my life. Which was pretty surreal to think about now, since I felt like I'd known them so much longer.

I watched my phone as my text went from *Sent* to *Delivered* to *Read*. The little dots started to jump around, and I held my breath, waiting to see Sebastian's response.

Sebastian: Work thingy?

I smiled to myself. I'd gotten his attention, but as I started to type back, I became nervous. Why? I didn't know. It wasn't like we were in an exclusive relationship or anything. Though to me, things with Sebastian weren't exactly casual, either. I regretted poking the bear even after I'd gotten exactly what I'd been after. How would I feel if Sebastian told me he had a date? *Ugh.* I needed to backtrack a bit . . . rewind and put Jack back in the box.

Sadie: Yeah. Just some research for an article.

But Sebastian wasn't having it.

Sebastian: A date?

Well, technically I had eight dates. Though I didn't think I needed to clarify that small point at the moment.

Sadie: Technically yes. Though not really. Just a new kind of speed dating for an upcoming article.

I braced myself, waiting for the response. While we'd been texting back and forth conversation-style, suddenly Sebastian went radio silent. It was a full ten minutes before my phone buzzed again. And when it did, my heart stuttered to a halt as I read his words:

Sebastian: Have a good time.

"So. What does Tyler do for a living?" Devin said, sipping her second Cosmo.

Tyler's friend Ethan answered. "He's a pilot. Does long hauls between here and Sydney."

"Wow. That's a cool job. Does Tyler get discounts for friends and family? If so, I might be willing to skirt the rules and give you Sadie's number right now."

We all laughed. It was our fifth date of the night, and Devin had gotten really into her role of vetting prospective dates. Though the fun of the evening had nothing to do with any of the men, because let's face it, I had no interest in any of them. The fun was the outlandish shit that came out of Devin's mouth. Maybe if I'd been more into the night, I'd have noticed how cute Tyler was.

"Does your friend have any nicknames?" Devin asked.

Tyler flashed Ethan a menacing warning look.

"Oh no you don't," she said. "Spit it out. Now we need to know."

Ethan grinned. "His nickname is Tink."

"Tink? Like in Tinker Bell?"

Ethan shook his head. "No, Tink because the first time he ever got drunk, we were about thirteen, and he got so shit-faced that he wet the bed after he passed out."

We all laughed while Tyler punched his friend's arm. "You're supposed to be helping me find a date, not scaring them away, jackass."

"What show does your friend watch that he wouldn't want you to tell me about right now?"

Ethan's smile grew wide again. Tyler just shut his eyes. This was going to be good.

"He watches that show *Something and the Restless*."

My eyes widened. "*The Young and the Restless*. The soap opera?"

Ethan cracked up. "We had a roommate in college who watched it. Tyler here was madly in love, but she had a boyfriend. He started to watch it just to spend time with her. For Christmas he even got her tickets to one of those fan meet and greets where you meet a celebrity at a bookstore."

"Aww, that's so sweet," Devin said. "What happened with her?"

Tyler groaned and mock banged his head on the table before Ethan answered. "She hooked up with the dude from the show after the meet and greet. The next day, she dumped the boyfriend and started to go out with the actor. Last I heard, they have two kids."

"Oh my God." I laughed. "Is he kidding?"

Poor Tyler just shook his head. "I wish he were."

His smile was lopsided and modest but adorable and seemingly genuine. I smiled back, and we shared a connection for a brief moment.

A minute later, the host yelled that time was up and instructed the women to move one table to the right. Tyler and I shook hands, and he caught my eye. "It was really nice sharing six incredibly embarrassing moments with you."

I laughed. "You too."

Shuffling to the next table, Devin bumped her shoulder with mine. "He was really cute. I hope we match with him."

The next three speed dates were on the painful side. One guy slurred his words, and the other two definitely didn't get Devin's sense of humor. I was thrilled to be done. Devin took out the match cards they'd given us when we walked in.

"I vote for one, three, and five," she said.

"I don't think the man you live with is going to be happy with three dates. Maybe you should cut it down to one."

She frowned. "I'm serious."

I sighed. "I don't want to go out with any of these guys, Dev."

"I know, honey. But you said yourself that you didn't know where things stood between you and Sebastian. So why not give some of these guys a chance? At least number five. He was adorable."

"I don't think so."

The host came around to collect the card that I was supposed to list my dates on. I handed it to him.

"You didn't fill it out yet."

I smiled. "Yes, I did. Thanks for a fun evening."

Outside, I hugged Devin goodbye and thanked her for coming with me.

"At least I can write a good article about it. This was actually fun. The other time I did speed dating, it was so awkward. But having your friend there keeps things so much more relaxed."

"It wasn't having me here that made it relaxed. You had no intention of going out with anyone before you even stepped foot in the place. So there was no pressure for you."

I shrugged. "Maybe."

"You know I was Team Sebastian from the very first day."

"I know. What happened? You went from encouraging me to go after him to wanting me to go out and date."

She squeezed my arm. "I don't want a heart that isn't available to love you to keep you from finding one that is."

I frowned. "I won't let that happen. I promise."

While I meant the words when I said them, the problem was, falling in love wasn't something I actually had any control over.

"Can I try one more time?" Birdie jumped up and down.

I looked at Magdalene, who had been a good sport all night, and she nodded. Birdie clicked the clicker twice then yelled, "*Speak!* Marmaduke. *Gib laut!*"

The overgrown puppy began to bark nonstop. Tonight we'd started to train him to bark on command. Since the doorbell was something that always made him yap anyway, we incorporated it into the training. Magdalene would go outside, and on the count of ten, she'd ring the bell and I'd click the clicker and tell him to speak. When he barked, I'd scratch behind his ears while telling him he was a good boy and rewarding him with a treat. After doing that five times, I could just click the clicker and yell for him to speak, and Marmaduke would start barking, even without the doorbell. The only problem was, sometimes we couldn't get him to stop. He'd take the biscuit, practically swallow it whole, and then go right back to barking again.

Which was exactly what had happened again this time. While the loud bark didn't bother Birdie at all, it was starting to drive me nuts, and poor Magdalene sat at the dining room table rubbing her temples again. Desperate to stop the piercing sound, I opened the end-table drawer, where we'd hidden the stuffed toys he had taken a shine to, and tossed a stuffed unicorn at him. He stopped barking but only because he was now too busy humping. I sighed. *Note to self: This week watch YouTube videos on how to stop barking once you get it started.*

Magdalene's phone started to ring, and she laughed answering it.

"Oh, hi, Mr. Maxwell."

My ears perked up more than Marmaduke's did when he saw the shell of a tortoise.

"Yes, sure. She's still here." She paused and then: "Hold on a second." I tried to look busy when Magdalene called to me. "Sadie, Mr. Maxwell would like to speak to you."

"Oh. Okay." My heart started to flutter as she walked over the phone.

"Hello."

"Hey."

His voice sounded tense. "Is everything okay?"

"I was trying to reach you, but you weren't answering your phone."

"Oh. It was . . . in my bag, I guess. I probably didn't hear it because of the barking."

"Barking?"

"We were teaching Marmaduke how to speak."

I heard Sebastian blow out a deep breath through the phone. "Listen. I was trying to get out of here by eight thirty so I could make it home before you leave. But that's obviously not happening. I could probably get out in an hour or two. Do you think you could . . . hang around until I get home? We need to talk."

My pulse quickened. "Sure. Of course. Why don't I tell Magdalene she can go?"

"If you don't mind. She's been staying pretty late all week. So that would be great."

"Of course."

"Let me run. We're down a few people."

"Okay. See you later."

I ended the call and handed the phone back to Magdalene. "Sebastian asked me to stay so we could . . . uhhh . . . talk about Marmaduke's training. Why don't you go home? He said you could use a night of getting out early."

She smiled and looked over my shoulder at Birdie, then leaned in to whisper. "Mr. Maxwell has been cranky this week."

"Has he?"

She nodded and winked. "Hopefully your talk about Marmaduke's training will have him feeling better."

"Oh . . . it's . . . not what you think."

She raised both her eyebrows.

I sighed. "Okay . . . so maybe it is what you think. But it's . . . it's . . . I don't know what it is, Magdalene."

She smiled. "He's a good man. Have patience with him."

I wasn't sure what to say to that, so instead I just nodded.

After Magdalene left, Birdie took a shower. She came out to the living room and asked if I could braid her hair. About nine thirty, she yawned, and I tucked her into bed. Then I sat in the living room waiting for Sebastian. I kept replaying what he'd said to me on the phone over and over. *"We need to talk."* No good news came after an opening line like that. A horrible feeling of dread loomed over me as I waited. I felt hurt, and he hadn't even ended things yet. To be honest, I wasn't even sure what exactly he would be ending. It wasn't like we'd defined anything. All I knew was that we had started *something*, and to me that something was special.

By ten thirty, I was still sitting on the couch but now bobbing my knee up and down, feeling like I might jump out of my skin. I hadn't heard from Sebastian again. On the phone, he'd said an hour or two, so hopefully that meant he'd be here any minute. Deciding I needed to calm down, I went in search of wine in his office.

I knew where the key was kept, because I'd watched Macie raid the locked cabinet last weekend. But when I went to grab it from the desk drawer, a framed picture snagged my attention. I picked it up and stared at a photo of Sebastian and Amanda. It had been taken in the hospital. Sebastian had one arm around his wife's shoulder while she cradled a newborn Birdie. They were both smiling and looked so happy.

Was this how it would be if we were together anyway? Framed photos of his first love all over the house? Living in the shadow of another woman? How exactly would that work if he got married again? Would the photo of his new bride slide into the frame right over the one from his first wedding? Maybe him dumping me tonight was for the best.

Yeah, definitely for the best.

"She was born three weeks early."

Sebastian's deep voice startled me and I jumped. Unfortunately, the frame slipped from my fingers and fell to the floor, landing facedown with a loud *clank*.

The hand that had been holding the frame flew up and covered my heart. "You scared the shit out of me."

"Sorry."

Nervous, I bent to pick up the frame. I felt nauseous when I turned it over.

Cracked. The glass was cracked.

I shook my head. "God, I'm so sorry. It's broken. I'll replace it."

Sebastian walked toward me and slipped it from my hand. "It's fine. No big deal." He set the frame facedown on his desk and our eyes caught. "Sorry I'm so late."

"I wasn't snooping. I just came in to see if you had any wine and . . . I guess the photo caught my attention."

Sebastian nodded. He walked around to where I stood and pulled open the drawer. Taking out the key, he unlocked the liquor cabinet and grabbed a bottle of red wine. He tilted it to show me the label. "This okay?"

"Does it have alcohol?"

He chuckled. "Got ya. Fill your glass to the brim."

"Thank you."

Sebastian uncorked the bottle and filled one glass, then stuffed the cork back in.

"Aren't you having any?" I said.

He handed me the very full glass. "Maybe later. I need to keep my head clear right now."

"Oh. Okay."

"Come on. Let's go sit in the living room."

Together we sat on the couch. While I sipped my wine and waited, Sebastian held his head in his hands and stared down at the floor. It made my heart hurt that he looked as pained as I felt. The man had been through so much; I needed to make this easy for him. So I took a giant gulp of liquid courage and set my glass down on the end table before moving closer to him.

"Sebastian . . . it's okay. I get it. You don't have to say anything. We had fun, but you don't want more than that. It's fine. You don't have to feel bad."

"Is that what you think? That I feel bad because I'm done with you?"

My brows drew together. "Isn't that what you're stressing over? Hurting my feelings?"

He started to laugh maniacally. Shaking his head, he pointed to the glass I'd just set down. "Give me that, will ya?"

I handed it to him and watched as he downed the entire contents of my glass. Offering it back, he said, "Fuck a clear head. I just need some balls."

Was he saying what I thought he was saying? I fought to not let my hopes get up. "I don't understand."

He raked his hands through his hair and turned to face me. "How was your date tonight, Sadie?" He'd said the word "date" weird, almost spitting out the "t," as if the word itself sickened him.

"It was . . . fine."

"Well, I'm glad. Then at least one of us had a good evening."

"You didn't have a good night?"

"Let's see . . . I broke the handle off an oven, burned my arm *twice*, put in three orders wrong, and almost fired a waitress who did nothing wrong. And that was all before six o'clock."

"I don't understand."

"I couldn't focus, Sadie. The thought of you going out with another man—*no less a half dozen men while speed dating*—makes me feel violent."

"It was eight actually."

He scoffed. "Thanks. That makes me feel a hell of a lot better."

I'd been so certain that he was coming home to break things off that even though he'd just told me he hated the thought of me dating anyone else, I still guarded my heart.

"If you didn't want me to go, why didn't you tell me that? Or better yet, why didn't you even call me this week?"

"Because I feel like I'm not *supposed to* want another woman all to myself."

I swallowed. "But you do? You want me like that?"

Sebastian looked into my eyes. "I want you in every way, Sadie. And that scares the shit out of me."

I smiled sadly. "If it makes you feel any better, you scare me, too."

"I want to move on. But I have so much guilt about doing it." He shook his head. "Did you ever play tug-of-war in school when you were a kid?"

"Sure. Of course."

"You know how they told you not to wrap the rope around your hand?"

"Yeah . . ."

"Well, that's sort of what I feel like I'm doing right now. I'm playing tug-of-war, only I have the rope wrapped around my hand really tight because I've been afraid to let go for so long. But now my circulation is getting cut off. And if I don't just let go of the damn thing, I'm going to cause more damage than I would if I just finally let go."

I looked down at Sebastian's hands. They were balled so tight, almost like he was physically hanging on to that imaginary rope. And I wanted to help him, even if it wasn't to tug him to my side and win the game. So I reached over and gently pried his fist open, then put my hand inside his and held on.

Sebastian stared down at our joined hands for a long time. "I want you to be mine, Sadie."

My heart thumped in my chest. "I'm pretty sure I have been from the start."

He smiled. "I'm sorry about this week. For acting like such a dick after our afternoon together."

"It's okay. Just talk to me next time. I get you're going to have mixed feelings, and I'll give you space when you need it."

He nodded. Bringing our joined hands to his lips, he kissed the top of mine. "So how does this work? It's been a long time since I went steady with anyone."

I chuckled. "Went steady? What are you, sixty?"

He tugged me from next to him up onto his lap. Pushing a lock of hair behind my ear, he said, "I know dating is part of your job. I won't ask you to give that up *yet*, but maybe we could have a few ground rules."

"Okay . . ."

"I'd like us to be exclusive, as far as anything physical goes."

"Of course. I'd like that, too."

"Anything else that you have to do for work, just don't tell me about it. Don't even mention you have a *thingy*."

I smiled. "I'll figure something out for work. I can do articles on different types of dating out there, interview people for worst-date stories . . . my research doesn't always need to be me trying out a different type of date."

Sebastian cupped my cheeks. "So we're going steady?"

I smiled. "We're going steady, you nerd."

We sealed the deal with a kiss. When it broke, I looked over my shoulder toward Birdie's room. "What about Birdie?"

"I'm thinking I should tell her. What do you think?"

I nibbled on my lip. "That's up to you. But I guess it's better to be honest than to have her find out by catching me sitting on your lap like this."

He nodded. "I'll talk to her tomorrow. How about after that, the three of us go out to dinner and a movie or something. Me and my girls."

My heart melted, and I couldn't contain my smile. "I like the sound of that."

"Good. Me too."

CHAPTER 21

Sebastian

This was definitely something I was going to have to wing. It wasn't like I had a handbook at the ready on how to tell your child that you're dating someone. Someone who wasn't her mother. I knew Birdie had wanted this, but I often wondered if her attitude about that might change once it actually happened. My palms were sweaty as I walked down the hall, headed toward my daughter's room. Birdie knew Sadie would be joining us for dinner and a movie tonight. She might have suspected something, but I needed to have "the talk" regardless.

Birdie was listening to music, bopping her head and lying flat on her stomach. Her long legs reached much farther than they used to. She was getting so big. It was hard to believe she'd be eleven soon. I couldn't even think about what having a preteen would be like.

I knocked to get her attention.

She looked up and took out her earbuds. "Hey, Daddy."

"Hi, pumpkin. You looking forward to the movie?"

"Yeah. And getting to hang out with Sadie, too."

That makes two of us.

"Good." I sat down on the edge of the bed. "So . . . that's actually what I wanted to talk to you about."

A look of concern crossed her face. "She's still coming, right?"

"Yeah. Yeah, of course, honey." Rubbing my palms together, I said, "What I need to tell you is that Sadie has become more than just the dog trainer. She and I . . . have gotten to know each other and, well, we really like each other's company."

The few seconds that passed felt like torture.

Her mouth curved into the slightest smile. "I'm not surprised."

My brows lifted. "Really?"

"You act sort of funny when she's around. Plus, she's pretty."

"How come you never told me that you suspected something?"

"I didn't want to get my hopes up."

"So it makes you happy that I'm dating Sadie?"

She nodded.

Feeling a sense of relief, I grinned. "You really like her, don't you?"

"Yes. I *really* really like her."

I grabbed one of her stuffed toys and looked down at it as I spoke. "You know it's important that whoever I spend time with be someone you get along with and who also makes you happy. I would never bring anyone around who didn't fit in with us."

"I know, Daddy."

"I also hope you know that just because Sadie and I are getting close, that doesn't change how much I loved your mother. Okay?"

Birdie glanced over at a photo of Amanda that hung on the wall, then said, "I know. Mommy's never coming back. You'd still be with Mommy if she were here. Mommy knows that."

That was an interesting comment, because I often wondered whether Amanda and I would have lasted had she not gotten sick.

Placing the stuffed animal back down, I said, "Do you have any questions for me?"

"Is Sadie going to live with us?"

Well, that was more direct than I was expecting.

"No. Not anytime soon. Maybe someday if things work out. This is still very new. That also means that there's a chance it might *not* work out."

"You mean you might mess it up?"

I chuckled at her assumption. *That's probably the more likely scenario, yeah.*

"That's not my intention, but adult relationships are complicated, and sometimes even though we don't intend for them to fail, they don't work out."

She had no clue that even her mother and I had struggled.

"Is Sadie still gonna go on dates for her job?"

Yeah. Sore subject.

"Not real ones."

"Because you're her boyfriend now?" She smiled.

I took a few seconds to let that word sink in. "Boyfriend." Jesus, I hadn't been someone's boyfriend in ages.

"Yeah. I guess I am."

"Is she still gonna train Marmaduke?"

Scratching my chin, I said, "I get the impression she likes spending time with you and the Duke, so I bet you can convince her to keep taking him out with you."

She sighed. "Alright, Daddy."

I squeezed her knee. "No more questions?"

She shook her head. "I don't think so."

"Okay." I leaned in and kissed her on the forehead. "I'll come get you to leave soon."

As I was walking out the door, she stopped me. "Wait."

"Yeah?"

"I do have one more question."

"Shoot."

"Can I get the big box of Milk Duds at the movies?"

I chuckled. "We'll see."

Another wave of relief hit me as I left her room. That had gone way better than I'd anticipated. I hoped nothing would happen to jinx it.

Birdie ended up really enjoying the Disney movie we watched. As for me, I really enjoyed holding Sadie's hand as I sat between them. Not to mention I'd been so busy taking care of everything over the past several years, I'd forgotten what it felt like to have someone who was looking out for me. Sadie would do subtle things like move the hair off my face or brush crumbs off my shirt. She definitely had a very protective instinct. And I had to say, I loved being looked after by a beautiful woman.

It was too soon to have Sadie spend the night with Birdie home, but I wanted nothing more than to have her in my bed tonight. I'd have to figure out a way to get alone time with her, whether it be in the middle of the day or by having Magdalene do a few overnights here and there.

When we left the theater and Sadie took Birdie down the hall to the bathroom, it occurred to me that it was the first time in ages that I didn't have to stand outside the door while my daughter used a public women's restroom to make sure she was okay. That was definitely one thing I'd taken for granted when Amanda was alive.

After the movie, the three of us went to a restaurant of Birdie's choosing and, as usual, she chose fondue.

My daughter dipped a piece of bread into the melted cheese as she looked up at Sadie, who was sitting next to her.

"Don't you like fondue, Sadie?" she asked.

Sadie seemed to be enjoying watching Birdie eat more than enjoying the food herself. "You know . . . you might not believe this, but I have never had fondue before tonight."

Birdie's eyes nearly bugged out of her head. "Whoa. How come?"

"I know. Seems crazy, right? I never really started going out to eat until I moved to the city, so I had a lot of catching up to do. Still catching up, I guess."

"Your daddy never took you out to eat?"

"We didn't have a lot of money growing up. So my dad preferred to cook at home."

"Your daddy could cook?" Birdie looked at me with an impish grin. "Mine can't."

My shoulders shook from laughter. "Thanks for that, sweetheart."

Sadie chimed in. "Yeah, but your daddy has so many other great qualities. He's smart and witty and an excellent businessman. So, if he could cook, that would make him, like . . . perfect . . . and no one is perfect." She winked at me, and it made me want to leap across the table and devour her beautiful lips.

"That's true," Birdie agreed. "He's smart and really nice and tells really good bedtime stories off the top of his head."

"See . . ." Sadie smiled.

Birdie's eyes brimmed with curiosity. "So, what kinds of things did your dad cook for you?"

"My dad has a really big garden, so he'd make all kinds of things with vegetables. Tomato sauce for homemade pizza, fried zucchini . . . stuff like that."

"Zucchini!" Birdie scrunched her nose. "I don't love vegetables. I only love olives."

"Birdie wishes *her* dad would grow *cookies* in the garden, right, sweetie?" I said.

Sadie pointed her finger to her chin. "Hmm, we'll have to find some creative ways to get you to eat your vegetables, Birdie." She raised her brow. "Do you like shakes?"

"I love them. Especially with ice cream."

"I'll bet you I can sneak vegetables into a delicious shake, and you won't even know they're there."

Birdie looked skeptical. "Really?"

"Yup. In fact, I make them all the time for myself, and I can't even taste the spinach."

Her mouth dropped. "Spinach?"

You'd think Sadie had uttered an obscenity based on my daughter's reaction.

"Yup. Wanna bet it's good?"

"Can you come over and make it tonight?"

Sadie looked at me like she wasn't sure how to answer that.

"I think Sadie has to work tomorrow," I said.

Sadie looked a little disappointed that I'd closed the door on her coming home with us. It wasn't that I didn't want her to. I just worried I might mess up tonight in front of my daughter. But I really did want her to head back with us, even if for a little while. So I added, "But if she wants to come over and make you a shake for dessert, I'll make sure she gets home safe."

I signaled to her with my eyes that I really hoped she came over tonight. The more I thought about it, the more I realized I *needed* her to come over so that I could at least kiss her good night.

Sadie smiled at me. "Okay, maybe I can stop by there for a little bit."

Birdie jumped up and down in her seat. "Yay!"

On the way home, we stopped at a market so that Sadie could buy the ingredients for what she dubbed her "magic shake."

Once we got to the house, she laid all the ingredients out on the counter.

"Now, I shouldn't even be giving out my secret recipe, but since I really like you, Birdie, I'm gonna show you exactly how to make my special shake."

Birdie watched with excitement as I got the blender out for Sadie. Then I rolled up my sleeves and leaned into the counter to just enjoy watching the two of them interact.

Sadie peeled a banana. "So the first magic ingredient is a really ripe banana. Because that makes the shake super sweet without having to add too much sugar."

Birdie looked up at her. "I love sugar."

"I know, Miss Cookie, but sugar isn't that great for you. I promise you that this will taste just as sweet as sugar, okay?"

My daughter shrugged. "Okay."

Sadie opened up a jar of peanut butter. "This is the next secret ingredient . . . which does have some sugar in it . . . but I'll let it slide." She winked.

"I love peanut butter. Especially peanut butter cookies," Birdie said.

"Why doesn't that surprise me?" Sadie chuckled.

My daughter eagerly hopped up on her toes. "What's next?"

"Next is a cup of vanilla almond milk."

Birdie scrunched her nose. "Milk made from almonds?"

"Yup. And it tastes kind of like vanilla ice cream."

She looked skeptical. "Hmm."

"Are you challenging me, Miss Birdie?"

My daughter giggled. It was nice to see her this engaged. Sadie made her so happy. She made *me* so happy.

"The next ingredient is . . . frozen blueberries." Sadie ripped open the bag of fruit.

"I love blueberries!" Birdie squealed.

Sadie walked over to the ice maker and placed a cup under it. "Next, I'm adding a few ice cubes to make the shake extra cold. Then, last but not least, comes the most important ingredient."

"What's that?"

"Have you forgotten? It's spinach, silly, remember? Veggies?"

"Oh yeah. I was hoping you'd forget."

"No such luck." Sadie added a handful of raw spinach to the blender.

"Are we done?"

"That's it!" Sadie put the top on. "Are you ready to blend it all up?"

"Can I?" Birdie asked excitedly.

"Yup. You do the honors."

Birdie pressed her little finger down onto the "Blend" button and watched as all the ingredients turned into a dark-green color, almost a purple with the blueberries.

"You know what I call this drink?" Sadie said.

"What?"

"The green monster."

"That's so cool."

Sadie stopped the blender and grabbed a plastic iced-coffee cup and straw from the cupboard.

"Are you ready to try it?" Sadie asked as she placed the cup on the counter.

My daughter nodded.

Sadie poured the concoction into the cup and fastened the lid before adding the straw. She slid it down the counter to Birdie.

Sadie and I watched with bated breath as Birdie tried it. After a hesitant first sip, she stopped and licked her lips, then took another, longer sip. She looked over at us.

Sadie rested her chin in her hands. "And?"

"It's really, really good!"

Sadie began to dance around in celebration. We high-fived each other. Birdie started giggling and proceeded to drink down a good portion of the smoothie.

Sadie poured some of the drink into another glass and handed it to me. "Something tells me even your dad can make this."

I took a sip and licked my lips. "Mm. Really good." I was sure she could tell from the look in my eyes that I wasn't exactly thinking of the shake when I'd made that sound. Although I had to say, the drink definitely didn't taste anything like spinach.

I looked over at the clock. It was late for my daughter to be up. "Birdie, it's way past your bedtime, and you have school tomorrow. How about you go get washed up, then come back and say good night to Sadie."

She looked disappointed to see this night coming to an end. I hoped there would be many more like it.

When Birdie finally disappeared down the hall, I wrapped my hand around Sadie's waist and pulled her in for the kiss that I'd been so incredibly hungry for all night. She moaned into my mouth, and that was confirmation that she'd wanted it as much as I did.

Pulling her into me, I bit her bottom lip and slowly released it. "You are so fucking delicious, you know that?"

"Oh my," she said, clearly noticing the growing bulge in my pants. "Wow. You'd better get that down before your daughter comes out to say good night."

"Yeah." I sighed. "This isn't exactly a scenario I'm used to."

Figuring it was a good idea to heed her warning, I took a walk down the hall and used the bathroom for a breather.

When I returned, Birdie was standing in the kitchen in her nightgown, her hair wet, looking up at Sadie.

"Can you braid my hair before bed, Sadie?"

Sadie looked over at me, seeming to want permission. I nodded.

"Sure. Let's do it," she said.

Sadie disappeared down the hall to Birdie's room and was gone much longer than I expected. When she came back out, I was waiting for her on the living room couch.

"That was a long braiding session."

Sadie sat down next to me and laid her head on my shoulder. "She's so cute. She just wanted to talk."

"Thank you for being so sweet to her." I kissed the top of her head. "You want some wine? What can I get you?"

"No. I'm good. I just want to lie here in your arms for a while if that's okay."

I adjusted my body so that she was completely enveloped in my arms. "That's more than okay."

After a long while, she raised her chin up to me and I took that as a cue to plant a long kiss on her lips. My dick rose to attention. I was horny as hell tonight but knew she wouldn't agree to spend the night even if I suggested it. This was a complicated situation. I knew she *shouldn't* spend the night, but I wasn't ready to let her go, either. As I thrust my tongue inside her mouth, her familiar taste ignited a need so intense that I wasn't sure I was going to be able to stop. When she moaned this time, I wondered if she was as wet as I was hard. The strongest temptation to slip my finger inside her panties to check consumed me.

"This is painful. I need to be inside you," I muttered over her mouth. "It feels like it's been forever."

I wondered if there was a way we could sneak into the bathroom, anywhere. I just needed her.

Sadie must have sensed that I was spiraling, because she pulled back from our kiss. "I'd better get going."

I let out a frustrated groan. "You know how much I don't want you to leave, right?"

"Of course, I know that. But it's better if I do." She stood up.

I wrapped my hands around her cheeks. "I'm not going to be able to stop thinking about you." My eyeballs moved from side to side as the wheels in my head turned.

"What are you thinking?" she asked.

"I'm trying to scheme a way for you to be in my bed tonight and disappear magically by morning."

"Except that's not possible. It's way too soon to risk anything. So I'm gonna go."

She was right. It just felt wrong to let her go for some reason. She felt like she belonged here.

I ended up calling her an Uber, and we spent every second until it arrived kissing like two horny teenagers.

After she got in the car and took off, she sent me a text.

Sadie: I forgot to clean up the green monster remnants. I meant to go back into the kitchen and do that.

Sebastian: The real monster is in my pants, and he's not able to be tamed tonight.

Sadie: LOL

Sebastian: No worries about the shake. I got it. I owe you for getting my daughter to eat vegetables. Seriously, that was some magical shit.

Sadie: I was so happy she liked it.

Sebastian: She likes YOU.

Sadie: That makes me so happy.

Sebastian: I might like you, too. A LOT.

Sadie: I like you, too, Sebastian. I might even be crazy about you.

Sebastian: I have a new story idea for you.

Sadie: Yeah?

Sebastian: Dating the Horny Single Dad.

Sadie: LOL. What does this assignment entail?

Sebastian: Several meetups in the afternoons at various places and lots of sex. You in?

Sadie: Definitely.

Monday morning, I still couldn't stop thinking about Sadie. So I decided to push what I'd mentioned last night about a daytime meetup.

Sebastian: Good morning. How did you sleep?

Sadie: Pretty good. I had a nice dream. You might've been in it.

I caught myself with a gigantic smile on my face as I went to text back.

Sebastian: What time do you go to lunch? Maybe I can swing by and take you out and you can tell me about that dream.

Sadie: That sounds great. Except . . .

My shoulders slumped waiting for what would come after the word "except." I assumed it would be something like *"except . . . I can't because I have too much work to do."* Or . . . *"except I have a meeting."* But the next text perked me up . . . some parts might've gotten more perky than others.

Sadie: How about you meet me at my apartment at 2, and I do better than tell you about my dream. We can act it out . . .

Fuck yeah. I couldn't type back fast enough.

Sebastian: I'll be out front of your building at 1:45.

Sadie: LOL. I like your eagerness, Mr. Maxwell.

Sebastian: Oh, I'm eager, alright. You should see what's going on in my pants already . . . with more than five hours to go before I arrive.

Sadie: You could . . . show me what's going on.

All the blood from my brain had rushed south with better shit to do than support logical decisions. So of course, it sounded like a damn good idea to oblige. Reaching down, I fisted my hard-on through my sweatpants, then snapped a pic and sent it in response to her text. Maybe it was the angle, but my cock looked pretty damn impressive, if I did say so myself.

Sadie wasted no time responding.

Sadie: OMG. Lunch looks delicious! I can't wait. Let's make it 1pm, instead of 2!

I laughed.

Sebastian: See you at 1, beautiful. Can't wait.

CHAPTER 22

SADIE

"I love this little dip."

Sebastian ran his finger up and down the arch between my lower back and the top of my ass as I lay on my stomach. We'd just ravaged each other, yet the slightest touch of his finger on my back had me already wanting him again.

"Oh yeah?"

He nodded. "Would it be too much if I poured the soup I brought with lunch and drank it out of there?"

I laughed. "Well, it might be hot, and I don't think you would be *drinking* it out of the dip in my back, more like lapping like a dog."

"Sweetheart, that soup is ice-cold by now. And lapping at you sounds absolutely fucking perfect."

He was definitely right about the soup not being hot anymore. Now I was glad that I'd told my office I needed to take a half day for a fake doctor's appointment. We'd been at it for close to two hours already, and the Chinese food that Sebastian had brought hadn't even made it out of the bag.

As if that thought reminded my body that it had skipped breakfast, my stomach growled . . . *loudly*.

Sebastian chuckled. "I guess that's one way of you telling me I should feed you."

"I'm actually starving. I usually eat a bar in the morning on the train, but some guy bumped into me and it fell on the floor after one bite."

"Why don't I go heat the food up, then?"

"Okay."

Sebastian got out of bed. He bent to grab his jeans, giving me a spectacular view of his very taut ass.

"Wait!"

He froze with one leg in the pants and turned to look at me.

"Don't get dressed," I said.

He flashed a crooked smile. "You want to eat naked?"

"Yeah. I do. Would it gross you out if I said I wanted to eat naked in bed with you?"

Sebastian chuckled. "No. But it might make me propose."

He kicked back off the pants leg and strutted out to the kitchen buck naked.

What a view. I sighed. Feeling content, I adjusted the blankets and pillows to sit up against the headboard.

A few minutes later, Sebastian returned with three containers and two sets of chopsticks. He climbed back into bed and passed me one of the cartons, then unwrapped the wooden chopsticks and snapped them apart before offering them to me.

"Thank you."

His eye dropped down to my exposed breasts and he shook his head. "Best fucking lunch ever."

I stuffed my face with Szechuan shrimp. "Mm. This is good. Where did you get it?"

"This little takeout place two blocks from me."

"I'm very picky about Chinese food. It's probably because I'm part Chinese."

Sebastian was midswallow and started to cough. "You're Chinese?"

"Four percent. I did one of those 23andMe DNA tests to find out my heritage two years ago, since I'm adopted. I'm sixty percent Italian, thirty-six percent Norwegian, and four percent Chinese. Ever since I found that out, I feel like I got better with chopsticks."

He laughed. "Interesting. My daughter is obsessed with those damn commercials ever since she made a family tree at school."

"I totally forgot about that! She told Santa she wanted one of those in her early letters."

Sebastian shook his head.

"What about you? What nationality are you?"

"My grandparents were from Sicily on my dad's side, and my mother was Welsh." Sebastian fished a piece of sesame chicken from his cardboard container and went to put it into his mouth. Halfway there, he fumbled, and the chicken landed on his abs. He picked it off using his chopsticks. "Must be because I'm not four percent Chinese."

I smiled. "Do you sing in the shower?"

Sebastian raised an eyebrow. "That's an odd question to ask."

I shrugged. "Maybe. But I think people's shower habits tell a lot about them. Like if you're in and out in five minutes, racing through the washing to get done, or whether you take your time and use your shampoo bottle as a mic when the mood strikes."

"I don't think I've ever used the shampoo bottle as a microphone. But I definitely whistle sometimes." His face fell. "At least I used to."

I set my container on the nightstand and then plucked Sebastian's from his hands and placed his lunch next to mine. Crawling over, I straddled his lap. "I think we can get you back to whistling in the shower."

He brushed hair from my face. "I think so, too. You make me feel happier than I have in a long time, *Gretchen*."

I rubbed my nose with his. *"Danke."*

It was another half hour before Sebastian and I got back to the Chinese food. We were just destined to eat it cold. But I couldn't care less. Playing cowgirl on my handsome boyfriend's lap beat warm food any day of the week.

After, we showered together, and Sebastian had to get ready to leave for the restaurant.

"What are you doing tonight?" He kissed the top of my head while I sat at my vanity brushing out my wet hair. "Any plans?"

"Actually, I have a hot date."

I watched Sebastian's face fall in the mirror. *Shit.*

"Gah! It's not what you're thinking. I meant I was going out to dinner with my dad."

He squinted at my reflection in the mirror. "Not funny. Considering your job."

I stood and pushed up on my tippy-toes to plant a kiss on his cheek. "Sorry. I wasn't thinking."

He finished buttoning his shirt. "Where are you going for dinner?"

"I'm not sure. We usually decide when he gets here."

"Why don't you come to the restaurant?"

I blinked a few times. "Really? You wouldn't mind meeting my dad?"

Sebastian shrugged. "Why would I mind? You're already one of my daughter's favorite people."

Warmth spread throughout my chest. Being with a mature man really made the men I'd dated over the last—oh, I don't know—*ten years* seem like such little boys. Sebastian wasn't afraid to meet my family and had welcomed me into his once he gave in to his feelings.

"I'd love that. I'll have to see if Dad already had his heart set on something else. But maybe we'll come."

"Sounds good."

I walked Sebastian to the door. "Thanks for . . . lunch."

He kissed me one more time, then grazed his thumb along my bottom lip. "Thanks for not giving up on me when you probably should've."

◆ ◆ ◆

"So you're serious about this guy?"

Dad picked up the folded napkin from the table and shook it out, laying it across his lap.

I looked over his shoulder. Sebastian had just gone to get us a bottle of wine from the bar. He winked from the other side of the room when he caught me watching him. I smiled and sighed. "I'm crazy about him, Dad."

"Then I guess I better get to know the fellow a little bit."

On the way to the restaurant, I'd filled Dad in on some of the story behind Sebastian and my getting together. He hadn't actually said much, so I wasn't sure what he was thinking. But that was Dad's way. Sometimes I would swear he wasn't even paying attention when I talked. Then a few weeks later, he'd surprise me by asking a follow-up question to some minor thing I'd casually mentioned. Dad was a listener more than a talker.

Sebastian came back with a bottle of merlot and opened it table-side.

Dad glanced around. "It's pretty busy. Think you'll have time to join us? I'd like to get to know the man who my daughter is spending time with. How old are you?"

"Dad," I scolded. "Sebastian is working."

Sebastian waved me off with an easy smile. "I'm just going to check on things in the kitchen and put in an order for you, and then I should have some time." He turned to my dad. "Is there anything you don't like to eat or are allergic to?"

My dad patted the little belly he'd developed over the last few years. "Does it look like there's much I don't eat?"

"Okay. Give me about ten minutes. When I come back, I'm all yours to interrogate, sir."

My father seemed to like that response, but I was embarrassed. As soon as Sebastian walked away, I said, "Dad, what the heck?"

"What?"

"Sebastian invited us here and is going out of his way and you say, 'Hey, nice to meet you . . . *how old are you?* What does it matter how old he is?"

"You said you're crazy about him. So I want to get to know the man."

"There's a difference between getting to know someone and being rude."

Dad took a breadstick from the center of the table and broke it in two. "You're involved with a man with a lot of baggage. A widower, a ten-year-old daughter, running this place . . . I read eighty percent of all restaurants fail within five years. I'm just concerned, sweetheart."

I sighed. I suppose it was only natural for a parent to be concerned about his daughter dating a man who'd already been married, especially one with a daughter. It made sense that he would see Sebastian's daughter as baggage, though I was certain that would change when he met Birdie.

"Okay. I get it. Just . . . be nice about it, please. Go slow."

Fifteen minutes later, Sebastian appeared at our table balancing four different plates. He set them down and then took a seat himself.

"We make the mozzarella fresh daily. It's our best-selling appetizer." He pointed to the other plates one at a time. "I also brought out salami-and-fig crostini with ricotta, homemade rice balls, and mini eggplant rollatine."

Not only did everything smell good but the presentation was gorgeous . . . drizzled dressing and decorative garnishes almost made it too pretty to eat. "Wow. Everything looks amazing."

Sebastian smiled. "I can't take credit for it. It's all the chef's doing. Though I might've threatened to fire him if these plates weren't perfect."

The three of us dug in, and Sebastian took my father head-on.

"So, Mr. Bisset, to get back to your question, I'm thirty-six, seven years older than your daughter. I married my college sweetheart at twenty-three and she passed away four years ago. My daughter, Birdie, is ten. I own a brownstone on the Upper West Side but only live in part of it. I rent the other half, even though I don't have to because the restaurant actually does quite well, but my daughter and I don't need all the space."

My father smiled sadly. "I'm sorry about your loss."

"Thank you."

"Pretty big coincidence that you and my daughter both lost someone to the exact same type of cancer."

Sebastian nodded. "I'm sorry about your loss, too, Mr. Bisset."

"It's George, please."

Sebastian looked over at me. "But yeah, there are a lot of things that Sadie and I have in common. I think that's one of the things that made us grow close so easily." He extended his hand for me to take, and I happily clasped mine with his.

My dad smiled. "Do you want more children?"

"Dad, isn't that a little personal? Sebastian is being so open, but I think that's taking it a little far."

Sebastian squeezed my hand. "It's fine. I guess I always assumed more kids weren't in the cards for me. Amanda got sick when Birdie was only four and a half, and I figured that part of my life was done. I have my daughter, and I'm grateful for that." Sebastian smiled at me. "But I'm not opposed to having more kids. I think I'd actually like it. Birdie would be thrilled, that's for sure."

Oh wow. I was excited to hear that Sebastian was open to having more kids. Family was important to me, and I'd always dreamed of having a big one.

My dad nodded. "Thank you for your candor, son."

After that, the three of us fell into easier, light conversation. My dad and Sebastian figured out they both loved fly-fishing and playing poker. Since neither appealed to me, but watching these two men bond fascinated me more than anything, I happily stuffed my face and listened. At one point, a waiter came over and told Sebastian that he was needed in the kitchen.

I leaned forward in my seat after Sebastian excused himself. "Satisfied you won't get denied grandkids?" I said.

My father reached across the table and took my hand. "Sweetheart, if you married a man with a kid, that kid would be my grandchild, no different from if you birthed your own. It's not about what I want. You've always wanted a big family, and your mother and I couldn't give that to you. I only want what you want."

I'd seriously hit the jackpot when it came to parents. I stood and walked over to my dad's side of the table to plant a kiss on his cheek.

"What was that for?" Dad smiled.

"Just for being you, Dad."

"Thank you for being such a good sport tonight."

After a three-hour dinner at the restaurant, Dad went home, and I hung around the restaurant waiting for Sebastian to finish up. Then he talked me into coming home with him for a little while.

We sat down on the couch, and Sebastian pulled off my shoes. He lifted my feet onto his lap and began to rub. When he dug his thumbs into the arch, I let out a little mewl.

"Oh my God. That feels so good. But you were the one up and down all night and on your feet. I should be the one giving you the foot massage."

He smiled. "My feet are fine. You get the massage just for wearing those sexy heels tonight. And your dad is great. The apple didn't fall far."

"He is pretty great. But I'm sorry he got so personal. He's never actually done that before."

"Did he meet a lot of the men you went out with?"

"Not too many, but a few. He's only ever made small talk with the ones he's met before. It's really unlike him to be so meddlesome."

Sebastian shrugged. "I'm sure hearing I've been married and have a daughter gave him reason for concern. Can't say I blame him. It's hard to even imagine a day when I couldn't protect my daughter anymore."

"I guess. Though I don't think it really had anything to do with you having been married or there being a Birdie."

"No?"

"I think he just saw something he'd never seen with me before."

"What's that?"

I bit my lip, thinking maybe I'd said too much. Sebastian noticed and stopped rubbing my foot.

"Talk to me. What is it?"

I shook my head. "Nothing bad. I think he just . . . saw the possibility of a future for me with someone."

Sebastian's eyes looked back and forth between mine. "Smart man. I see the same thing. There's a future here, sweetheart."

A future here.

Sweetheart.

I let his words seep through me, enjoying the warmth in my chest that spread to my fingertips and toes. A huge smile spread across my face.

Sebastian crooked one finger at me. "Come here, smiley."

I sat up and inched closer to him on the couch.

He cupped both of my cheeks, and his eyes roamed my face for a long time before he sealed his lips over mine. Emotions bubbled to the surface as we kissed. I started to get lost in the moment. Until a voice snapped us both back to reality.

"Daddy . . ."

◆ ◆ ◆

"I better get going."

Birdie had woken up from a noise outside her window, and she'd caught us making out on the couch. If it had bothered her, she definitely hid it well. Sebastian bribed her with a cookie to go back to bed, and she asked if I would tuck her in, which I did.

Sebastian groaned. "I hate this."

"Me too. But we have to set an example for her."

"Can't we just sneak you out before she gets up?"

I pushed up on my toes and planted a kiss on his lips. "She's a smart girl. I don't think it would take too long for her to figure things out."

Sebastian hung his head and pouted. "Fine. I'll call the damn Uber."

"Thank you."

"But I want a night, a whole one. One where I get to fall asleep with you in my arms and wake up and roll over and slip inside you. I'm going to ask Magdalene if she can stay over one night soon."

I smiled. "I like the sound of that."

A few minutes later, the Uber arrived and Sebastian opened the door. "Hey," he said, grabbing my hand as I went to walk out.

I backed up. "Yeah?"

"I'm crazy about you."

My insides melted to a pile of mush. "I'm crazy about you, too."

CHAPTER 23

SEBASTIAN

The following morning, my daughter seemed like she was expecting to see Sadie.

Her eyes were groggy when she walked into the kitchen and asked, "Is Sadie here?"

I put down my coffee. "No, honey. She went home last night."

"Oh. I was hoping she would make me another green monster."

"You really like that shake she made the other day, huh? You weren't just saying that to be nice?"

"No. I loved it!"

"Want me to make it for you?" I winked. "I think I can handle it."

"Yes, please."

I swiftly got up. "You got it. One green monster coming right up."

Birdie looked preoccupied as she sat on one of the stools by the counter.

"Everything alright?" I said as I reached for the blender.

"I think Santa brought Sadie to us."

Her comment caught me off guard. I paused, unable to concentrate on gathering the rest of the ingredients.

"Say what?"

"I never told you this . . . but I started writing to Santa back in June."

Knowing the story behind *who* Santa actually was, I felt almost uncomfortable as Birdie was confessing this to me. She went on to tell the full story of all her letters to "Santa." I was unsure what compelled her to admit it to me now.

"Anyway, I told Santa that I wanted a special friend. And I think Sadie is his last gift to me."

I had to ask, "What makes you so sure that it's Santa . . . and not just luck?"

"Well, Mommy believed in writing to him."

Mommy?

"What do you mean?"

"The only reason I started writing to Santa was because Mommy used to read the letters that people wrote in to Santa. That's why I first wrote to him—at the address in the magazines Mommy kept."

"Your mother kept articles of people writing to Santa?"

"Yeah. You know that big box of dolls you gave me that used to be Mommy's?"

"What about it?"

"That's where the folder was. With all the Santa articles and stuff."

I had no idea what she was talking about. "Do you still have it?"

Birdie nodded.

"Can I see it?"

"Sure." She ran to her room and came back with a worn manila folder. Articles were bulging from it. It had to be at least two inches thick and had a fat rubber band tied around to keep it closed.

I took the folder, confused. "Why wouldn't you tell me about finding these?"

She looked down. "I thought you'd get mad at *me* for writing to Santa. Because I really don't need much. And that's, like . . . greedy. I know. I just wanted a special friend for us . . . and some socks for you."

"It's okay, sweetheart. I'm not mad. Why don't you go take your shower and get dressed, and then we'll take the Duke to the park."

"Okay, Daddy!"

Birdie took off, and I stared at the folder for a long time, unsure of why it wasn't sitting right with me. So what if Amanda kept a box of Santa clippings? She probably hadn't been hiding them. Perhaps the folder had been in the box with a bunch of other files, and that one had been on the bottom. She'd taken them out to use the box for something else and hadn't noticed she'd left one behind. I was certain there was a logical reason.

Yet that gnawing feeling in the pit of my stomach wasn't going away.

Trying to shake it off, I slipped the rubber band off the file and opened the folder. There had to be a hundred articles snipped from magazines in here. Sifting through, the first twenty or so were all from the Santa feature. It seemed Amanda had kept each of the weekly articles that ran throughout November and December and for quite a few years. I guess she really had been a big fan. But as I dug further, I noticed there were other articles, too. A few dozen on makeup tips, then a bunch that seemed to be about women in business—dealing with office politics and stuff like how to dress for success. Amanda hadn't been big into makeup, and she definitely never worked in an office. So it all seemed pretty random. Since they were clippings, not all of them had a date. But some did at the top. She'd cut out these articles over years. But why? And why hadn't she ever mentioned her little collection?

Then it hit me.

Makeup articles.

Business etiquette.

Santa letters.

They weren't random. They had one thing in common.

I flipped back through the columns and searched each for the name. I hadn't noticed the writer listed on my first look. The *Holiday Wishes* articles had the writer listed only as Santa Claus.

But the other articles, the ones on makeup and business etiquette, each and every one of them were the same.

Sadie Bisset.

Years and years of articles written by Sadie.

And *only* Sadie.

What the fuck?

Sunday afternoon, Birdie talked me into taking her and two friends to one of those trampoline places. Sadie came along, and we planned to go to the Barking Dog restaurant on the Upper East Side afterward. It was one of the few dog-friendly, dog-themed restaurants in the city. Though my daughter was disappointed when I'd said Duke couldn't come. That crazy dog wasn't ready for that type of outing yet. Actually, I wasn't sure he'd ever behave himself enough to go into a restaurant.

Sadie and I sat having coffee in the waiting area while the kids did their hour of jumping. I'd been anxious to say something to her about the articles that I'd discovered. I wasn't sure why, but I couldn't just chalk it up to coincidence and let it go.

"So . . . Birdie told me about her writing to Santa yesterday."

"Oh. Wow. I'm glad she finally came clean about that. I hope you were able to act surprised."

I nodded. "She had no idea I already knew."

"Good."

"But something interesting came up during our conversation."

"Oh? What's that?"

"She said she wrote to you because her mom had liked the Santa column."

Sadie's jaw dropped. "Her mom?"

I nodded. "She found your Santa articles in a file. Amanda had clipped all of them out from the magazines and saved them."

"So all of this"—she motioned with her hand back and forth between us—"happened because her mom was a fan of the column?"

"Apparently so."

"That's kind of odd, isn't it? Basically your wife, who's been gone four years, is responsible for us getting together, then."

"That's not the oddest part."

"What do you mean?"

"There were other articles in the folder, too. Written by you. They dated back to when you first started with the magazine, or close to it. Apparently Amanda had saved all of them."

"Wow." Sadie shook her head. "That's . . . I can't believe that."

I don't know what I'd been looking for, but I watched Sadie's face closely. She was genuinely surprised. Maybe even more shocked than I'd been yesterday.

"Just my articles? Or other writers', too?"

"Just yours. Years' worth of them."

Her brows knitted together. "I don't understand. You mean she was a fan of mine?"

I sipped my coffee. "I guess so. Do you get a lot of those? Fans who collect your articles?"

"I have gotten some fan letters over the years. People who say they've followed my articles in the magazine and stuff. But that's just a freaky coincidence, isn't it?"

"That's what I thought."

We both sat quietly for a while, mulling it over. Eventually, Sadie spoke. "So your wife read all my articles and kept them in a folder. Birdie found that folder, which in turn made her write to me. My impersonating Santa led me to your door. Where I happened to find a little butterfly barrette that caused me to then impersonate Gretchen.

We also both lost someone we loved to the same type of cancer." She shook her head. "I don't think I've ever heard of fate opening so many doors to make things happen before."

I smiled. She was right. It was fate. I felt like an idiot now. While I hadn't suspected anything in particular, I'd just had a terrible feeling that something was working against me, instead of accepting it for the gift that it is. But maybe that was because of my track record. Every time Amanda and I had been happy, something happened. I'd learned to wait for the other shoe to drop. I needed to stop doing that shit and enjoy what I had, no matter how it came my way.

Reaching over the table, I took Sadie's hand. "I had another act of fate happen today."

"Oh my Lord, what now?"

"When I picked up Melissa, the little curly-haired blonde we brought with us, her mother asked if Birdie wanted to go apple picking upstate with them tomorrow. There's no school, since it's Veteran's Day."

Sadie's brows drew together. "Well, that's nice. But I'm not sure how that's fate. Unless you mean that Birdie and I are both off for the holiday tomorrow."

I shook my head and grinned. "Nope. They're driving three hours upstate. Fate is that they're leaving at six in the morning to beat traffic."

"Okay . . . I'm still missing the fate here."

"Because they're leaving so early, Melissa's mom asked if Birdie could sleep over tonight. Which means I'm alone for almost twenty-four hours."

Sadie's eyes lit up. "Oh wow. That does sound like fate." She grinned. "But what will you do with that much time on your hands?"

I reached out for the bottom of Sadie's chair and dragged it closer to me. "You. I'm going to do you . . . over and over again."

CHAPTER 24

Sadie

With the house all to ourselves that Monday morning, we'd definitely gotten carried away fast. I kept expecting that maybe Sebastian would pull out of me to get a condom on at some point, but he never did. He knew I was on the pill, so it wasn't a big deal, but he'd always been diligent about the extra protection every time we'd been together.

But having him inside me with no barrier felt incredibly good. The feeling was so intense that I could feel myself coming much faster than I'd anticipated. Our bodies just seemed to be in sync because as soon as I started to orgasm, I felt him quake. We rocked together as our orgasms shot through us simultaneously. There was nothing more beautiful than the guttural sound Sebastian made when he climaxed. I felt it vibrate throughout my entire body.

"Sebastian," I called out over and over as he came inside me. "Sebastian . . ."

It was the best sex we'd had thus far. I wasn't sure if it was because we'd grown that much closer recently or what. I just knew I'd never felt more connected to a man in my entire life.

He rested his head inside the crook of my neck. "I'm sorry. That felt too good. I should've stopped it."

Reaching down and squeezing his ass, I said, "It's okay. I'm on the pill."

He let out a relieved breath. "I know. But I've never been irresponsible like that. You just make me a little crazy, Sadie."

"I've got you." I smiled.

He looked into my eyes and said, "Yeah. You definitely do . . . have me."

Deliriously happy, I returned his sentiment with a huge smile.

"What do you want to do?" he asked. "We have the whole day."

Doing a whole lot of nothing sounded good to me. Hanging out in his bed like this was such a rarity.

"Can we just lie here for a bit? I love not having to rush out of bed or worry about getting caught."

He frowned at my statement. "I'm sorry that I can't have you here all the time with me."

"It's okay. That just makes being with you even more special, when we can have days like this."

He used the bedsheet to playfully pull me toward him. "What am I gonna do with you? You've totally knocked me on my ass, Sadie Mae."

I narrowed my eyes. "Sadie *Mae*? Where did that name come from?"

"Yeah." He laughed. "Not sure where it came from. 'Mae' just seems to go with your name. But what's your *actual* middle name now that we're on the topic?"

"It's nothing you'd ever guess."

"What is it? Tell me."

"It's George."

His eyes widened. "Really? After your father . . ."

"Yep. My mother thought it was funny to give me my dad's name. Definitely not feminine but I love it. It's different." I grinned. "What's your middle name?"

"Rocco."

"Really? I love that. Where does it come from?"

"My grandfather."

"Cool name."

He moved the sheet to gaze at my naked body. I loved the way he looked at me.

Sebastian seemed like he was pondering something. "You know, the fact that I didn't think to stop when we were having sex is really telling. I'm usually so responsible. And I think part of why I slipped is that I'm just so damn comfortable with you." He blew out a breath. "But I'm sorry I didn't check that it was okay with you first."

"I would've stopped you if I was worried. But if you want . . . we can just forego condoms now that you know." I winked.

"I think I'd like that . . . a little too much." His eyes then landed on a scar on my abdomen. It was the first time he seemed to notice it. Sebastian traced his finger along it. "What's this?"

I looked down at myself. My heart raced a little because telling this story might lead to me admitting other things.

"My appendix burst when I was a teenager. I had to have an emergency surgery."

"Shit. That must have been scary."

"It really was. It actually . . . caused some complications for me."

A look of concern crossed his face. "How so?"

"It's a bit of a long story."

"I have time," he said as he gripped my hip and pulled me toward him.

I wasn't sure if it was too early in our relationship to be bringing it up. But this was the perfect window to talk about it. His not knowing had actually been eating away at me a little bit. I didn't think he would judge me. But regardless, I still felt like it was something that I needed to tell him. Since we were on the subject, there was probably no better time than the present.

I took a deep breath in. "A few years after my appendix burst, I started experiencing pain. I was in my late teens. I went to the doctor to get it checked out, and when they examined me, it turned out I had scar tissue blocking my fallopian tubes as a result of the appendix rupture. That meant that basically down the line, I might have trouble getting pregnant."

His expression darkened. "They couldn't do anything for you?"

"Well, I ended up getting surgery to repair them, but they couldn't remove all the scar tissue, so there are no guarantees. I was told that in the future, they could become blocked again. It's possible that I won't have a problem, but at the time, I really became quite worried that maybe I wouldn't have any luck getting pregnant someday when I was ready. My doctor knew how anxious it was making me. So she encouraged me to consider having some of my eggs harvested. That way, if one day I reached a point where I couldn't conceive naturally, I would have young, healthy eggs for IVF."

Sebastian blinked a few times to process that information. "So you froze some of your eggs . . ."

"Yes. But . . ." Here was the part I needed to brace myself for. It was something I'd never told anyone I'd dated before. "Shortly before the procedure, I started to think about everything that my mother went through . . . losing her ability to conceive from the cancer and struggling to adopt. It all worked out in the end, because she got me. But not everyone is as lucky as we were. I'd always wanted to do something to honor her. So an idea came to me . . . since I was going in for the harvesting-eggs procedure anyway." I swallowed and continued. "My doctor expected to get a good amount of eggs because I was young and healthy. I wondered if that might be my only opportunity to donate some to a family in need, in honor of my mother."

His eyes slowly widened. I couldn't gauge what he was thinking.

So I continued. "It made me feel like I was not only doing something to protect my future fertility but to also help someone."

Sebastian blinked a few times. "Wow. That's . . . certainly an honorable decision for someone so young to have made."

"Yeah. I mean . . . I didn't want to ever have to do it again. I figured since I was going through all the trouble, if there was ever a time to make that kind of decision, that was it. So I bit the bullet." I shook my head. "Anyway, I don't even know why I was so compelled to admit this to you now. It's just . . . you asked me about the scar, and I felt like this was the right time to let you know." I looked into his eyes. "I hope you don't think any differently of me because of my decision."

The seconds that passed where he didn't immediately say anything were excruciating.

Then he cupped my face. "I would never judge you for making a decision that helped someone else. Don't ever think that. It's definitely . . . surprising . . . but not something that makes me think any differently of you, Sadie. If anything, I admire you even more for doing that."

I let out a long, relieved breath. Not sure why I expected that to be harder than it was. I supposed I didn't have to admit anything to him at all, and he would have never known about that decision I made all those years ago. But deep down, I think it would have bothered me to not know how he might have felt about it or whether he would have looked at me differently.

"So . . . these eggs . . . ," he asked. "Did they go to different people?"

"No. I didn't want that. I wanted them to all go to one person in need—a cancer survivor like my mother. And I didn't want to know who that person was. It was important to me that there be no contact at all. I just wanted to help someone. So I made sure it was all anonymous. To this day, I have no idea whether anything took . . . whether there was a baby who came from it."

"Wow. Okay." He squeezed my side. "Thank you for opening up to me. I know you didn't have to do that." Then he stared off for a bit.

We lay in a sort of awkward silence after my admission—until Sebastian got out of bed abruptly and said, "How about I order us some lunch?"

I sat up against the headboard. "That sounds great."

"Why don't you take a hot shower? I'll go pick something up so that it's ready for when you get out."

Things were seeming brighter by the second. I smiled and lifted myself off the bed. "Okay."

By the time I got out of the long shower, though, while the hot Thai food was waiting in containers on the table, Sebastian made an unexpected announcement.

He looked upset. "I have to head to the restaurant. The chef called in sick and the substitute has never worked with us before. I have to make sure he knows what he's doing, oversee things."

"Oh no. Does that happen often?"

"Only a few times before. It always works out in the end, but it's nerve-racking."

This sucked.

"Okay . . . um, well . . . can I do anything?"

"Birdie isn't supposed to be home for a while. But you can hang out here or head home. Whatever you prefer."

"Will you let me know if you need me to head back here for her or something if you can't make it back in time for her tomorrow?"

"Absolutely. Thank you for offering to do that."

After he left, I couldn't help wondering if there was more to his departure than the story he had given me. I knew that was probably ridiculous paranoia. It just seemed like the entire mood changed after I admitted to him that I'd donated my eggs. I could see how that might freak someone out. I remember watching stories on the news about sperm donors whose children came to find them years later. One guy had, like, twenty kids. My situation was different, of course. I didn't do it for money. It was to honor my mother and help one family in need. But still, maybe he'd had some sort of a delayed reaction to my admission.

Anyway, I was probably reading into it too much. I tried to put it out of my mind for the rest of the day.

CHAPTER 25

SEBASTIAN

I was being ridiculous.

Right?

To suspect such a thing would be absolutely crazy.

It had honestly taken a while for my mind to conjure up the wild theory that Sadie's news brought about. First, it shocked me to hear what she'd been through, how scared she'd been, and how it led her to make that very bold decision to harvest her eggs at such a young age. But it wasn't until she mentioned the egg *donation* that the alarms started going off inside me.

It was hard to fathom where my mind was going with this. And yet . . . how could it not? How could I not wonder? There was a very good chance that all of this was just one big coincidence. But what if it wasn't?

Pulling on my hair as I sat alone in a café around the corner from Bianco's, I honestly had no idea what to do. I'd felt bad lying to her about the situation at the restaurant, but I had to be alone to process this. She would have definitely suspected something in my behavior if I'd stuck around.

Think.

Think.

Think.

Okay. When we had been given the information for our donor, all they gave us was a profile of her looks, health, and general background. But . . . they'd also told us that our eggs came from a woman who had donated them at no cost to help another family. I suppose that could be a coincidence, too. But the articles. Why did Amanda have them? And how could she even have found out the donor's name? The process was supposedly completely anonymous. And why not tell me if she somehow found out? And why save the articles and not do anything else about it? What was the benefit in that?

Maybe Amanda just liked those articles.

Maybe this was all one big coincidence.

Maybe I really needed to let this whole thing go.

Forget I even thought it in the first place. But how? How could I just move on from this without knowing for certain if there's any correlation?

What if Sadie ended up being Birdie's donor? Wasn't that an intrusion on Sadie's privacy? She didn't intend to ever find out whom she had donated to. It wasn't fair to bring this upon her. *My God. This is so fucking crazy.*

Burning up, I took off my jacket and rested my head in my hands. There was no way I could broach the subject to Sadie without proof. I'd once mentioned that Amanda and I had some fertility help, but I had yet to even tell her that we'd had to use a donor egg because of the cancer treatments. Eventually, I would've told her and then what? She might have wondered the same thing I was wondering right now. Eventually, we'd have to face it.

If Amanda hadn't saved those articles, none of this would even be happening. But it was too suspicious not to consider. There was no way I could alarm Sadie without proof, though. I needed to figure out a way to confirm things beforehand.

◆ ◆ ◆

"Daddy, why are you looking at me funny?"

I hadn't even realized I'd been staring so intently at my daughter as she sat across from me eating her pasta the following evening. All day, I'd been looking for signs of Sadie in her. They had the same blonde hair, but Birdie's face, well . . . it was mine. She looked just like me, so her facial features weren't going to be able to give me much of a clue.

"I'm just thinking about how beautiful you are," I said. "And how lucky I am to have you. That's all."

"Oh." She twirled her spaghetti. "When are we gonna see Sadie again?"

"Not tonight. But hopefully soon. Actually, Magdalene is coming over in a little while to babysit you so I can pay Sadie a visit."

"Why can't she come here?"

I had no good answer for that.

"We can do dinner some night this week here, okay?"

She shrugged. "Okay."

Several minutes passed before she called me out again.

"Daddy . . ."

I blinked out of my daydream. "What, sweetie?"

"You're looking at me funny again."

I sighed. "I am, aren't I?"

Not only was Birdie sensing that something was off, but I couldn't risk fucking everything up with Sadie if all this worrying was in vain. Would I be staring at her like this, too? I needed to figure out a way to keep my cool with her tonight.

After Magdalene arrived, I headed over to Sadie's apartment as fast as I could.

When she opened the door, I got the unexpected urge to pull her into my arms and just hold her. Because no matter what the truth was,

I cared so much about this woman. I didn't want her to end up feeling hurt or violated. Any decision she had made in the past was out of the goodness of her heart, and I knew that.

"What's that for?"

Speaking into her neck, I said, "I was just thinking about how crazy I am about you. I also want to apologize for having to abruptly end our date yesterday."

"You never have to apologize for something like that. You have so much going on. Honestly, I admire how you handle it all."

Pulling back to look in her eyes, I said, "You know what, Sadie? I was handling it before you came along, going through the motions of life with little to look forward to for myself. Handling it all is so much easier when you have someone by your side, someone who brings you joy. Don't ever doubt what you've brought into my life. I know we haven't been together that long, but I haven't been this happy in a very long time."

She looked like she might cry. "You know you don't have to say stuff like that to get in my pants, right?" She playfully smacked my shoulder. "Seriously, though, thank you for saying that. I feel so lucky to have met you. This is the first time in ages that I wouldn't change a thing about my life."

Cupping her face in my hands, I leaned in and took her mouth in mine and closed my eyes, cherishing every movement of our tongues, every taste. I didn't want anything to change. Everything was perfect just the way it was, without anything happening to turn both our worlds upside down.

Impulsively lifting Sadie up, I carried her into her room and placed her on the bed. She reached over to my waist, undoing my buckle and throwing the belt to the side. My rigid cock sprang forward as I pushed my boxers down and lowered myself down to her. Within seconds, she'd spread her legs wide open for me and I was inside her.

Sex with Sadie was different each and every time. Sometimes it was rough, other times slow and sensual. This time was pure passion, a manifestation of the words I'd just admitted to her minutes earlier. The feel of her warm flesh against my bare cock as always was almost too much to bear. I lasted all of a few minutes before I lost control, emptying my cum inside her faster than I wanted.

"Shit. I'm sorry," I said as I continued to move back and forth inside her.

It pleased me to feel her muscles tighten around my cock seconds later. There was nothing more beautiful than feeling her come all around me.

With my dick still buried inside her, I muttered against her neck, "What did I ever do before you?"

"I hope you never have to remember." She smiled.

We held each other for a long time, and Sadie actually nodded off soon after that. She must have had a long day. My plan had been to return home by eleven, at which point I'd call an Uber to take Magdalene home.

It was 9:00 pm now, and I had no idea how long Sadie would be asleep. I knew this might be my only opportunity to do something I really needed to—as wrong as it felt and as much as I didn't want to have to do it.

Slowly and carefully lifting myself from the bed, I walked over to her kitchen and looked around. I found a stash of Ziploc bags and took two out of the box.

Quietly venturing into her bathroom, I swiped her toothbrush before placing it into one of the bags. Opening the drawer below, I grabbed a wad of hair off her brush and placed it in the other bag. My understanding was that hair needed to be pulled from the root for DNA testing, so I doubted it would take but hoped that at least the toothbrush would suffice.

Jesus.

Am I really doing this?

I felt like a thief.

A piece of hair and a used toothbrush might not be of any monetary value, but what I'd done was stealing nonetheless—I'd stolen Sadie's right to privacy. And I'd felt like shit since the moment I'd done it.

Standing in the post-office lobby, I hung my head as I leaned on the counter and blew out a shaky breath. I'd just mailed off the DNA testing samples I'd collected and couldn't possibly walk home yet. My head pounded, my chest felt tight, and I had a sinking feeling in the pit of my stomach. Normally, I'd take Motrin for a headache, but I didn't deserve any relief. I was a piece of shit who deserved to feel like someone had chiseled into his temples.

Even though I'd been sick about what I'd done since yesterday, it still hadn't stopped me from being the first one in line at the post office when it opened this morning.

When Sadie had told me about her egg donation, she'd said she never wanted to know who the recipients of her generosity were. In fact, she'd made sure the entire process was anonymous before going through with it. And for some reason, I didn't think she'd ever had contact with her own birth parents. At least she'd never mentioned it. So I was pretty sure she didn't want to know if she had children out there.

But I *had* to know.

Plus, what were the odds that Sadie was our donor? The fertility center had never even told us what state the person was from, only that she was a US citizen. There are over three hundred million people in this country. I'd have a better shot of winning the damn lottery. Sadie would probably think I'd lost my mind for even thinking it was a possibility—three hundred million people in the country, and my daughter just *happens* to write her biological mother a letter. The more I thought about it, the more I realized she'd probably be right—I *was* a little nutty for even considering it could happen.

The fucked-up thing was that I'd never once wondered about who my daughter's biological mother might be before the other day, even though I knew she was out there somewhere. I'd thought a lot about that over the last forty-eight hours. Why was I so compelled to know now when I hadn't been the least bit interested in knowing just a few days ago? The answer was obvious—because it was Sadie. But what was I hoping for with these results?

Did I want Sadie to be Birdie's biological mother?

Or did I want to go back to not knowing who the egg donor was?

I grappled with those questions the most. Deep down, even though I didn't want to admit it, I think a part of me wanted Sadie to be Birdie's mother. My daughter lost her mom at such a tender young age, and I'd give anything so she could have her mother again. But did that *anything* I'd give include forcing a woman I loved to acknowledge a child she'd never planned to know?

I blinked a few times.

A woman I loved.

Did I love Sadie?

My shoulders slumped, and I let out a heavy sigh of defeat.

Fuck.

I did.

I went and fell in goddamn love with her.

Great. Just great. I betrayed a woman I love.

I was pretty sure I was never going to forgive myself. But that was okay. I deserved to beat myself up over what I'd done . . . and then some. That wasn't even a question. What was most important now was, would Sadie ever forgive me?

CHAPTER 26

SADIE

Sebastian had been acting odd the last few days.

He was quieter than usual and seemed really distracted. Tonight I'd cooked dinner for him and Birdie at their house, and then the three of us took Marmaduke to the dog park. As usual, Birdie talked nonstop, keeping us entertained with stories from school today. But once she'd gone to bed, it became really noticeable how far away Sebastian's mind was.

I'd just told him all about an article I was working on for my column, where I'd interview men and women after their first blind date with each other and see how different their answers were to a set group of questions. So often, one person thinks things went great, while the other leaves feeling like the date was a complete bust. I'd rambled on for a solid ten minutes, and my gut told me that Sebastian hadn't actually heard one word. He was looking right at me, but his eyes weren't focused. So I decided to test exactly how far his mind had wandered.

"So . . . ," I said. "We thought it might be fun to ask the post-date questions naked. You know, to keep the article interesting and all."

I stopped speaking and waited for Sebastian to answer. He blinked a few times, and it seemed like he just figured out it was his turn to speak.

"Oh. That sounds great."

I frowned. "Yeah, it's perfect. I won't sleep with more than two or three of them. So don't worry."

He started to nod. "Okay, great . . . Wait . . . what did you just say?"

"Oh, hi, Sebastian. It's nice of you to join me in this conversation."

"What are you talking about?"

I rolled my eyes. "I'm talking about that you haven't listened to a word I said in the last half hour. Your mind is obviously elsewhere. What's going on with you? Is everything okay?"

He looked down. "Yeah. Everything is fine. Just a lot on my mind."

"Like what?"

He continued to avoid eye contact. "I . . . uh . . . I still haven't hired a new manager at the restaurant."

I knew in my gut he was full of shit. "Look at me."

His eyes jumped to meet mine.

"What else is going on?" I said. "I feel like it's something more than just work."

Sebastian's eyes shifted while he shook his head. He tried to keep eye contact but couldn't do it. This man was not a good liar. Ever since he noticed my appendix scar, he'd started acting strange. I didn't think the timing was a coincidence. I had a feeling that his mood shift had something to do with the conversation we'd had about my eggs. To be honest, ever since we'd talked, I hadn't been able to stop thinking about things, either.

I took his hand. "Is there any chance that what I told you the other day upset you? About my harvesting eggs and donating some?"

Sebastian's eyes widened, but he again quickly diverted them before shaking his head.

His reaction pretty much confirmed that was it, yet for some reason he still didn't want to admit it. Last year I'd done a dating article titled *Deal Breaker* where I interviewed a few hundred single men and women on what things would rule out a potential relationship with someone they otherwise really liked. Both sides listed spiritual beliefs among their deal breakers. I knew Sebastian was Catholic, and the Catholic Church was against IVF, so perhaps that was it. Or maybe the fact that I'd basically given away my eggs to a complete stranger freaked him out a bit.

"Do you . . . have religious beliefs against artificial insemination?"

Sebastian's brows drew together. "Religious beliefs? What? No. Of course not."

"So what is it, then? You haven't been yourself since we talked about it."

He sighed and pulled me to him for a hug. "I'm sorry. I didn't mean to make you feel like you'd said or done something wrong. I think what you did, harvesting your eggs to avoid a possible future conception issue and donating some in honor of your mother, was extraordinary."

I pulled back to look him in the eyes. "You do? Are you sure?"

He nodded. "It was a very selfless act. Hearing about what you'd done just confirmed that you are undoubtedly one of the most kind-hearted and compassionate people I've ever met in my life."

I exhaled with a sigh. "I'm so glad you feel that way. I really thought maybe what you'd learned made you think less of me."

"Why would I ever think less of you for what you did?"

"I don't know. I guess I was worried you would think it was weird that I gave away my eggs, which could very well have grown into children." I shook my head. "You know, the fact that I may have children out there that I have nothing to do with."

Sebastian was quiet for a moment before speaking again. "What if . . . with all the genetic testing that has become commonplace these days . . . what if you found out that you had a son or a daughter out there? Would you want to know them?"

I shook my head. "I don't know. I guess I'd leave that up to the child. As someone who was adopted, I never wanted to know my birth parents. A lot of adopted children have a sense of abandonment and resentment toward their birth parents, but I never did. Oddly, I don't see the decision my mother made as having anything to do with me. They didn't even know who I was yet, so I don't take it personally. Though I wouldn't belittle someone who felt that way, either. I guess if one of my little eggs made it to become a real live person, and he or she wanted to know me, I'd be okay with that. But the decision should be the child's when they are old enough to make it. Not mine."

Sebastian face was so solemn, but he shook his head. "You're truly a beautiful person, Sadie."

I laughed. "I don't know about that. But I do still feel good about what I did. So I'm relieved that it didn't upset you. Though if it's not that, I really would like to know what it is that's been bothering you."

Sebastian shook his head. "It's nothing. But you're right—I haven't been in the moment the last few days. And I'm sorry about that. I didn't mean to make you worry."

"It's okay. We all have ups and downs. I just hope you know I'm here to listen if something's on your mind. It doesn't matter what it is."

Sebastian cupped my cheeks. "I know. And that's why I'm crazy about you."

I smiled. "I'm crazy about you, too."

Everything seemed to go back to normal after that, though Sebastian had to work even more than usual, since he no longer had a manager. I guess it made sense that it had been weighing on his mind. Since he was so busy, I'd volunteered to help out more with Birdie so that Magdalene wasn't working eighty hours a week. Tonight I came straight from the office. I brought an arts-and-crafts project for the two of us, figuring it was Friday, and Birdie could stay up a little later. We sat at the dining room table after dinner, making friendship bracelets. The kit came with enough colorful string to make ten. Birdie was on her second and had already figured out how to weave designs.

"Wow. That one looks awesome," I said.

"I'm making it for my best friend."

I smiled. "She's a lucky girl. You know, when I was your age, we made friendship bracelets with safety pins and beads. Everyone was giving them to their best friends at school. So I made one and gave it to my friend Darren. He lived next door, and we played together after school every day."

Birdie laughed. "Your best friend was a boy?"

"Well, I thought so. But when I walked up to him at school to give him the bracelet I'd made, he was with his friends, and he acted all weird about it. He stuck it in his pocket and made it seem like he had no idea why I'd given it to him. Apparently, it wasn't cool for a boy to be best friends with a girl, and I was the only one who didn't know it."

"Did you feel bad?"

I nodded. "I did. Over the next few days, he came over to see if I wanted to play, and I said I didn't. I guess he got sick of having no one to hang around with because a week later, he started wearing the friendship bracelet at school. We never talked about it, but I started playing with him again."

"I'm going to give the first one I made to Jonathan at school."

"Oh? Is he your best friend?"

"No. But Suzie Redmond likes him, and he told Brendan Andrews that he doesn't like her, because he likes me."

Oh wow. Boys? Already? She was only ten. "Do you . . . like Jonathan, too?"

Birdie wrinkled her cute little nose. "Definitely not." She shrugged. "Plus, Dad said I can't like boys until I'm thirty anyway."

I chuckled. That sounded like something Sebastian would say. Oddly, I was thinking maybe he was right about this one.

"Can I ask you something, Sadie?"

"Of course, anything."

"Dad's your boyfriend, right?"

"Yeah, I think he is. Why do you ask?"

"So . . . if Dad is your boyfriend and I call you Sadie, what would I call you if you and Dad got married someday?"

My hands had been weaving a bracelet and froze. "Umm. Dad and I aren't getting married anytime soon."

"I know. But if you do, what would I call you? Would I still call you Sadie?"

God, I had no idea what the right answer was to that question. "I'm not really sure, sweetie. I guess you, your dad, and I would sit down and talk about it all together. And it would probably come down to whatever you felt most comfortable with."

"But you'd be my mom, right?"

Heaviness settled into my chest. This . . . *this* was the reason why I'd always felt so connected to Birdie. I knew what it was like to long for a mother.

"Well, your mom will always be your mom. Technically, if your dad and I got married, I'd be your stepmom. But I don't have to be married to your dad for you to be special to me." I leaned over and brushed my hand down Birdie's hair. "You know you're special to me, right, Birdie?"

She forced a smile, but I could see she was still troubled.

"What's wrong, sweetheart?"

"Well, what happens if you and Daddy don't get married and you meet someone else and marry him?"

"Oh, honey." I shook my head. "Please don't worry about that." It was on the tip of my tongue to say I'd always be here for her. I felt that strong of a connection to Birdie. But honestly, that kind of a commitment was something I'd need to run by Sebastian before making. I wouldn't want to make her an important promise like that unless I knew I could absolutely keep it. "Would it be okay if we talked about this again another night? I want to think about some of the questions you asked me. Because they're important questions, and I want to give you the right answers."

Birdie smiled. "Sure." She went back to weaving her friendship bracelet and then stopped again. "Sadie?"

"Yeah, sweetie?"

"As long as you're going to be doing some thinking, I have another question."

Oh boy. "Sure. What's up?"

"How does Santa get into our house? Daddy puts one of those caps on our chimney so the squirrels don't get in, remember?"

I laughed. "You're filled with tough questions tonight. Let me give that one some thought, too."

And just like that, our serious conversation was over and things went back to normal. An hour later, we packed away the arts and crafts, and Birdie went to get ready for bed. She brushed her teeth and changed into her pajamas and then came back out carrying one of the bracelets she'd made.

"That one came out really nice. I think it's my favorite of the five you made. You said it's for your best friend, right?"

She nodded.

"What's her name?"

Birdie held the bracelet out to me. "Her name is Sadie, silly. It's for you."

"Hey, sleepyhead." Sebastian pushed a lock of my hair from my face. I must've fallen asleep on the couch watching TV.

I stretched my arms over my head. "What time is it?"

"Almost one. I'm sorry. I really need to find a new manager. I can't keep doing this to you and Magdalene."

I sat up and rubbed my eyes. "It's fine. I don't mind at all."

"I know you don't. But I hate you trekking home at such a late hour. I was actually thinking earlier . . . Magdalene has slept over before, on nights that I had an event or an emergency at the restaurant. She slept on the pullout couch in my office. What if I talked to Birdie and told her that you're going to stay over sometimes, at least on the nights I have to work late? I'll sleep on the couch, and you can take my room."

"That might be a good idea. But she couldn't wake up to me in bed with you."

He nodded. "I know. I'll talk to her tomorrow." Sebastian noticed the bracelet tied around my wrist and looped his finger through it, giving it a tug. "New jewelry?"

"Birdie and I did crafting tonight. She actually told me that she was making it for her best friend, and then right before she went to bed, she brought it out and gave it to me."

He smiled. "My kid's got good taste in women. She takes after her old man."

"Yeah. I thought it was so sweet. She actually struck up an interesting conversation tonight."

"Oh yeah? About what?"

"Well, first she wanted to know what she would call me if we got married."

Sebastian's brows jumped. "Shit. What did you say?"

"I basically sidestepped. I told her that if that happened, the three of us would sit down and have a conversation about it."

Sebastian raked a hand through his hand. "Good call. I'm glad she asked you that and not me."

"Then she asked me what would happen if we broke up and I met someone else and got married to him."

He frowned. "Does she know something I don't know?"

I laughed. "No. But I think she really wanted me to make a commitment to her that we'd stay friends, or whatever we are, even if things don't work out between you and me. Loss is obviously weighing on her. For whatever reason, she's concerned she might lose me, too."

Sebastian sighed. "You're the first woman she's connected with since her mom died."

I nodded. "Yeah. I realize that. That's why I thought we should discuss it a bit before I made that kind of a promise to her."

Sebastian's gaze grew serious. "You want to promise her that you'll always be friends, regardless of what happens between us?"

I nodded. "I do. I know I've only known her a few months, but she's really special to me. I love her, Sebastian. So if you'd be okay with me keeping contact with her if we split up, no matter what—even if, say, you go out with someone else and she doesn't like your ex-girlfriend coming around once in a while—then I'd like to make the promise to always be there for her."

Sebastian swallowed. His eyes became glassy and he cupped both my cheeks. "Sadie Gretchen Bisset Schmidt, I freaking love you. I've known it for a while, but I was too chicken to admit it to myself. Yet you and my ten-year-old daughter are completely fearless with giving love." He shook his head. "You both put me to shame. I wish I had half the balls you two do."

My heartbeat quickened and warmth flooded my chest. "You really love me?"

"I do. I love you, Sadie."

My hand covered my heart. "I love you, too, Sebastian. And I've known it for a while. In fact, I can prove it to you!"

The corners of his lips twitched. "How?"

I smiled from ear to ear. *"Ich liebe dich!"*

CHAPTER 27

SEBASTIAN

Saturday morning, the doorbell rang just as I was getting ready to leave for work.

"I got it, Magdalene!"

A young guy in a UPS uniform held out a tablet. "Sebastian Maxwell?"

"Yes."

"Sign here, please."

I scribbled my name, assuming it was the new iPads I'd ordered for the restaurant. Our entire system was electronic, and since we broke another one two days ago, now we were down to one. After I signed, the driver handed me a small envelope.

"Have a good day."

"You too," I said.

I shut the door and started to walk back into the house, still thinking nothing of what was in my hands. Until I saw the logo on the packaging.

Holy shit.

I froze midstep.

I knew that logo.

The lab.

But they'd said seven to ten business days, and it hadn't even been a full week yet. An overwhelming sense of dread washed over me.

Fuck.

I stared down at the envelope. My entire life could be turned upside down by what was inside. I felt sick, completely nauseous.

Birdie came skipping to the front vestibule where I still stood. She looked at my expression and down at the envelope. "What's that?"

"Uh . . . nothing." I shoved it into my back pocket. "Just a bill for something I got delivered to the restaurant."

"Sadie is coming this afternoon, right, Daddy?"

My chest hurt even thinking about Sadie anywhere near this envelope. "Yeah, honey. She said she's going to come about five."

"Could we come to the restaurant for dinner?"

I had no idea how I would be able to look either one of them in the face by that time. Yet I nodded. "Sure. If it's alright with Sadie. You're always welcome."

Birdie jumped up and down. "I'm going to ask Sadie if we can get all dressed up fancy!"

I smiled and leaned down to kiss the top of her head. "Okay. I need to get going. I'll probably see you later, then."

"I love you, Daddy."

"I love you, too, my little Birdie."

By the time Sadie and Birdie showed up to Bianco's, I was a wreck. Unable to concentrate, my being here wasn't even helpful to anyone. I kept giving wrong directions, and the managerial candidate I was training probably thought I was on drugs.

Sadie waved over to me as she and Birdie were seated by the hostess at a table close to one of the fireplaces. My heart was practically bursting from my chest as I looked at them—my two girls. They were done up like they were about to attend a freaking ball. Sadie's blonde hair was tied up into a bun, exposing her elegant neck. I'd never seen it like that before. Even as fucked-up as I was tonight, I imagined sinking my teeth into her skin.

And Birdie. My daughter looked adorable. Her hair was done exactly the same as Sadie's—except she had a little tiara on. Sadie wore a long black evening gown while Birdie donned a purple dress with a frilly hem.

"Look at you beautiful ladies. You weren't kidding when you said Sadie was gonna get you all dressed up."

"Sometimes a lady needs to live like the princess she is." Sadie winked at Birdie.

"Don't we look pretty, Daddy?"

"You'd better put a napkin over that beautiful dress, Birdie. I know how messy you normally get when you're eating your Bolognese."

I took a deep breath in. The anxiety in my chest was starting to suddenly build again. Anytime I would think about the envelope that was sitting way in the back of my closet in a box I kept old CDs in, I freaked. I hadn't opened it. I just hadn't been ready. Not only that, the more I thought about it, the more I realized it was a major violation of Sadie's privacy. I still had no idea what to do. But this was eating away at me, and I knew I couldn't last like this for very long.

As I stood there ruminating in front of my girlfriend and daughter, I was apparently doing a horrible job of hiding my continuous panic.

A look of concern crossed Sadie's face. "Seb, are you okay?"

I blinked several times. "You know . . . I haven't been feeling well all day."

Not a lie.

I pulled out a chair and sat down with them, downing the water that had been placed in front of Sadie.

Sadie put her hand on mine. "It's stress. You've been so worried about the staffing shortage here. I know it's been getting to you."

"Yeah. That's probably it." I placed my other hand over hers and squeezed it, forcing a smile to ease her worry.

She felt my forehead. "You're actually freezing. I don't think you have a fever."

Birdie pouted. "Daddy, can you stop working and just eat with us? I bet you'll feel better after a big bowl of Birdie's Pasta Bolognese."

I needed to get my shit together. I needed to sit down and have a normal meal with them and quietly figure out how to handle the situation without giving myself away.

Get your shit together.

"You know what? I think that might be just the medicine I need. Let me go put the orders in." I turned to Sadie. "What do you want, baby?"

She looked over at Birdie and smiled. "Why don't we make it a Bolognese triplicate."

I nodded. "Three Birdie's Pasta Bologneses coming right up."

As I retreated to the kitchen to put the order in, I inhaled deeply, relishing the break from having to look Sadie in the eyes. As I stood there amid the chaos of the kitchen, listening to the clanking sounds of pans, watching the steam emanate from the stove, all the sounds became amplified. Even the chopping of the salad felt like a banging inside my head. It became clearer and clearer by the second that I couldn't handle this alone. My fear wasn't about the end result of that DNA test. It was about losing Sadie for what I had done, going behind her back and stealing her things. I knew I needed to tell her before I ever opened that envelope. The choice wasn't mine. It was Sadie's. It was all hers.

Wiping my brow, I took a deep breath in and returned to the table.

"Dinner should be ready shortly." I smiled, looking between them.

"Okay." Sadie reached across the table and took my hand, then reached out and offered her other one to my daughter. "Birdie, honey, I want to talk to you about something."

Birdie placed her hand into Sadie's. "Are you going to tell me we can't have dessert? Because I really can't stop thinking about these rainbow cookies they make here. They're so soft with some kind of jam in the middle, and the entire outside is made of chocolate. I was going to ask if we could have them before dinner, but I figured Dad would say no."

Sadie chuckled and shook her head. "Definitely not what I was going to say. But as long as we're talking about rainbow cookies, I think we should order two helpings of those." Sadie looked up at me, smiled, and squeezed my hand. "What I wanted to talk to you about is something you asked me the other day. You asked what would happen if your dad and I broke up. I've been thinking a lot about that question and even discussed it with your dad. So I thought I'd give you a better answer now that we've had the time to think about it." Sadie glanced at me again and then leaned closer to Birdie, looking her directly in her eyes. "No matter what happens between your dad and me, I'm not going anywhere when it comes to being your friend. So I guess what I'm trying to say is, you're sort of stuck with me, kid. No matter where life takes any of us, I'd like to be a part of your life." Sadie looked up at me. "And your dad is good with that, aren't you, Sebastian?"

I'd gotten choked up watching the two of them together and had to clear my throat before speaking. "Absolutely. Sadie will always be welcome in our family."

Birdie got up out of her chair and stood before me. She tucked her chin to her chest and said, "Daddy, can you take my tiara out of my hair for me?"

My brows furrowed, but I did it. Untangling a few pieces of hair that were stuck, I slipped the sparkly crown from atop my daughter's head and handed it to her. She then walked over to Sadie.

"This is our special friend crown. It's my most favorite thing I have. One time I thought I lost it, so my dad went and bought me another one just like it. So I have two. I want you to take this one. It means more than just a friendship bracelet."

Sadie smiled wide and lowered her head for Birdie to place the crown in her hair. When she was done, my daughter practically leaped into Sadie's arms. The two of them shared a long hug, and then Birdie went right back to asking about dessert. She wanted to make sure I set aside two helpings of her cookies so they didn't sell out. But while my daughter snapped back to business as usual, I felt like I'd just had my world rocked, and I needed a drink to calm myself down a bit. So I called the waiter over to bring Sadie and me a bottle of pinot noir.

After, I looked over at my two princesses and prayed that tonight after Birdie went to sleep, the revelation I would make didn't leave me with only one.

Sadie brought Birdie back to her room to help take her hair down and get her ready for bed. In the meantime, I paced. And paced some more. Sadie still suspected something wasn't right with me despite my best efforts to put on an act during dinner. Her demeanor clearly showed that she was onto me. I doubted I would even have to be the first to start addressing my behavior once she came out from Birdie's room. I knew she'd call me out on it once my daughter was safely out of earshot. Honestly, I *hoped* she did. Because I had no idea how I was going to even begin to broach the subject if she didn't.

Still pacing in the living room, I watched as Sadie slowly closed Birdie's bedroom door. Sadie looked so beautiful with her hair now down in loose tendrils. Her evening gown was a little wrinkled. The sight of her leg exposed through the slit on the side of the dress managed to make me aroused despite my mood.

Her expression was sullen as she slowly walked over to me. She placed her hands around my face and positioned me to look into her eyes.

"What's happening? Am I losing you?" she asked. "Is this too much?"

My heart sank as I closed my eyes and took both of her hands to my mouth. "No. No, Sadie. The last thing I ever want is to lose you. I can promise you that." Blowing a deep breath out, I found the courage to add, "But I'm afraid I stand a very good chance at that after what I'm about to tell you."

A look of alarm flashed across her beautiful face as she pulled slightly away from me. "What is it? You're scaring me."

Reaching my hand out to her, I silently led her back into my bedroom. We needed to be as far away from my daughter's room as possible for this conversation.

After leading her onto my bed, I turned the lamp on. I lay across from her as we faced each other and looped my fingers in with hers. It took a few seconds to conjure up the strength to get the first words out.

"You were worried that my attitude had changed after you told me the story about your egg donation. You weren't off base about that. But the reasoning behind my reaction is something you couldn't possibly know."

She swallowed, seeming both scared and eager for what I might say next. "Okay . . ." Her hands started to tremble.

"I never told you that . . . Birdie . . . well, she was the result of an egg donation herself."

I paused to note any changes in her reaction, but her expression remained frozen, aside from her eyes searching mine. She hadn't seemed to make the connection based on that one sentence. So I continued.

"Amanda . . . like your mother . . . had been unable to conceive naturally because of her cancer treatment at a young age. I knew it when I married her, and I always knew that it wouldn't matter. We'd find a way to have a child one way or another. When she told me that she'd prefer to try IVF with a donated egg, I definitely had my reservations." I sighed. "At first, I couldn't understand how my sperm and another woman's egg made *our* baby. But she was insistent that our child be related by blood to at least one of us and that she be able to experience the pregnancy. After much debate, I agreed."

I stopped to examine Sadie's face. Again, no realization had hit her yet. Or at least it hadn't seemed to compute. So I went on.

"Honestly, seeing her carry that child, it was the most beautiful thing. Once the pregnancy happened and we were experiencing that joy, I knew I'd made the right decision. She was getting to live out something she thought she'd never have an opportunity to. And it was all because of a selfless person who'd decided to give a part of herself to us. It was surreal and amazing. And it only got more amazing once we laid eyes on our beautiful daughter, who happened to come out with my face." I chuckled. "It was clear from the very beginning that this *was* our child. It didn't matter how she came to be biologically. She was Amanda's. She was mine. She was ours. She was from God."

Sadie's face curved into a slight smile. "That's beautiful."

I cleared my throat. "So, you see, I never thought to make it a point to spell all of that out to you. I didn't want to give you the impression that how she came to be mattered. Of course, I knew it was something that would have come up eventually. But it just didn't happen before you told me *your* story."

I intentionally stopped talking to really give it a moment to set in with her.

Taking both of her hands in mine, I whispered, "Sadie, baby, do you know where I'm going with this?"

Her face was still frozen, and then at one point her eyes slowly widened as she stared off. Then, when she looked at me, I knew. The wheels had finally started turning in her head. She saw where I was going with this. She gripped my hands tighter as her eyes flitted from side to side.

Then her words finally came.

"The articles . . . Amanda's saving those articles . . . of mine . . . you think . . . you think . . . she thought it was . . . me?" Her chest was heaving.

"I don't know. She never told me a single thing. If she'd gone looking for the egg donor, she certainly didn't want me to know about it."

Sadie exhaled, never letting go of my hands. I couldn't tell what she was thinking. She just looked numb and a little scared. Which made it all the more difficult to admit what I needed to.

"When the possibility hit me, Sadie, I freaked out. I decided I needed to know the truth before I even addressed this with you. I didn't want to cause you any unnecessary alarm. So I made a very hasty decision to take your toothbrush and hair and send them to a lab along with Birdie's DNA."

Sadie's face reddened to a color I had never seen before. Her breathing became rampant. "What?"

"It was the wrong decision," I said. "It was made out of fear. Not fear of the result. But fear of losing you, Sadie. I love you. And nothing would make me happier than to know that the loving, wonderful human who gave a part of herself to us . . . is also the woman I love. Make no mistake . . . there is nothing that scared me about the thought that my daughter could actually be a part of you and me. But the entire decision to find out? That wasn't my decision to make. So I didn't open the envelope. It's still sealed. And I won't open it without your permission. We never have to open it, in fact. It won't change anything between us or in your relationship with Birdie. You have every right to the privacy you were promised. And I want to sincerely apologize for allowing my fear to control the decision I made."

I swallowed hard, waiting for her next reaction.

She straightened up against the headboard. "The envelope . . . it's . . . here?"

My heart pounded. "Yes. I got the results earlier in the mail. They came this morning, which is why my behavior at the restaurant was so erratic."

Her voice was shaky when she asked, "Do you . . . think it's me?"

"I don't know, baby. Honest to God, I just don't know."

"Are we going to find out?"

"I felt obligated to tell you about the possibility. But in the end, this isn't my choice. It never was. And I never want to do anything ever again that would hurt you or violate your privacy. I will happily rip up that envelope if you want me to. Or you can take it. We can open it up together or forget it ever existed. We don't have to find out. Birdie loves you. Amanda's her mother. Nothing has to change."

I hated that I'd placed this burden on her. I didn't know what else to do or say. But I felt the weight lift off my chest now that she knew the truth. I just had absolutely no clue what she was going to do with it.

CHAPTER 28

Sadie

This felt like a dream. As I continued to sit across from him in shock, I honestly couldn't even move, let alone know what to say.

Amanda might have been following me. If she had been given my identity, how was that even possible? I had been assured that the process was anonymous, which was the only reason I had agreed to it in the first place.

"I'm sorry . . . I . . . still haven't wrapped my head around this," I said.

Sebastian leaned in and took me fully into his arms. My breathing immediately relaxed. Despite the uncertainty and shock, I felt safe. I felt loved. And I knew that no matter what happened—he had my back. To know that he fully supported any decision I made about this meant everything. Because I certainly had no idea at this point what the right decision was.

"I don't blame you for doing what you did," I said. "I can understand how freaked out you must have been."

He exhaled. "Thank you. I now realize I should've talked to you first, but at the time, I thought maybe I could rule it out before having to scare you." He shook his head. "But it was wrong. Because . . . if . . .

you know . . . it turns out you *are* . . . that's not my place to know before you. Or to know at all."

"I don't know what the right answer is."

"You don't need to make a decision now. Or ever."

I blew out another shaky breath and just kept nodding. "I've always felt so connected to her."

"I know. This whole thing . . . it's been like some sort of magic from the start. But maybe there was more to it than that."

"Suppose Amanda did look for me. Then there's always the chance that they might have given her the wrong info, right? Or maybe . . . my articles just resonated and gave her hope and this is all just a weird coincidence. I mean, they *are* public articles. Anything is possible, right?"

"Of course. That's why I debated even telling you at first. I thought I might be crazy for even thinking it. It seemed so hard to believe."

A tear finally formed in my eye, rolling down my cheek as the realization hit me in waves. Not just because I had no clue what to do but also because it hit me that if Birdie *were* my biological child, that she was *our* child. Sebastian's and mine. Made from us. I could have inadvertently made a human with the man I love before I ever even knew him. The emotions that thought brought about were some of the strongest I'd ever experienced. But stronger than anything was the thought that if this were true . . . how could I ever tell Birdie? She'd already lost her mother. And this would be like losing her all over again in a sense. For what? So I could have some kind of validation? It wasn't fair.

Shaking my head repeatedly, I said, "I have to think about this."

"Take all the time you need. I mean it. We can pretend it's not happening until then. I have no problem doing that. Just tell me that this won't break us," he pleaded.

I looked into the eyes of the beautiful man before me and gave him the assurance he needed. "The only thing I *am* sure of right now is that I need you more than ever. I love you, Sebastian. I love you so much."

He reached for me and spoke into my neck. "I don't want you going home tonight. I need you here with me. In my bed. It's time."

I wasn't going to argue with that. I couldn't imagine going home alone right now with the weight of this decision wearing me down.

We didn't have sex that night. Sebastian just held me until I fell asleep in his arms, so confused and scared—yet safe and loved.

The following morning, it might have seemed like any normal start to a day as the three of us sat in the kitchen having breakfast together. But it *felt* far from normal. I couldn't stop staring at her. Her blonde hair . . . was it from me? Her nose . . . it wasn't exactly like Sebastian's. Did it look like mine?

"I was surprised to see you here," Birdie said to me. "You're never here for breakfast with us."

Sebastian cleared his throat. "Sadie spent the night last night. How do you feel about her doing that more often? Maybe every weekend?"

Birdie shrugged and smiled. "Duh."

Sebastian and I grinned at each other as he reached across the table for my hand.

I was in a total daze. As much as I wanted this dilemma to go away, I knew that the decision wasn't going to come easy or soon.

Birdie and I ended up taking Marmaduke to the park after breakfast, enjoying the late-autumn beauty of the city.

When we returned to the house, we were alone, since Sebastian had been gone at the restaurant most of the day. After Birdie retreated to her room to read a book for a school assignment, I wandered the house aimlessly until I landed right in front of one of the photos of Amanda in Sebastian's room.

I lifted the frame and stared into her smiling eyes.

It felt natural to speak to her even though I knew she wasn't really here to listen. "What did you intend? Why did you collect those articles? Were you trying to find me or were you hoping to leave a trail? Were you just curious about me?" I sighed. "Or maybe we have it all wrong. I wish I could ask you what you would want me to do right now." A tear escaped down my cheek.

If Amanda's intention was to find me, why wouldn't she have actually contacted me? She knew she was dying. She apparently knew where to find me. And she never did. So why stalk my articles? I would never know what she wanted. Sebastian had left the decision to me. On one hand, I appreciated that he'd done that. On the other, it might have been easier if someone could just tell me the right thing to do.

"I'm sorry, Amanda. I'm so sorry. I hope you're in a better place. I promise you I'll look after Birdie. I'll protect her and make sure she has a female role model. Thank you for bringing her into the world. And thank you for leading me to Sebastian. I know it's awkward for me to be thanking you for leading me to your husband. But I promise to love him and to cherish him and to never try to take your place. I truly feel that you would want him to be happy, even if he seems unsure of that. Woman to woman, I know in my heart that you wouldn't want him to be sad and alone."

"Hey."

I jumped when Sebastian entered the room.

"You're back early," I said as I put down the photo.

"What were you doing?" he asked.

"I was . . . talking to Amanda. Asking her for guidance. Is that crazy?"

He smiled. "I do it all the time. All the freaking time."

"Does it ever help?"

"Sometimes I hear her swearing at me, telling me to man up and stop complaining to her." He chuckled.

"I'm . . . no closer to a decision on what to do. I think I really need to take some time to think about it."

"Take all the time you need."

"I think I need to go visit my dad."

"Does your father know you donated your eggs?"

I nodded. "Yeah. I told him before I was going to do it. He wasn't exactly thrilled, but he understood. And in the end, he supported my decision."

"Your dad's a great guy. Maybe he can help you decide what's best. I think it's a good idea to talk to him."

Nodding, I wiped my eyes. "I'll probably head out there next weekend."

He placed a soft kiss on my forehead. "Sounds like a plan. Let's sit on this until then."

CHAPTER 29

Sadie

"That's some crazy story." My father shook his head and rubbed the back of his neck. I'd just spent a full hour unloading the entire unbelievable tale, from how I'd come to meet the Maxwell family because of Amanda clipping my articles to how they'd received a donated egg. He'd known some of it already, but not the entire crazy thing. Honestly, saying it out loud truly made the whole thing sound like something from a soap opera. It had been a week since Sebastian had told me everything, and it still felt surreal.

"I know. So many things had to happen for everything to wind up where we are today. I mean, let's say it turns out that I was their egg donor and somehow Amanda found out my information and started keeping tabs on me. Someone was going to be the recipient of my donation, so that's not even the outlandish part. Though of course I realize the donation itself probably isn't something that is commonly done. But even if that happened, Birdie still had to find her mom's clipped articles in the bottom of a box and write to Santa on her own. And then I had to decide to start playing Santa Claus, which eventually led to me being nosy and walking by their house. Birdie had to lose a tiny little butterfly clip on the ground, which I happened to have stumbled across. Not to mention, when I attempted to return it, I was stricken with a sudden case of insanity and decided to pretend to be a dog trainer . . . one who trained in *German*. And let's not forget that the *actual* dog trainer had to coincidentally not show up that day because she happened to have had an emergency on the exact same morning I walked by. And even then, after every one of those crazy chain of events actually did somehow transpire, Sebastian and I still had to fall in love. What are the chances of all those things happening, Dad?"

"You know I'm practical to a fault. I believe most things in life come from our own doing. You don't find a five-dollar bill on the ground because you're lucky. You find it because you're paying attention to your surroundings. But this story here, it's making me think there's more to it than that. Your mother was more religious than I am. I believe that if you work hard, you get to put food on the table for your family. While your mother believed God takes care of the people who serve him. I gotta say, sweetheart, right about now, I'm feeling like maybe I should be going to church on Sundays."

I smiled. "What do I do, Dad? Do I open that envelope?"

"Would it change anything today if you did?"

I thought about it and shook my head. "I love Birdie already, so it won't change how I feel about her. And I'm not sure it would be the right time to tell her now. You and Mom never hid it from me that I was adopted. I don't remember a time that I ever didn't know. So I never felt like one day you pulled the rug out from underneath me by dropping a bomb that you weren't my biological parents. I always knew who I was, and I would think Birdie would feel like she suddenly didn't anymore, if that makes any sense."

Dad nodded. "We struggled to decide how to handle that. But in the end, we felt that the truth always comes out. And often that happens when it's not a good time for it to appear. We didn't want you to believe something your entire life and then find out that everything you knew had been a lie. Your mother and I were afraid that could lead to you having trust issues."

I sighed. "Yeah. That makes a lot of sense, and I'm glad I always knew. But in Birdie's case, things are a little different. She's ten years old already. The fact that her mother isn't her biological mother has been hidden from her for a long time now. So she would feel like her world got turned upside down. And you're absolutely right, she might not trust anything her dad, or me for that matter, tells her after springing something like this on her. It's almost like the damage has already been done for ten years. That can't be changed."

"When we were debating how to deal with letting you know, we asked the adoption agency for their opinion. You know what the woman said?"

"What?"

"She said if you have to sit down with your child and tell them that they've been adopted, you waited too long."

I blew out a deep breath. "I think you're right. Since it's already been kept from her, the focus needs to be on when the best time to come clean is. Is that now or when she's more mature? Or is it not at all?"

"It sounds to me like you already know the answer to that question."

I smiled sadly. "Yeah, I guess I do. Thanks, Dad."

He patted my hand. "There's something I want to show you. Come with me."

I followed Dad into his bedroom, and he took an old shoebox down from the top of his closet. He dug around for a minute and then pulled out something. "Here it is. Take a look."

It was a wrinkled-up piece of paper with one line of script on it. The handwriting I knew was my mother's. I read it aloud.

"When two people are meant to be together, God makes it happen."

I looked up, confused. "What is this?"

"You know that I was in the military when your mom and I met. I'd come home on leave and met her. We spent every moment we could together for two weeks, but then I had to fly back to where I was stationed overseas. I still had six months left of my tour."

"Yeah, I knew that."

He took the paper from my hand and smiled looking down at it. "We said goodbye the morning I had to ship out. I was crazy about her, but six months is a long time. I was afraid I'd come home and she'd have moved on." Dad winked at me. "Your mom was quite the catch, especially for an average guy like me. Anyway, we said goodbye, and I spent the next eighteen hours traveling back to base. That night, when I got changed, this here note fell out of my jacket pocket. Your mother had shoved it in there without my knowing about it. I kept it on me every day until I could get back to her." He paused and then looked up at me. "Then the day we brought you home, your mother was sitting in that rocking chair she loved so much, cradling you in her arms. And I couldn't stop watching her."

My heart squeezed. It was such a beautiful thing for him to say, but it also made me sad, too. I leaned my head on my dad's shoulder and looked down at the paper with him.

He cleared his throat. "Anyway . . . your mom caught me staring one time too many and asked me what the heck I was doing. You know what I said?"

"What?"

"When two people are meant to be together, God makes it happen."

I swallowed and tasted salt in my throat. *"Oh, Dad . . ."*

He folded the piece of paper in his hands and tucked it into my pocket. "Keep it. Share that wisdom with your child someday. Whether that turns out to be Birdie or some other lucky little kid."

I couldn't sleep that night. So I texted Sebastian and asked him if I could come by at almost eleven o'clock.

"Hey." He opened the door before I even knocked.

"How did you know I was here?"

Sebastian smiled. "I was watching out the window for your Uber."

"Oh. Okay." I took off my coat and hung it on one of the hooks in the entranceway. "Sorry to come over so late."

When I turned around, Sebastian immediately pulled me into a hug. "I'm glad you're here." He kissed the top of my head. "I'm just hoping the urgency I felt in your text wasn't because you needed to come dump my ass and get it over with."

I pulled back. "What? No. Why would you think that?"

He let out a ragged breath. "I haven't heard from you much over the last couple of days. I thought maybe you came to your senses."

I smiled sadly. "I'm sorry. I just needed some time to think."

"Of course. Come on, do you want some tea or something?"

I shook my head. "No thanks." We walked into the quiet living room. "Birdie's sleeping, I'm assuming?"

"Yeah." He held up his wrist where there was a friendship bracelet tied on. "She made me take her to get another kit, and then she interrogated me about whether Santa Claus was real while she taught me how to weave these things. I made one for you."

I smiled. "You did?"

"Yeah, but don't get too excited. I suck at it."

I laughed. "Okay. Well, it's the thought that counts."

"Keep thinking that when you see how lumpy your new jewelry is."

I nodded toward his bedroom. "Why don't we go talk in private? Just in case she gets up."

"Good idea."

Sebastian led me into his room before sitting up against the headboard of his bed, and I settled in facing him, tucked between his open legs. I took his hands.

"So I've been doing a lot of thinking, and I don't think we should open the envelope."

He held my eyes. "You sure?"

I nodded. "I think at this point, it's Birdie's decision. When she finds out how she was conceived, she may or may not want to find out who her biological mother is. I've never wanted to know mine, because I have my family, and I just didn't need anything else." I shook my head. "Maybe my decision was born out of an allegiance to my parents. I'm not really sure. But it was my decision, and I think this is Birdie's, not ours."

Sebastian dragged a hand through his hair. "Okay. But do we give her that decision now?"

"Ultimately, I think that's your choice as her father. You know her better than anyone. I feel like it would be better to wait until she's older. But really, it's your call."

He went quiet for a long time before he spoke again. "What about you? Won't it be difficult for you to not know if I put off telling her?"

"Sometimes a difficult thing is also the right thing to do."

Over the next two hours, we debated all the pros and cons of telling her now or in the future. I shared my honest opinions, and Sebastian listened and told me all his fears. One thing was for sure—I didn't envy him for having to make such a tough decision. The hardest questions are always the ones that don't have a wrong or a right answer.

Eventually, he shook his head. "We'll put the envelope in my safety-deposit box tomorrow. I don't know when we should tell her, maybe when she's eighteen . . . I'm not really sure. I guess we'll figure out when the time is right when it's time. At least I hope so."

I smiled. "Yeah. I think we will know."

"But I want to discuss something else. I hate to be morbid, but one thing the both of us have learned is that life changes in the blink of an eye. If something happens to me, and you're her mother . . . she should be with you, Sadie. Right now, my will has custody going to Macie."

"Oh wow. Okay. Yeah, I guess I hadn't thought about that."

"I think we should go to my lawyer and get a consult on how it should be handled."

"That makes sense."

We looked into each other's eyes for a long time. "Well, I guess it's settled, then," I said.

Sebastian smiled. "I guess so."

I took a deep breath in, and my shoulders relaxed for the first time in days. He cupped my cheeks.

"I don't know if it's fate or a series of crazy coincidences that brought us together. But whatever led me to you isn't as important as what will keep you here. I love you with all my heart, Sadie."

"I love you, too."

He smiled. "Good. Now. *Umdrehen.*"

"Umdrehen?" My brows furrowed. "Roll over?"

Sebastian did some stealth move and I went from sitting up to flat on my back.

His eyes twinkled. "You know, deciding not to open that envelope until years from now works in my favor in another way."

"Oh yeah? How's that?"

"It'll give you a reason to stick around and find out the answer."

I smiled. "You mean *another* reason to stick around."

He seemed genuinely confused. "What's the first reason?"

"You. I never needed any other."

CHAPTER 30

Sadie

Four weeks later

"Coffee?" Devin sashayed into my office and plopped down two rubber-banded stacks of mail onto my desk. Each had to be three inches thick. *Even more letters than yesterday.*

I looked down at the piles. "I think I need caffeine for this. Can you grab me my usual, a grande iced, sugar-free vanilla latte with soy milk?"

"Yup. One cup of no-fun coming up."

I went into my desk drawer and pulled out my wallet. Devin held up her hand. "Nope. It's my turn. I'll be back in a bit. Put aside the nuttiest letters for me to read."

I laughed. "Always."

Two days ago, the magazine had run a snippet stating that the *Holiday Wishes* feature would be starting back up next week. I couldn't believe how much mail I'd received in only forty-eight hours. One of our interns usually helped sort through the letters. She'd pull out the ones she found interesting for consideration, but I also liked to rummage through and open a few myself. Sometimes it was random, maybe the first few letters on the top of the pile, and other times I'd pick by the last name listed on the return address or an interesting place that the person lived. Even though the magazine was only distributed in print in the US, I'd always get some readers from across the globe. Yesterday I'd picked Janice Woodcock because, well, who wouldn't be curious what else a woman with that last name could possibly need for Christmas? I also picked a person who lived in Bacon, Indiana. Because, well . . . bacon.

I sat back in my chair, took the rubber band off one of the bundles, and started to shuffle through today's letters. Scanning the names and addresses, nothing seemed to jump out at me, until I got to one particular envelope and froze.

B. Maxwell.

Holy shit. Birdie wrote to Santa again?

I couldn't rip the letter open fast enough.

> Dear Santa,
>
> I'm not sure if you'll remember me or not, but my name is Birdie Maxwell. I wrote to you a few months ago and asked you to bring my dad and me some stuff. Don't worry, I'm not asking for more already. I have everything I need. But here's the thing: I don't think you're real anymore. It wasn't too hard to figure out.
>
> You see, in history we're studying population. My teacher, Mrs. Parker, said the population of the North Pole is zero. She said that humans can't survive the temperatures and pretty much only narwhals live there. Zero people at the North Pole where you're supposed to live!
>
> Then there's Suzie Redmond, this girl at school. I told you about her before. She saw her mom putting out the presents Christmas morning last year. Also,

if you make the toys in your workshop, why do the dolls I got last year say *Made in China*? Something's fishy with that.

Oh, and I did the math. Mrs. Parker said there are 1.9 billion kids in the world living on over two hundred million square miles, and the average family has 2.67 children. That would mean that you'd have to go 5,083,000 miles per hour to visit everyone on Christmas Eve. How can that old wooden sleigh go so fast?

Plus . . . you can't get in our fireplace! Duh!

So, since I'm pretty sure you're not real, you're probably wondering why I'm even writing at all. Well, I've decided that when I grow up, I want to be a writer, just like my special friend Sadie. Sometimes she comes over so that my babysitter can go home early, and we sit at the dining room table doing our work together. Like right now, she's on her laptop typing across from me, and I'm pretending to do my homework. But really, I did my homework in class while the teacher was talking about something boring today, so I'm writing to you just to practice my writing.

I covered my mouth with my hand and started to crack up.

What a little twerp. We did sit across from each other when I came over early and had work to finish. I had no idea she wasn't doing homework. Still laughing, I went back to finish her letter.

Anyway, it's okay that you're not real. I have everything I could ever want. My dad smiles all the time now. That's pretty much because of Sadie. She makes me smile, too. Even if you were real, I wouldn't ask for any presents for me this year. Well, except maybe for Sadie to say yes to what Dad's going to ask her on Christmas.

Love,

Birdie Maxwell

My eyes widened.

To what Dad's going to ask me on Christmas?

Christmas Eve had me on pins and needles. This was going to be perhaps the biggest night of my life. I carefully selected my wardrobe, choosing a red dress that I knew Sebastian loved based on the one time I'd worn it before. If he was going to be proposing to me tonight, I wanted to make sure that I was dressed for the occasion.

The plan tonight was for Sebastian, Birdie, and me to have an intimate Christmas Eve along with my dad, who would be coming down from Suffern to spend the night in Sebastian's office, which doubled as the guest room. I couldn't wait to show Birdie some of Dad's and my Christmas traditions and to spend a cozy evening at home with the people who mattered to me most.

After catching an Uber to Sebastian's house, I stopped to really take in the cold night air as I exited the car. A few small snowflakes started to appear. *Could this be any more perfect of a night?* On top of everything, we were getting a white Christmas, too? Was this the last time I'd be standing on this sidewalk as a nonengaged woman? *Wow. Let that set in for a moment.*

I clutched my coat and looked up at the already darkened sky, thanking the man above for making this life possible, for leading me to this family, and for granting me the opportunity to have them as my own.

Sebastian opened the door before I had a chance to ring the doorbell.

"What are you doing standing out here in the cold, beautiful?"

"I was just thanking the stars above—literally—for everything. I feel like the luckiest woman alive."

He nudged his head. "Get in here so I can kiss you."

Once up the stairs, Sebastian enveloped me in his arms. The warmth of the sweater he wore brought immediate comfort. He smelled so good, like a blend of juniper and sandalwood. He kissed me long and hard, and I could actually feel his heart beating through his chest. I wondered if he was nervous about what might possibly be happening tonight.

"Sadie! You're here. It's about time!" Birdie came running out.

She wore what many might deem an ugly Christmas sweater with cats on it and had her hair in two pigtails.

The three of us fell into a group hug.

"I'm so excited for tonight," I said. "Are you ready to get started in the kitchen?"

Birdie clapped and jumped. "Yes!"

Sebastian removed my coat. He took a moment to ogle me in my dress and groaned subtly as he shook his head. I fully looked forward to him taking this dress off me later. We'd need to be quieter than usual with my father in the room next to us, but there was no way I wouldn't be getting some Christmas Eve lovin' tonight.

Birdie ran ahead of me to the kitchen. The doorbell rang before I even had a chance to follow her.

"That must be Dad."

Sebastian went to open the door. My father wore his famous winter hat with the furry flaps on the ears.

"George! Glad you made it safely." Sebastian patted him on the back.

Dad's cheeks were red from the cold.

"How was the train ride?" I asked as I pulled him into a hug.

"Uneventful." My father looked around. "Where's Miss America?"

"I'm right here!" Birdie said, returning from the kitchen.

She ran to give my father a hug. "Sadie's daddy!"

"Merry Christmas, sweetie. It's so wonderful to meet you."

He hugged her extra tight. I knew Dad must have been thinking the obvious: that she could be his granddaughter.

Sebastian took my dad's coat. "What can I get you to drink, George?"

"Some of my daughter's delicious rum punch would be nice."

"I was just about to go make that, Daddy. Making a nonalcoholic version for Birdie first, then adding the rum to ours." I winked.

Birdie and I ventured into the kitchen to start working on the evening's fixings. We roasted chestnuts, made punch, and prepared trays of cut-up vegetables with various chips and dips.

Sebastian had had the chef at Bianco's prepare a special lasagna for us, which was sitting in the fridge waiting to be put into the oven later.

At one point, Birdie fell into a daydream. Then she said, "My mom used to make little gingerbread men on Christmas Eve."

My heart clenched. The fact that she was thinking about her mother right now had a profound impact on me. Here I was doing the best I could to be motherly tonight when in fact I'd never be able to replace Amanda.

"Really?" I said. "Gingerbread men. I love that."

"I don't remember everything she used to make. But I remember those and Mickey Mouse pancakes." She shut her eyes momentarily, then said, "I don't want to forget. Sometimes, I'm afraid I will when I get older."

In that instant, I knew exactly what we needed to do.

"We won't forget. Do we have the stuff to make gingerbread men?"

Her eyes brightened. "I think so? I know we have cookie cutters in the drawer."

"I think we need to make them. And if we don't have the ingredients, I'll go out right now and get them, okay? I think we should make them every year in honor of your mom."

She beamed. "Thank you. Mommy would like that."

I ended up having to run out to the market down the street for a couple of the ingredients. Thankfully, it was open.

After I returned, we made the gingerbread men and frosted them.

Just as we were finishing, Sebastian walked into the kitchen.

"Just checking on things in here." His eyes landed on the gingerbread cookies lining the tray. "You're making gingerbread men. Now it makes sense why you ran out to the store."

"Yes. Birdie informed me that her mom always made these on Christmas Eve."

"Yeah." He smiled. "She sure did."

"I told her we need to make them every year."

He stared at the cookies for a few seconds before looking up at me and mouthing, *"Thank you."*

"Of course," I mouthed back.

My father walked in. "Are those roasted chestnuts I smell?"

The four of us gathered around the island, noshing on all the delights along with the punch.

After carrying some of the items over to the coffee table in the living room, we gathered around the tree as my father told Sebastian stories from my childhood.

"So what did you ask Santa to bring you this year, Birdie?" my dad asked.

"Nothing," she answered. "I have everything I need. Plus, I don't know if Santa's real anymore."

We all looked at each other, unsure how to respond to that.

Sebastian tackled it first. "How do you explain all the presents every year, then?"

"I don't know. Maybe it's you. Maybe some of it's real, but not certain parts? Like the chimney? I wrote to someone I thought was Santa. I told you that, Daddy. I used to think it was Santa answering me, but I don't know if it was anymore." She shrugged. "But good things have happened ever since."

We fell into silence.

"I believe in good people," she finally said. "But I'm still hoping for olives and a glam nail stamper this year." She winked at Sebastian.

I sighed. Our little girl was growing up.

Our little girl.

Either way, she was. My girl. No matter what the truth was.

Sebastian got up from the couch. "Well, Birdie, you have to wait until Christmas morning to open your presents, because *Santa* wasn't prepared tonight. But maybe now is a good time to give Sadie the gift we bought her?"

She jumped up and down. "Yes! I'm so excited!"

Is this it?

My heart raced. Was Sebastian about to propose to me with Birdie by his side? Were they going to ask me officially to be part of their family? I started to get a little choked up as they walked together to the bedroom.

My father smiled over at me. I couldn't tell 100 percent, but he seemed like he might know something.

Is he in on it?

Sebastian might have asked his permission.

Birdie was skipping down the hall next to Sebastian as they returned to the living room. Sebastian carried a box wrapped in shiny red paper with an elaborate gold bow.

He took a seat next to me before handing it over. "We thought long and hard about what to get someone who means so very much to us. Ever since you walked in that door, our lives have been richer and full of joy. This gift represents our gratitude to you for being a part of our world. We love you."

My hands shook as I worked to open the box.

Then my heart fell a little when I realized it wasn't a ring. I closed my eyes, needing a moment to calm my nerves, because I had been so certain. I opened them. Then, when I caught sight of what it was and it registered, my emotions went from disappointment to complete awe.

Inside the box was an exact replica of the butterfly barrette that had led me to Sebastian's doorstep that day, except it was encrusted in diamonds and hanging from a white-gold chain.

My mouth fell open. "I have no words."

"I mentioned to Birdie that you told me how much you admired her barrette." He winked at me, knowing full well that only he and I knew the full story about that barrette and how it had led me to the dog-training gig.

He continued. "We took to it a jeweler and asked him if he could replicate it in diamonds. I think it came out perfect. I hope you love it."

Getting choked up, I said, "Are you kidding? This is the most thoughtful, heartfelt, stunning present anyone has ever given me in my entire life."

After I hugged each of them tightly, Sebastian took the necklace out of the box.

"Let's put it on you."

The feel of Sebastian's hands on my skin sent a shiver down my spine as he placed the necklace around my neck.

My dad smiled from ear to ear. "Looks beautiful, pumpkin."

Birdie's eyes were wide as she took in the bauble. "Now you can think of me every time you wear it."

I hugged her again and said, "Honey, I don't need a necklace to think about you. You're always on my mind. But I will cherish this so much. It means more to me than you could ever know."

There ended up being no ring in sight that Christmas. And that was just fine by me. I'd rather Sebastian not rush into such an important decision. Was I a little disappointed? Sure. But I still felt like the luckiest woman on the planet.

CHAPTER 31

SEBASTIAN

"Marmaduke, look at me."

The dog raced around the room, his paws scratching against the hardwood floor.

"Stop, you horse!"

He continued to scurry. I then remembered the German command for "stay."

"Bleib!"

That worked. He stopped in front of me.

"Show me what you did with it."

Ruff!

I held out the mangled, empty box and pointed inside. "What did you do with the ring?"

Ruff!

If the past few days were a movie, they would have been dubbed: *The Year the Dog Ruined Christmas.*

The morning of Christmas Eve, I'd been standing in front of the mirror in my room, practicing all the poignant words I would recite when I got down on one knee and asked Sadie to be my wife. I hadn't been sure when exactly I was going to pop the question—either it was going to be Christmas Eve or Christmas Day. I only knew it was going to be at some point during those two days, when the moment felt right.

Birdie knew everything and had planned her own little speech to recite to Sadie when *we* proposed. With Sadie's father in town to witness it all, it was supposed to be epic. That is, until I decided to leave the ring on my end table while I took a shower. When I emerged from the bathroom, the box was gone.

There was no one else to blame but the Duke. He was the only one home at the time and he'd been in and out of my room moments before my shower.

I ended up having to tell Birdie. She and I'd spent the entire day scouring the house for the ring box. We finally found it—empty. Our dog had lost a $20,000 Tiffany diamond.

I supposed I could've still proposed without it. But I'd wanted everything to be perfect, and without a ring, well, that would have pretty much sucked. Thank God I'd also had the idea to have that pendant designed, because at least I had something to give Sadie. What a nightmare.

So here I was, the day after Christmas, with no ring, just a crushed empty box, and I was talking to the dog expecting an answer like a lunatic—as if I could somehow negotiate with him to tell me what he'd done with it.

The fact that we'd turned the entire house upside down and still couldn't find the ring was very discouraging to say the least.

If it didn't turn up in the next few weeks, I'd have to cut my losses and purchase a new ring. But I still hadn't given up 100 percent hope yet.

It was strange, too. I sensed something in Sadie when she left this morning, like a disappointment. I wondered if she'd been secretly hoping I'd pop the question. That made all this so much worse—because I desperately wanted to put that ring on her finger.

Birdie walked into my bedroom as I continued to negotiate with the dog.

"Any luck, Daddy?"

"No. You?"

She shook her head. "No. I even went through all my stuffed animals, thinking maybe Marmaduke was playing with them and might have had the ring there. But I didn't find anything. Is there anywhere else we could look?"

Looking around and scratching my head, I said, "I feel like we've searched every corner of the house."

Birdie knelt in front of the dog. "Marmaduke, please tell us where you put Sadie's ring." He just proceeded to lick her face. Even my daughter couldn't work her magic with him when it came to this situation.

The doorbell rang. My heart sped up a bit because I knew it was Sadie arriving back at the house for our afternoon plans. She'd only run home for a change of clothes. We'd be taking Marmaduke to the park, then heading to Bianco's for an early dinner. Then later, we'd watch a movie back here.

I opened the door to let her in. "Hey, sweetheart," I said as I leaned in to kiss her.

Sadie's cheeks were rosy from the cold. "Hey."

"Your dad make it home okay?"

"Yeah. He just called. He's safely back in Suffern."

"Good. It was nice getting to spend quality time with him."

"Yeah. He really enjoyed you guys, too." She smiled.

Birdie entered the living room with her coat already on. "We're ready whenever you are, Sadie!"

"Hey, Miss Birdie." She hugged my daughter. "Did you miss me in the three hours I was gone?"

"Tons!" She giggled.

The three of us embarked on our outing with the dog walking *us* as usual instead of the other way around.

When we arrived at the park, we let Marmaduke run around for a bit while we sat on a bench and listened to Birdie go on and on about the kids at school. Meanwhile, the entire time I kept thinking about the damn ring. I hoped my lack of attention wasn't too obvious. I'd hate to have to lie to Sadie when she called me out on being preoccupied.

After twenty minutes, Marmaduke finally got tuckered out. We got up from the bench and began the trek home to drop him off so we could head out for dinner at my restaurant.

A few blocks down the street, the dog stopped under a tree. We knew what that meant. So we waited while he squatted down. Sadie had been holding the cleanup bag, so she bent down to pick up his droppings.

She suddenly froze.

"What's wrong?" I asked.

Sadie's mouth hung open.

She could hardly speak. "Um . . . there's a . . . diamond . . . ring . . . in his poop!"

Birdie squealed and began jumping up and down. "Yay!"

Me? I literally just stood there on the sidewalk with my eyes bugging out in total disbelief.

No fucking way.

Instead of explaining, something unexpected happened. I just started laughing uncontrollably. It must have been the few days of stress catching up with me. It was apparently contagious because Birdie fell into a laughing fit as well. Sadie was the last to give in. Eventually, she lost control and began cracking up too. Marmaduke then started barking at us.

Once I got over my hysteria, I realized Sadie was still standing there looking down at the large, oval diamond—and everything that came along with it.

I held up my index finger. "Stay right there. Don't move."

"Yeah . . . not going anywhere at the moment." She laughed.

Thankfully there was a store on the corner. I ran inside, asked the man at the register for a couple of plastic bags, and thanked him profusely.

I rushed back, then used one of the bags to cover my hand in order to carefully pick the ring out before placing it in the other bag.

Sadie then discarded everything else and tied the other bag she'd been holding.

Now collectively over our laughing fits, the three of us just stood there. I needed to acknowledge the ring but didn't know quite how to do it. So I did what felt right in that moment.

Kneeling, I said, "Sadie, this is probably going to go down in history as the shittiest proposal in the history of proposals. But now that you saw what you did, I can't erase it. The surprise is already ruined, so I'm going to run with this." I took a deep breath in. "I wanted so badly to propose to you over Christmas. Birdie and I had been planning it for some time. Then, as you've probably been able to figure out, the ring went missing. We scoured the earth for it. And now it's clear why it never surfaced." I looked up at the sky to gather my thoughts before I met her gaze again. "I was devastated, because I thought the ring was an important part of the process and chose to delay something that in my heart I really didn't want to put off. This was apparently the universe's way of showing me that the ring wasn't the most important part. The most important part of a proposal is the expression of love." I put my hand on my chest. "I love you. Birdie loves you. Please say you'll be a part of our family forever?"

Tears covered Sadie's face, her words barely coherent as she nodded. "Yes! Of course, it would be my honor. Yes!"

Then I stood to kiss my lady hard—my lady, who was still carrying a poop bag. But somehow none of that seemed to matter right now. My daughter jumped and clapped while Marmaduke continued to bark at us. Birdie came between us and we hugged her.

We'd gone from laughing to crying in unison. If anyone had been watching this episode on the sidewalk from start to finish, I could only imagine they were either thoroughly confused or thoroughly entertained.

"I promise to get the ring properly disinfected," I said.

She wiped her eyes. "It is so beautiful from what I could see of it."

I turned to the dog. "You could've choked on that, you crazy animal."

Sadie laughed. "I guess it was fitting that he somehow be a part of this, seeing as how he had a big part in us becoming a family."

Birdie excitedly proclaimed, "And now I can tell everyone my dog poops diamonds!"

EPILOGUE

SADIE

Eight years later

Christmas break had become my new favorite time of year. As I waited at the door for Birdie to arrive home from college for the holidays, I could hardly stand it. I'd missed her so much.

Over the years, Birdie had become like a best friend. Our relationship was different from a typical mother-daughter one. It was born out of a conscious choice and desire to be in each other's lives. We weren't stuck together by blood but rather by some unnamed magical source that felt even stronger.

Blood. That word immediately reminded me of one of the hardest days of my life, the day we'd told Birdie the truth. Sebastian and I had decided that when she turned sixteen, we would tell her about the egg donation. A few months after her birthday, we sat her down with the envelope and told her the story, not only about the donation but about all the circumstances that led me into their lives and finally about the possibility that I could be her biological mother.

She'd sat there in silence as we laid it all out. I remember thinking she must have been in total shock because out of everything she could've said, the first question out of her mouth was, "You pretended to be the dog trainer?"

When the reality had started to set in, it was hard. That was certainly an intense and emotional day, one I'd never forget for as long as I lived. Her emotions ran the gamut from shock to confusion to sadness to eventually—understanding. It took about a full year for things to feel normal again after that, though. But eventually, they did. And if anything, telling her made our relationship stronger. Ultimately, as crazy as our story was, all the pieces of it were still bound together tightly by love.

After the revelation, it had taken her almost that full year as well to come to a decision on whether she wanted to definitively find out the results of the DNA test. We decided that if she wanted to, we would get a traditional blood test just to be sure of the accuracy. Birdie ultimately came to the conclusion, however, that knowing whether we were related by blood wouldn't change how much she loved me. She also believed that Amanda might not have wanted her to find out. So she felt it best to continue not knowing. Sebastian and I fully respected her decision, and once she made it, a sense of relief came over our household. We were able to finally move on.

Sebastian, Birdie, and I ended up taking the infamous envelope that had been stashed away in Birdie's room and burning it outside.

And that was that.

Would a part of me always wonder? Sure. But in the end, it didn't change anything. And that was what was important.

Ironically, after all these years, letters had become a part of our relationship again. Writing to me was Birdie's favorite way to keep in touch while away at school. She said it was sort of like journaling—the only difference was that she'd share her thoughts and feelings with me rather than keeping them private. It made me so happy that she considered me not only a mother figure but a friend. I looked forward to every single one of her letters.

My son came up behind me, startling me out of my thoughts.

"What are you wearing on your head, Mommy?"

I pulled him toward me as I continued looking out the window. "Oh . . . this is my special crown. Your sister gave it to me a long time ago."

"It looks too small for you."

I laughed. "Is that your way of telling me *you* want to wear it?"

Seb wrinkled his adorable little face like he'd just smelled bad fish. "No! Crowns are for girls."

"Actually, I think anyone can wear a crown." I leaned in and rubbed my nose against his. "But I'm glad you don't want to wear mine, because it's my most favorite piece of jewelry I own."

Seb Junior was born six years ago as a result of artificial insemination with one of my stored eggs after Sebastian and I had tried unsuccessfully for a couple of years to conceive naturally. Like his sister, Seb had blond hair and Sebastian's face.

"She's not here yet?" I heard my husband say from behind.

"No. Her car must have gotten stuck in traffic."

Sebastian placed his hand on the small of my back. "God. I keep thinking that Marmaduke is going to be so excited to see her, and then I remember he's gone."

A tear started to stream down my cheek at the thought of that.

Our precious dog passed away from lymphoma earlier this year, right after Birdie went away for her first semester at Stanford. That day—having to call her and tell her Marmaduke was gone—was the second-hardest day of my life.

We'd gotten his dog tag made into a necklace for Birdie as a Christmas gift. We wanted her to always have something to remember him by, since their relationship was so special.

"There she is!" Seb Junior proclaimed excitedly when he noticed Birdie's Uber pull up.

Sebastian ran to the door. My son and I scurried behind him. It was like a race.

Birdie stepped out of the vehicle. Just the mere sight of her put a huge smile on my face. Recently she'd developed a style that was very bohemian chic. Her long blonde hair was tied into a side braid, and she had on a flowy skirt that hung to the ground. But it was what was on top of her head that made me well up. I covered my mouth, feeling emotional. My Birdie had her crown on top of her head, too. I couldn't believe it. Though I probably shouldn't have been so surprised. We'd somehow always been on the same page, right from the very start.

Birdie ran up the steps and into Sebastian's waiting arms.

He hugged her tightly. "My baby girl is home."

"I'm so freaking glad to be home." She moved down to rustle her little brother's hair. "Hey, squirt. Thank you for holding down the fort for me."

When she stood up, she wrapped her arms around me. "Smommy! You have yours on, too! I missed you so much."

"Smommy" was the name she'd given me shortly after Sebastian and I got married. It was short for Sadie-Mommy. Honestly, it was perfect for us. I wasn't her actual mommy. I was her Sadie-Mommy.

She looked around, and then I saw the tears form in her eyes when the realization hit that our big lug of a dog wouldn't be running to greet her. It was the first time since she was ten that she was walking into this house without him.

"I can't believe he's gone."

I wiped my eyes. "I know, honey."

"It's literally the only reason I didn't want to come home."

Sebastian rubbed her back. "He was like your soul mate. He'll always be with you, Birdie."

"Can we go to the graveyard tomorrow?"

"Of course," I said. "We were planning to do that at some point during your break."

She shook her head. "Okay. Happy thoughts. Happy thoughts." She turned to me. "I'm starving."

"Well, I just happened to make your favorite kale salad, and Dad brought a tray of Birdie's Pasta Bolognese home from the restaurant today."

She pumped her fist. "Hell yeah."

The four of us ventured into the dining room, where I'd already had the table set.

"Will Magdalene be stopping by?" Birdie asked. "I was hoping to see her."

"She'll be visiting tomorrow for Christmas Eve to say hello."

"Oh cool."

Magdalene no longer worked for us but was still like family. We kept in touch, and Birdie made sure to write to her all the time from college. Magdalene had informed us a few years ago that she needed to step back to take care of her ailing husband. It was perfect timing, really, because I had been considering quitting the magazine to stay home with Seb. So it worked out for everyone.

That decision in retrospect was a good call, considering I was about to give birth for a second time in a few months.

Birdie paused to look at my belly before serving herself a heaping plate of salad. "You've really popped, Smommy."

I rubbed my belly. "I know. It's crazy, right?"

It's funny how life works sometimes. Sebastian and I tried for years to get pregnant before our son and ended up turning to artificial insemination. Then once we accepted the fact that we were probably done having kids, I got pregnant naturally. We were surprised but ecstatic.

"Are you finding out the sex?" Birdie asked.

"I don't know," Sebastian said. "Smommy and I were talking about that. What do you think? Should we keep this one a surprise?"

"This family is really good at *surprises*," she said sarcastically. "So yeah, maybe!"

Birdie spent the next several minutes shoveling food in her mouth. She finally stopped long enough to say, "So . . ."

I tilted my head. "Yes?"

"I have a visitor coming over tomorrow night for Christmas Eve."

Sebastian's brow lifted. "Visitor?"

"Yeah. My . . . boyfriend." Birdie looked like she was bracing herself for his response.

I could literally see the vein popping in Sebastian's neck. "Boyfriend . . ."

"Yeah. You know . . . I am almost nineteen."

"What's his name?" I asked.

"Don't laugh." She wiped her mouth with a napkin. "It's Duke."

"No way!" I said. "That might be a good omen."

"Or it could mean . . . he's a dog," Sebastian deadpanned.

"Dad." Birdie rolled her eyes. "He's a good kid."

"I'll be the judge of that!" Seb Junior shouted out of nowhere. He totally got that line from Sebastian, who said it often.

We all turned to him and laughed. He was so smart for his age, like a little adult. Even at six, he sure was protective of his big sister.

Sebastian sighed. "I'll try to be on my best behavior."

"His family lives in Brooklyn. It's a coincidence that we're both from New York."

I reached my hand over to hers. "Well, we can't wait to meet him."

Over the next hour, we polished off all the food as Birdie told us stories from her first year at school. I'd made gingerbread men cookies for dessert. Not a year went by when I didn't make them in honor of Amanda over the holidays.

Birdie finished taking a sip of water before she lifted her index finger. "Oh, I forgot to tell you guys. In my genetics class, we were studying genotypes and traits. One of the perks of the course is that students get a big discount on one of those DNA tests. You know, the kits you order online and send in a saliva sample? Remember, Dad, I used to put one of those on my Christmas list every year, but Santa never brought me one?"

Sebastian glanced over at me, then said, "Yeah, I remember."

"Well I got mine done, finally. The results were really intriguing. I'm basically a mutt. But you know what's really interesting?"

"What?" I smiled.

"I'm part Chinese."

My smile faded as her words set in. I felt a rush of blood course throughout my body.

Sebastian and I just looked at each other.

And we just . . . knew.

Now we knew.

Wow.

Just wow.

We hadn't been seeking the truth, but it seemed the truth found us. And like every single part of our journey—it was magical.

Free for our Readers!

Dear Readers,

We hope you've enjoyed reading *Happily Letter After*. As a thank-you to our readers, we have *two* free stories for you, both available exclusively to our mailing-list subscribers.

"Dry Spell" is a short story—a fun, twenty-minute beach, bath, or bedtime read.

And

Jaded and Tyed is a novelette—meant to be read in an hour or two. It's perfect for anytime!

Click to sign up now, and you'll receive these exclusive stories.

www.subscribepage.com/2FreeBooks

Much love,
Vi and Penelope

Acknowledgments

Thank you to all the amazing bloggers who helped spread the news about *Happily Letter After* to readers. We are so grateful for all your support.

To Julie—thank you for your friendship and always being up for our little adventures!

To Luna—thank you for your friendship, encouragement, and support. Today the magic number was 70. Can't wait to see what it is when you read this.

To our super agent, Kimberly Brower—thank you for putting up with us!

To our amazing editor at Montlake, Lindsey Faber, and to Lauren Plude and the entire Montlake team—your excitement about this book started at the summary and kept us motivated the entire way through. Thank you for making *Happily Letter After* shine.

Last but never least, to our readers—thank you for allowing us into your hearts and homes. We are honored that you keep coming back to take this publishing journey with us. Without you, there would be no success!

Much love,
Penelope and Vi

About the Authors

Photo © 2019 Irene Bella Photography; Photo © 2016 Angela Rowlings

Vi Keeland is a #1 *New York Times*, #1 *Wall Street Journal*, and *USA Today* bestselling author. With millions of books sold, her titles have appeared on more than one hundred bestseller lists and are currently translated into twenty-six languages. She resides in New York with her husband and their three children, where she is living out her own happily ever after with the boy she met at age six.

Penelope Ward is a *New York Times*, *USA Today*, and #1 *Wall Street Journal* bestselling author of more than twenty novels. A former television news anchor, Penelope has sold more than two million books and has appeared on the *New York Times* bestseller list twenty-one times. She resides in Rhode Island with her husband, son, and beautiful daughter with autism.

Together, Vi and Penelope are the authors of *Dirty Letters*, *Hate Notes*, *Happily Letter After*, and the Rush Series. For more information about them, visit www.vikeeland.com and www.penelopewardauthor.com.

NO LONGER PROPERTY OF
SEATTLE PUBLIC LIBRARY